MSG FREE

An Italian's way of dealing
with the artificial

ELEONORA THOMAS

MSG FREE

For information contact: Eleonora Thomas Author

Front cover illustration by Angelique King

Typeset by Green Avenue Design

Editor Bianca Iovino

Co-editor Patrick Thomas

Unless otherwise indicated, scripture quotation is taken from:

Holy Bible, New International Version®, NIV® Copyright ©1973, 1978, 1984, 2011 by Biblica, Inc.® Used by permission. All rights reserved worldwide.

A catalogue record for this book is available from the National Library of Australia.

ISBN: 978-0-646-80431-6 (Paperback)

ISBN: 978-0-6487257-0-1 (eBook)

Imprint: Independently Published

First Edition 2019

Dedicated to ME.

Select your relationships judiciously. Some people may offer you a five-star dining experience, when in fact they're feeding you takeaway.

– Eleonora Thomas

CONTENTS

INTRODUCTION..vii

CHAPTER 1
Round And Round We Go..*1*

CHAPTER 2
Little Miss Plain Ugly..*10*

CHAPTER 3
MSG Causes Heartburn..*21*

CHAPTER 4
Saints And Sinners..*31*

CHAPTER 5
Good Stuff Grows Between Tomato Plants.........................*38*

CHAPTER 6
Forgive Me Mary For My Sins...............................*46*

CHAPTER 7
One Door Closes Another Opens..*54*

CHAPTER 8
Expectations Versus Perceptions.............................*61*

CHAPTER 9
Faking Doesn't Work...*68*

CHAPTER 10
The Letter F...*77*

CHAPTER 11
Fun Girls Eat Yiros..*83*

CHAPTER 12
Hip Hip Hooray 89

CHAPTER 13
Bee Makes Three 97

CHAPTER 14
Soup Is Real Italian Medicine............................104

CHAPTER 15
The Gospel According To Dave.........................110

CHAPTER 16
Fortune Cookies Are Misleading........................118

CHAPTER 17
Big Girls Don't Cry 125

CHAPTER 18
Intelligence Is A Curse 132

CHAPTER 19
Xavier's Parable...141

CHAPTER 20
Sisterhood 147

CHAPTER 21
How Do I Love Thee? 153

CHAPTER 22
Scar Diversity 159

CHAPTER 23
Freshly Roasted 165

CHAPTER 24
Hello Man In The Hat..172

CHAPTER 25
Time To Say Goodbye *177*

CHAPTER 26
With Death Comes Life *184*

CHAPTER 27
Choices Simply Not Enough *190*

CHAPTER 28
Vegetarian Moussaka *197*

CHAPTER 29
Peaking Duck *203*

CHAPTER 30
Abracadabra *211*

CHAPTER 31
With Age Comes Grace *218*

CHAPTER 32
Knock Knock *226*

CHAPTER 33
Salute! Cin Cin! *232*

ACKNOWLEDGMENTS 239

AUTHOR'S NOTE 241

ABOUT THE AUTHOR 242

INTRODUCTION

Happy New Year. They say that January is the carry-over month from December, the carrying over of rubbish in one's life and that the New Year doesn't start until February. Well, mine just kept going.

I'm Emanuela Smith, Emmie for short. I can't really say that I suit my name. There is nothing wrong with being a 'Smith', it is just something that I have struggled with in my adult life. I feel like I should be an 'Emanuela Donatello' or something more culturally exotic. I mean, one's heritage and culture are more socially accepted now than it was 30 years ago, and diversity is embraced.

I have big apple green eyes and long dark hair with pouty lips. When I think of my name, Emanuela Smith, I think of fish and chips by the beach. Instead, it should be golden strands of handmade spaghetti alle vongole, washed down with fine red wine. I was born to Italian parents, therefore carbohydrates are a part of my constitutional makeup, and I wouldn't have it any other way.

Life leads us all in various directions. It hands out lessons, like standing at the counter of an Italian patisserie shop. Should I have that extra chocolate chip encrusted ricotta cannoli or not? Knowing you cannot stop at one, you order it anyway. Was it the right decision? Will it make me fat? Where is my willpower? Am I being foolish? It's okay, it's no big deal. We are always trying to justify our actions.

The carryover of rubbish in one's life into the next year, and perhaps many more years to follow, will not end. If we do not learn our lessons, they will keep repeating. How do I know this? Well it just so happens I ordered an extra Greek lamb yiros once and the tzatziki sauce repeated on me for years. You see, my eyes can be a lot bigger than my stomach at times, and if we don't stop ourselves or recognise the signs it will keep on going…year…after year… after year.

Social media and its users are rapidly taking over the world, so much information readily available. It's become an addiction. We have meltdowns when our phones stop working. People turn psychotic when they cannot access their daily prescription of who is doing what. We hit spell check and pull out our phones to calculate simple mathematical equations. What happened to a basic knowledge of maths and English? We eat out and spend more time taking photos of our meal and posting them than actually enjoying the food itself.

Society places so much emphasis on who we should be, what is or isn't politically correct, how we should think, how we should dress and how many 'likes' we get.

Have we all gone mad? Have we lost our way? We seem to relive the past, hope for a better future and overlook the very moment.

I thought I had lost my way once. I was told I had to find myself. Spend time finding out who I really was in solitude. I am here to tell you all, you already know who you are. You do not have to spend time in isolation to discover this, unless you want to. Go climb Mount Everest if that's what takes your fancy. I know who the fuck I am. I'm not perfect nor do I pretend to be.

My journey or yours should be just that, independent of one another. Support and motivation from friends and family are what empowers and inspires me to continue throughout life, not judgemental antidotes, or what the latest self-help remedy is. It comes from within. We all know who we are, what make us tick, and *that's* authenticity, something I value.

Friends come and go. Family tree branches die, reproduce, and bear new fruit. The fountain of youth leads the way. We are all role models to someone in life, we may or may not realise this.

How we see ourselves and how the person you pass walking down the freezer section at the local supermarket sees you are completely different. Should it matter what people think of you? No, it should not. So why do we care so much?

There is so much emphasis on self-discovery, self-respect, self-worth, self, self, and self. Therefore, I am here to say to *myself*, start living. Forget about the bullshit in your past and start living the way you would like regardless of other people's expectations. You cannot change something that has not happened yet, and worrying about it will only reinforce something that does not exist.

Let's not become confused between our minds and our hearts. It's our thoughts that need observing. Expectations lead to disappointments and I am keeping mine real. I have punished *me* enough. Broken hearts heal.

CHAPTER 1

ROUND AND ROUND WE GO

"**H**APPY NEW YEAR!"

"Thanks Jess." Jess Thompson and I have been friends for many years. Jess runs her beauty salon at the local shopping centre and that's how we met. I have been a client of hers for years. Our friendship consists of coffee and cake and seeing the occasional blockbuster movie when time permits. We do not live out of each other's pockets, but we do call one another now and then to touch base on life. She and I both know we are there for one another no matter what. Jess has blonde hair, blue eyes and is always perfectly spray tanned, so much so, her nail polish on her toes look fluorescent.

"Did you hear the news? Nguyen is getting married! He's getting married! Some gold digger has finally snapped him up," Jess said, half laughing.

"I mean if it wasn't for his financial status you wouldn't look twice at him, right?"

And there we had it. Those three words. The three words that will lead me on the way to my journey of self-discovery.

He's getting married...

The heat began to rise from the pit of my stomach. I felt like I had eaten a second bowl of tortellini alla panna when I knew I shouldn't have, and I washed it down with a glass of corked red wine. The acid churning the warm cream.

Within seconds I threw up, my face poking into a lavender bush. The flowers brushing up against my skin. Still holding on to my phone, up it comes, the lavender scented acid. Funnily, I had not even eaten, yet I was throwing up a smorgasbord of food. I was not expecting to fertilize my lavender bush with vomit after I had only finished watering it.

"Emmie, Emmie are you okay, what's going on?" Jess asked.

I didn't know how to tell Jess I had been dating Nguyen for nearly two years. I had even moved in with him for a short time. I had hidden this from her and others. Nguyen kept me away from my friends, then dumping me via a text message in November. Now he was getting *married*. It was only two days into January. I was so ashamed. I was so hurt. My mind and my vulnerability allowed this man to control me in such a way. I had my reservations at first, but at the time I went with the flow. I made poor choices and now I was paying the price. Humiliation.

I had found out Nguyen was in a new relationship on Christmas day. Nguyen is the type of man who required his daily dose of one hundred and ten plus likes and word spread quickly. Needless to say, that was one Christmas I will never forget. No Christmas turkey for me that day, rather a large lump in my throat perfectly positioned to stop me from sobbing.

"Jess, I was with Nguyen. We were in a relationship until he dumped me in November." I said between sobs.

"What the hell are you saying?" I could hear the surprise in Jess's voice.

"Jess I love him." I said, trying to convince the both of us.

"You *think* you love him!" Jess snapped.

"Emmie, he broke Amanda's heart. Four years on, and she's still not over him. What made you think he wasn't going to break yours? His relationships have a very short life span," Jess said sternly.

Jess was right, I was more upset at the fact that Nguyen had used social media as an avenue to spin his little web to suck me in, and lacked the dignity and honesty to provide me with a face to face explanation at the end of our relationship. I guess he was simply a cowardly keyboard warrior after all.

Jess listened intently as I filled her in.

"I'm coming over to see you tomorrow, I think I need to fill you in on *our* Nguyen," Jess said sarcastically before we ended our phone conversation.

What is love without self-respect? Not much at all. Having no self-respect could be compared to a doormat. People use this to wipe their dirty feet on before they walk through the door.

I met Nguyen Xin through Jess. We were all mutual friends. Jess lived next door to him and his family when they were growing up, so she'd known him for quite some time. Jess would often innocently post pictures of us out and about on social media. Hence the friend request that leads to my journey down the path of Asian fusion and the spring rolls with sweet chilli sauce repeating on me. You can never just stop at one. It's one of those frozen foods you use when entertaining large crowds, it's a much cheaper option.

Nguyen had sent me a friend request two years prior. I still remember that day. I was lying in bed when I heard my phone ping. Sunday morning sleep in. I reached for my phone. I had to look twice, I wasn't too sure who the request was from. I was not a fan of social media, but hey, once I recognised who it was, I was okay with that. He was cute I guess, I was curious and now we were 'officially' friends. I hit accept faster than I could blink. I mean what harm was there in a simple friend request?

Checking out his profile was impressive. Single, gym junkie, sports fanatic, great social life, great sporting accolades, a human rights lawyer, lots and lots of friends. Who has over nine hundred friends? Where do you find so many friends? I felt modest with my one hundred friends. I could spend hours and hours researching this person via the information he voluntarily posted. He had lots of female friends.

It started with random likes from Nguyen, and then it went on to the random comments on posts. Days went by, the comments became more frequent, and then they found a new home. We began to chat via private messages. These became more common, and then they became daily. Was I excited? Of course, I was! Who wouldn't be? He was so seductively confident.

"Hello beautiful how's your day?" Nguyen messaged.

"Hi! Good thanks how about yours?" I replied.

"Yes good, doing things with the kids, work has been busy, can't stop thinking about your beautiful big green eyes, I just want to kiss you." He messaged.

"I think about you too." I replied.

"I miss you Emmie." He messaged.

Does he miss me? Does he want to kiss me? Wow, Nguyen misses me! I hardly knew him. He liked to move at a fast pace, but I thought I really liked him. I like risk takers. I liked the excitement and confidence Nguyen fed me. I like honesty, he missed me.

Nguyen was quite the charmer. In fact, he was so good he made me feel like I was the only woman in his world. Was I fooling myself? Could it be possible he was juggling more than one woman in pseudo-relationships? I am an educated woman, god damn it. I am forty-four years old. I am mid-career, working as an adviser to a female politician. If someone was going to play me, I would see the signs, right? Wrong! I was caught up in this pipedream called love. A fucking make believe fairy-tale where the narrator is an expert at not so happy endings. If it's too good to be true it most likely is!

We have been led to believe love makes the world go round. We all need it and we all want it. We seek it out as if it is something so unattainable. It is already there, within us. However, we need reminding. If I had reminded myself about self-respect, self-love, and most importantly, self-awareness with Nguyen, I may have recognised the signs earlier than I had, perhaps saving my chest cavity the scar it bears today.

He showered me with attention. Each message began with "Hello beautiful." I was beautiful! I will take that, thank you very much. No one had ever called me beautiful before. I began to feel like more than *just* a mum, or *just* a wife whom I was relentlessly giving to an ongoing difficult relationship.

There we have it lesson one in life, self-respect should not include the word 'just'. We are not *just* anything. We are all and more.

"Hello beautiful, I'd really like to see you, I'd really like to catch up for a drink, I can't stop thinking about you," texted Nguyen.

"Sure! I'd love to, why don't we meet at your local pub? We can have a few there." I replied.

"I can't wait to see you beautiful." He messaged.

"I can't either Nguyen, see you there." I replied.

Nguyen's eyes are so intense, dark, and mysterious. I could see the sadness they carried. I have always believed you can tell a lot about a person through their eyes. Why was this person sad? He had no reason to be, well not according to his social media profile.

He is a serious person, but I liked that. I liked the intensity. His sense of style is average, neat and tidy, nothing spectacular like I'd imagined a lawyer would dress. He has gorgeous shiny black hair. His quirky hairstyle reminded me of a cross between a sulphur crested cockatoo and the troll doll my cousin Renata used to have as a kid. He has a very trim athletic body and his legs a little on the thin side. He has the most beautiful hands I had ever seen on a man. So refined, they seemed like they belonged to a surgeon and not a lawyer, repairing and easily sewing up an artery with exact surgical precision. Each finger so perfectly defined he looked like he should be playing Mozart Piano Concerto No. 21 showcasing them.

I sat there in awe. Elbow on the table with my head tilted to the side. My chin was cupped in my hand listening to him, like a child listening to *Strega Nona* for the first time.

My hamster wheel went into overdrive, *he is so well educated*, I thought to myself. Listening to every word that came out of his mouth strung together like it was a golden thread. *I am so lucky to be here with him.* I thought to myself. *Why? Why am I the lucky one?* I then wondered, briefly observing my thoughts.

We had our regular hangouts, quiet little pubs, not too many people around. Intimate. Why should I care who sees us anyway? Was I that worried? I couldn't explain it. Was it guilt? Perhaps, but why? I deserved happiness in my life. I began to justify my newly found happiness. I was beautiful and that was all that really mattered.

"Nguyen, what happened between you and Amanda?" I asked.

I knew Nguyen had been dating one of Jess's friends before me.

"She's too needy and I can't handle needy women!" he said with such a cutting tone.

I sat up-right now, elbow down, the bar stool sticking to me making me feel six inches taller. I do not like men who label women. I am someone who fights for women's rights. Protesting with banners in hand, waving them above my head for all to see. Where is my banner now?

"Needy?" I waited with bated breath. I wanted a reasonable explanation so I could put my imaginary banner down. He is too nice to be disrespectful to women, right? He has a mother and she is a woman. He is intelligent, he must understand women surely?

"She has no idea, she's a victim of her own circumstances, and she can't cook," he said with tone.

What did I just hear him say? My imaginary banner was flapping in the wind at this one comment, flapping so hard that it ripped in half!

"Oh really? What happened? Nguyen why are you so upset?" These were simple questions I was beginning to regret asking.

He went on to explain. He said her steaks were always overcooked, he preferred his rare, and she never put enough butter in her mash potatoes. Her kids were annoying, she didn't discipline them. She would overcompensate with giving her attention to them and not enough to him. Her children didn't have much contact with their biological father. Nguyen felt like he had to solve Amanda's problems and he couldn't be bothered anymore. His explanation was undertaken with such precision and persuasion that I readily accepted it. In a total of fifteen minutes, I was stargazing into his eyes. Explanation sufficient. It was like he fed me the most perfectly prepared crème brûlée. I ate it all up. He had been hard done by Amanda, it was all her fault.

I was on the road to love again. Nguyen made everything sound so much better. I thought he was so smart. I admire an intelligent man. I mean he had enough sense to pursue me, right?

"You, beautiful, are different. You are strong and resilient and you are not needy at all," Nguyen said convincingly.

Nguyen simply idolised me. He was so encouraging and caring. I was *all* and more.

Jess would mention Amanda and Nguyen in conversation when we had our coffee catch ups. Our discussions around relationships and others were a common topic amongst us. She would tell me how bad things were between them. How the pressures of the modern world influenced single mothers and how they were never going to work together as a couple due to his lack of understanding around this. She was busy raising a family on her own and he was busy pursuing his dreams. She would fit into his schedule when an opening became available.

So why should 1 care what happened in their past relationship? This was my future sitting right in front of me. I wanted to support Nguyen now and Amanda had her chance. This was my opportunity. I am the only woman in his life now. Like Nguyen said, "*She* was too needy."

"Let's have another drink, beautiful. We can look forward to better times ahead." He said, as he got up to order another bottle of wine.

"Sure, let's." I beamed.

The wound healed very quickly with Nguyen. The scar however, remains to serve a purpose. It is there to remind me about forgiveness. To forgive oneself is the ultimate success to the journey of self-discovery. If you can stop your thoughts spinning the hamster wheel, then you're off to a good start.

Self-respect. Loving thy self. If you love yourself, you do not need to seek love from others. Bullshit. We want our cake and to eat it too. Set boundaries, find what your values are and stick to them. Never bow down to have someone in your life, if they kick you to the curb, then walk away. The universe will push you off the wrong path beyond a shadow of doubt and set you on to the right one…eventually.

Loving relationships should include compromise, understanding, compassion, forgiveness, empathy, sex, balanced point of views, respect, effective communication, honesty, trust, direction and shedding the 'F' word, fear and introducing 'G' gratitude! Be grateful for what you have, and you will begin to see the bigger picture. You already have the right tools to work with.

Nevertheless, how do I apply all of these together? I was never good at swimming. I was so uncoordinated, I was afraid of drowning, how was I ever going to practice all the above at the same time? Keep practising…even if you have to develop your own swimming style!

Love yourself first before you go looking for someone else to fill your void. It is not rocket science. Otherwise, you will be forever chasing your tail attracting the same lesson over and over. Don't chase that pipedream that is not worthy of your love. Cupid had shot his arrow and it was headed right for me. Nguyen was everything I *thought* I had missed out on in life and that I now so deserved.

CHAPTER 2

DRAMA WAS A subject I chose to study in high school, but little did the teachers know I was already an expert at it. Thanks to my childhood I had become an A+ student. My Italian upbringing involved drama to the highest degree. From waking up in the morning to going to bed at night, nothing was short of drama. Speaking in a normal quiet tone was unheard of in my home. There was only one volume on our dial and that was loud. Each morning before school my mother would brush my long dark hair and would put it up in a ponytail, pulling out the ribbon box to select my daily satin bows. Multi-tasking at its best. I was an only child therefore appearance was very important to her.

"Mamma mia! Ma perché?" (Why?) My mother would ask in Italian. *Why what?* I would be thinking to myself each time my mother went off at something. If she was not arguing with my father, and by arguing, I mean having a simple discussion, she would be extremely annoyed at something or someone else.

"Don't play with your bow, leave your hair alone!" my mother would scold me.

My father, on the other hand, was a quiet, reserved man. Quiet, but deadly in the sense that one look could kill. Did he have superpowers? I think he did, because that 'one' look would freeze me dead in my tracks like playing a game of Simple Simon Says outdoors with my cousins.

"Finish your dinner," he would say to me with his stern look, sitting at the head of the table as the king of the castle. While I was trying to force down the last bit of pasta fagioli (pasta with broad beans) in red tomato sauce and proudly not vomiting.

My parents had very strong work ethics. They arrived from Naples to Australia as young adults seeking a better life of opportunity. Discipline was enforced at a young age. I was raised in a household evading flying shoes hitting the back of my head to being threatened with my father's leather belt. Threats came and went. Scare tactics were a large part of my upbringing. No stranger danger here, I would have welcomed a stranger enticing me into his car with a chocolate doughnut and strawberry milk any opportunity to take me away from that madness.

"Don't go swimming after you eat," my mother would yell at me from the kitchen window as I was about to step into my blue plastic wading pool filled with 20 inches of water. "You'll die!"

"Stop blowing up that plastic ball, you'll get dizzy and you'll die!"

"Don't touch the power point with wet hands! You'll get electrocuted and you'll die!"

"Don't eat so fast!" she would say as she was removing my plate from the table so she could wash the dishes before I could get the last meatball in my mouth.

"You will choke, and you'll die!" she'd say pointing to the print hanging in the dining room of Jesus and the Last Supper.

Therefore, I learnt very quickly at a very young age if I did the *right* things and followed the rules enforced by my parents I would not die.

"Se sei una brava ragazza non morirai," my mother would say. In other words, "If you are a good girl you won't die." Because as a young child I really didn't want to die, so I had to be *good*.

There were religious portraits of Jesus in nearly every room of the house as a reminder for me to be good. Each time I would walk into a room I felt like he was watching me and his eyes were moving with me. I was always too scared to walk down the hallway where the holographic picture was hanging. It would change when I looked at him as I was moving past. I was fearful of ever being 'bad'. I didn't want to be nailed to a wooden cross. Not only did I feel like my parents had eyes in the back of their heads, and they watched my every move, but so did Jesu Christo.

My mother Ida Sopracasa, the lunatic Italian, is so pretty, a classic beauty. I was mesmerised by her perfect lips encased in bright red lipstick and her flawless skin. She always wore an apron tied around her waist to keep her clothes clean. Appearance is something she takes quite seriously and with pride.

From the hands up in the air waving about to her hands in her hair whilst screaming at me. She would put her hand in her mouth and bite on it, and the deeper trouble I was in, the higher her mouth would travel up her arm. If it hit the top, I knew she would refer that incident to my father. She would put her hand in her mouth if I did not tie my shoelace up correctly and she would have to bend down to re-tie it. If I fell over and began to cry, she would put her hand in her mouth and bite on it, as if I had fallen on purpose. She didn't like being interrupted when watching her daytime soapies consisting of doctors and nurses secretly kissing in cleaning rooms. However, to me, this was the norm. I didn't know any different. I was a little girl raised in *my* world of multiculturalism in Australia. I was like any other kid, so I thought.

I have the same green eyes as my father, Gino Sopracasa. He had a perfectly chiselled jawline. He had dark hair and fair skin. He was very much into social justice, helping others less fortunate. When he was not working, he would spend time in the back shed. He also enjoyed nurturing his organic vegetable patch, or inviting strangers over for a meal. He was a rescuer, not limiting this to injured animals. He was no stranger to drama either. He was a religious man who had a very strong faith. When he argued with my mother he would yell out "Jesu take me away from this terra," (earth) so I guess when the going got tough, my father wanted to leave us and die. Death to Italians represents respect. You honour the memory of those who have passed, thus they live on forever.

Religion in our Catholic household was to be respected. Statues of Jesus, saints and famous naked figurines proudly displayed everywhere. Bottles that contained holy water were kept by our bed. If I became unwell, my mother would pop open a bottle sent to her via the Vatican and sprinkle it on me. If she had an argument with my father, she would sprinkle it in the room they were in after he left, cursing under her breath calling him, "Stupido" and praying at the same time. Church on Sundays and Sunday school were also expected of me. Respect God respect your parents, respect, respect, and more respect. Regardless of your situation, good or bad, respect anyway and do right by others and all will be fine, you will be loved.

Our house was immaculate. My mother was always in constant cleaning mode. To Italians of that era, there was no such thing as mental illnesses and obsessive-compulsive cleaning disorder was a normal thing. This was the disorder all good Italian women aspire to have. It's a cultural necessity to be a sufferer of the disease. There was nothing more satisfying than watching my mother clean the house and wash windows all on the same day.

Our home consisted of two of everything. Two kitchens, two lounge rooms and then there was the 'good' room. Off limits to all, completely out of bounds, this room was the golden room, the room reserved for The Queen of England only. It had a special name 'il salotto' (the formal lounge room).

"Non andare lì," my mother would say to me. In other words, "Keep out!" The one and only room in the house that no one could step foot in. As a child I would carefully plan my visit. I would wait, look around, listen if anyone was coming, like crossing a main arterial road alone. Look left, look right, look down the hallway, no one there, RUUUNNN! Even the lampshade hadn't had the plastic removed from it.

This was the museum room that housed all the famous reproduction statues our very own Sistine Chapel, straight out of an Italian factory. These were personally selected and transported home by my father on his return visits from Italy. An intriguing room filled with various paraphernalia. These were the toys that I played with. I didn't have dolls like other kids. This room was where my imagination unleashed, my main source of entertainment.

My favourite one of all was my biblical hero David, Michelangelo's masterpiece. The crowning glory of statues, he sat proudly on the intricately carved bar, each panel a slightly different shade of walnut coloured wood. He was surrounded by alcoholic jars of maraschino cherries preserved in liqueur and bottles of Italian spirits. When I pressed the little button on his back alcohol would dispense from his penis. I loved it! I was so flabbergasted a man that urinated alcohol I doubt it got much better than this.

"Hello baby Jesus, meet David, he can't afford clothes like you either." I would say, playing pretend in the museum, moving all of the figurines around as my imagination grew by the minute.

Alcohol was not off limits in our home. My father produced his own wine. We all had to help during wine season. The back-shed wall was lined with three oak barrels. Freshly made salami hanging from the rafters, drying out, and ready to eat on special occasions. I could smell these as soon as I stepped from the back door of our home.

Each morning my mother made me a warm beverage for breakfast consisting of egg yolk, sugar, milk, and marsala.

"Bevi," (Drink) she would say as she pushed the fine porcelain Royal Doulton Bunnykins mug with pictures of rabbits chomping carrots on it towards me.

"Why do I have to drink it?" I would ask.

"Bevi, ti dà forza!" "Drink, it will give you strength," she bit back.

Drinking an alcoholic beverage at age six, first thing in the morning was going to give me strength? According to my mother, it would. I drank it anyway, it tasted like a warm dessert in a cup.

I didn't eat toast in the morning, we only had continental bread and according to my father this bread was simply too good to dry out on purpose. In fact, we didn't own a toaster. If you wanted bread in the morning you broke off a chunk and you would dip it into your warm milk with Italian coffee. There was no age limit in an Italian household when it came to drinking and eating. Espresso coffee was always put into warm milk. Once I finished my breakfast, my mother would stick a woollen crochet poncho over my head and send me on my way to school. No hand holding, just me and my little school bag, swaying down the road.

If I ever became unwell, my mother would make me drink an alcoholic liqueur made with an extract taken from the artichoke plant. It was revolting, it was incredibly bitter. Needless to say, I wasn't unwell too often. No over the counter cough medicine for me, but the variety found over the bar. When she ran out of the alcoholic version, she would pick chamomile flowers straight from the garden, boil and strain them, add a little honey and make me drink it. I preferred the little white flowers out of the garden as opposed to the hairy artichoke drink.

Dinner time we had 'Italian cola', homemade red wine and lemonade.

"Bevi, ti fa bene," (Drink, it's good for you) my father would say. Sure, why not, I've still probably got my morning cocktail running through my veins, intoxicated from breakfast but hey, it's supposedly good for me like my father said. I mean, he had made it himself. He would make his own wine every year. Entirely organic ingredients and exclusively the colour purple.

However, the piece di résistance was black pudding tart. I was tricked into eating pig's blood set in a shortcrust pastry that looked like a perfectly baked chocolate tart.

"Mangia!" Both my parents would say, whilst shovelling spoonful's in my mouth. I would close my eyes and swallow it trying not to think about our own blood bank in the refrigerator with glass recycled drink bottles housing this red liquid. This was no ordinary chocolate tart! It tasted like a combination of chocolate and orange.

So there we have it, my first taste of 'strength'. Eating and drinking all of this traditional Italian food was supposed to make me strong! Problems are solved with food, and emotions are expressed through food. Food is everything to Italians. No preservatives, no additives, what you see is what you get, no hidden surprises. If you could handle it then you're 'strong', and I very rarely vomited. Resilience, on the other hand, had not arrived yet. It was quietly sitting, waiting around the corner.

Growing up in the '70s to Italian parents was difficult. I was born in Australia, therefore, I thought I was already an Aussie kid. But I wasn't, I was the Italian kid. However, when I visited my nonna in Italy, over there I was the Australian kid. This confused me. There was a cultural imbalance at school. The scales tipped 98 per-cent to two. I was one of the two. I hated recess and lunch. I was teased relentlessly, as soon as I pried open my Mary Poppins lunch box, I had an audience.

"Ew, look at what Emanuela is eating today!" the kids would say, all waiting eagerly to see. I like my eggplant parmigiana panini. The Aussie kids sitting near by with a round white bread roll, burrowing into it like some badger trying to get away from a dachshund. They then stuffed it full with some curly orange Twisties or potato chips. What was this foreign food they were all eating?

YUCK, I'd think to myself. Then there were the other kids, picking tall yellow flowers on the school oval, sucking on the green stems like a hummingbird sucking out nectar from a flower. Were these kids poor, like David and Jesus? People walked their dogs on the school oval. I didn't understand any of this at all, I had real food. I was confused and satisfyingly full. My mother even included a paper napkin in my lunch box.

I didn't mind sitting alone at recess and at lunch. I hoped the kids playing around me would not notice me and leave me alone. Some days I was not so lucky. I had become accustomed to being spat on and to being taunted because of my ethnicity. I was surprised Aussie kids knew how to spit as well as my mother.

I was not as confident as some of the other kids. Most of the girls at school had blonde hair and blue eyes. I was different. I was probably the only student with bright green eyes and dark hair. I was not as adventurous as some of them. I didn't do callisthenics or gymnastics, hence why I kept away from the monkey bars in the playground. I preferred to view the world the right side up not hanging upside down from my legs. My parents did not have time to bring me to weekend sports. My mother had to clean the house and my father worked. I had my books and that is all I required. My books and my imagination.

This day, I was really looking forward to going to the school library at lunchtime. The new Nancy Drew book *The Clue in the Old Album* had arrived and Miss Sullivan the librarian was holding it for me. I spent a lot of my time there. I loved reading so much, my imagination would introduce me to many friends.

I was walking across the courtyard making my way there with my piggy tails swinging freely side to side, held together with red and white polka dot ribbons when bang! I hit the asphalt with an almighty thud. I had been pushed from behind. It felt like a freight train had hit me. I felt many hands on my back.

"Emanuela, you're so ugly! Stupid wog girl." I heard.

I could hear laughter behind me, but I could also begin to feel something warm trickling on my skin. I looked down, and saw blood pouring out of my left knee with tiny flecks of asphalt sticking to my skin. Oh God, what was that white thing sticking out? I thought I was going to faint, why does it hurt so much? Was that my knee bone? Yes, it was my knee bone! My imagination worked overtime. I sat there, crying, cradling my knee into my chest like a mother cradling her newborn baby. Rocking back and forth with tears streaming down my face.

Italian number two ran over with Mrs Goodings. I didn't see Italian number two much, he had better hiding places than me. Italian number two lived in fear for his life so he was not in any hurry to share his hiding spots, even with me. Trust no one.

They picked me up and took me to the sick room where I was patched by the school nurse. I was still crying. I wanted my mum. Why couldn't my mum come and get me? Oh, I remember now, my mum was at work. She was always at work.

Mrs Goodings came in to check up on me. She sat by me on the sick bed and put her arm around me.

"Emanuela, you are different than all the other children at school, you are a very brave and obedient little girl. You are extremely patient and kind, and they're all very good qualities to have," she said as she smiled down at me.

"I have something for you," and she handed over my reserved library book. She had gone to get it for me.

"Thank you, Mrs Goodings," I said, through teary eyes.

That afternoon I walked myself home as I did each day, alone, but this day I hobbled. My knee hurt and I missed my mum. I hobbled all the way home, a lump perfectly positioned in my throat to stop me from crying. Holding hands with resilience. My new found friend.

I met strength and resilience during these years. It took some time to make our acquaintance, but I am glad we did. Because from that day on, I had decided no one would ever hurt me again. But I had to change. There was one thing that stuck with me like a big red neon sign flashing in the middle of the night, lighting up the empty streets. My name.

Emanuela Sopracasa. I hated it. I hated the sound of my name, I hated hearing it. It sounds like an Italian smallgoods salami. It caused me grief in class when the student roll was read out by the teacher. I was teased because of it.

"Emanuela so-stupid-arsa!" the kids would yell. I did not want some long winded Italian name nobody could pronounce or spell. I wished they would stop teasing me! I wished I could change my stupid name. I wanted to be inconspicuous. I wanted to be like the rest of the kids at school. Uncomplicated and straight forward Aussie plain Jane.

CHAPTER 3

NGUYEN IS A very busy man, however that's understandable. I had my life, and he had his, I was happy to see him when I could and when it suited his schedule. As a human rights lawyer, he fights for refugees to obtain residency and remain in this country of opportunity. Escaping death or persecution from where they once called home. They were leaving behind countries in violation of basic human rights. Some were lucky enough to escape human trafficking syndicates and criminal gangs, terrorist attacks, revenge killings, detention and torture in custody. However, others who were lucky enough to have escaped had to leave their families behind.

This was nothing in comparison to what we would ever experience in Australia. Helping and ultimately protecting individuals, enabling families' freedom of speech, education, health care, the list goes on and on. Many of his cases have avoided deportation which under any given circumstance would cause an uproar in our country. This man saves people's lives.

Nguyen and I had conversations around how we could make a difference to the world together. He told me I was the smartest woman he had ever met. He had finally found someone intellectually equal to him. He seemed so authentic. I was surprised by this as his ex-wife is a chemical engineer and surely poses a high degree of intelligence? We discussed working in a small remote village in a third world or developing country. Two intelligent individuals giving something back to those in need. We both seemed to be on the same page with civil rights issues passionate and driven. I appreciated having these sorts of discussions, but the thought had crossed my mind Nguyen may have been entertaining himself with grand ideas and unrealistic future plans that would lead to nowhere. When push came to shove, I doubted he would move to some small remote village where there would be no internet connection.

Communication was not a strong point of his. Funnily, that is what his occupation required mostly of him. Advocating for the rights and basic democracy of others. With me, he preferred to text message rather than call. Together we are a mix of Chinese hot chilli chicken served with steamed rice. You need one to cool down the other. I liked it when he rang me spontaneously and unexpected.

"Hello beautiful, would you like to go out to dinner on Friday night? I will book for us," he said.

"Sure! I would love to. I'll come around to your place at 6 o'clock, see you then." I said excitedly.

Nguyen liked nice restaurants and fine wine. He had a disposable income, quite a large one at that. I loved how he showed initiative and took the reins, he booked the restaurant and sorted the taxi. He was so thoughtful. He never let me pay for anything. He was so romantic and generous.

What colour is love? If I had to associate it with a colour, what would it be? Red, pink, blue. I looked at Nguyen with red hearts in my eyes, so my glasses were tainted red. Nguyen likes red, red wine …in fact he *loves* red wine.

I walked through his door and he had a wine and cheese platter waiting for me. He was so considerate. He had incense burning in the background. The house smelt like subtle tones of sandalwood and musk. Nguyen was seemingly on his third glass. Depending on how much he poured prior, I could see a near-empty bottle sitting on the kitchen bench by his glass, less than a quarter full.

"Nguyen, I really appreciate this drink. I've had a rough day. Dave isn't coping with our discussions about splitting our assets and he's making things hard for me. I feel so stressed. He's finding letting go very hard to deal with." I said.

"You never listen to me Emmie. I've told you what to do, and you never listen." Nguyen said hastily.

"People who don't listen to me are stupid! I'm sick of dealing with stupid people, they are not worthy of my time or my energy!" he snapped.

"Just stay with him. Go back home to him, you're better off! The grass isn't any greener on the other side!"

Maybe he's had a rough day I was thinking to myself treading cautiously and taking a big step back.

Dave Smith is my estranged husband. Nguyen had been divorced for ten years so I guess he knew the process I should be undertaking with Dave. Nguyen and I shared many similarities in our lives. I looked up to him. I took his advice on board. He became my best friend. Nguyen was going to help me. Note to self, listen to Nguyen.

"I'm sorry for not listening. I didn't mean to upset you." I said.

"You are smart Emmie you need to sort yourself out and I can't promise to always be here for you," he said.

I was standing there a little confused. *I think he may have insinuated I was stupid, unworthy of his time. What am I supposed to sort out? Ultimately, he may not be around anyway,* I thought to myself.

I felt like he was trying to provoke me in some roundabout way. I was deep in thought. We were finishing off our wine when his phone pinged. He was always on his phone. I trusted him, I had no reason not to, and it was probably his work. Although, my instincts were telling me something different. I think they liked toying with me.

Nguyen has an impressive friends list. The majority were women. He would quite often share stories to me about them and the women he had once dated, their names, nationalities, and occupations.

"Nguyen, why have you got your ex-girlfriends on social media?" I piped up.

"Why not?" he asked.

"I guess because they're an ex for a reason." I stated cautiously.

"I like to keep in touch with them. A few have mental health issues, and when I broke up with them, they didn't cope well. I've explained this to you already, you're being too sensitive again, and you're making a big deal over nothing. I like to see how well they are now doing, end of story."

When Nguyen spoke like this it was best not to challenge him. I referred to my notes and tacked on another, do not challenge Nguyen.

Then his mood changed, instantaneously. Like a dark cloud coming in from the east. He opened his second bottle of red wine and started pouring. I could see his jaw tighten as he clenched his teeth. His gorgeous tanned skin was now changing a slight shade of rosé.

However, Nguyen had met his match with me. My Italian mouth began to open and there was no stopping it. I struck like a hot puttanesca sauce with extra chilli thrown straight in his face. I could not hold back. Maybe that was the start of my undoing, speaking my mind. The words flew out like candy from a piñata. The harder I hit, the more came out.

"Why do you drink so much? Maybe you should ask someone else to go out to dinner with you? Ask an ex, you've got plenty to choose from!" I threw out there.

Here we were, standing in the middle of his cluttered kitchen Asian versus Italian, a culinary standoff. My imagination was filling with unthinkable thoughts. Do I go for the chopstick to the eye or the Italian coffee percolator over the head? I was beginning to feel like Sophia Loren in the movie *Houseboat*, when she slaps Cary Grant after he insults her. But then she still stays in the apartment with him. The sexy runaway Italian clearly attracted to the handsome intriguing American. Cinzia simply can't resist him.

His dark eyes were so intense. Mine, lighting up my face. My anger began seething from the top of my head, my scalp going into itchiness overdrive from the emanating heat.

"Emmie you are beautiful, you have nothing to worry about." He said with such conviction.

"Let's go out." He took my hand, looked directly into my eyes, kissed it, we made our way to the front door. The magician had waved his magic wand yet again.

Insecurities, what are they? Self-doubt, self-contempt, self-hatred, don't all these words mean the same thing? They lead to the same person. Me. Why was I so insecure? Self-respect? Had I met self-respect? Had it introduced itself to me yet? Because I felt like I was running out of time.

Nguyen was throwing me scraps of attention here and there and I was eating it up like seagulls eating chips out of a rubbish bin at the beach. I didn't trust him, but yet I found myself still wanting to be around him and wanting him to like me. I was putting more effort into him than he was with me.

"What you put out there stays there," I'd say to Nguyen.

This is why I take such a dislike to social media. Nothing is safe, the information is sitting right there in front of you. I mean, if you're going to use it, at least familiarise yourself with the 'advanced settings and locations' first. I can navigate my way around any site, any post, like I navigate my spoon around a bowl of leftover chocolate Italian cream custard, executed with attention and care. I had started to play the game of detective.

Nguyen would be online all hours of the night. Nothing lies more than an active green dot. He would be chatting online, liking posts from ex-girlfriends, writing encouraging little comments, supporting all their social online needs quite eagerly. Or on the other hand, was it more than their online needs he was supporting? Was he baiting them or me? Was I being too sensitive, as he quite often reminded me?

If someone is truly 'into you' they do not surround themselves with ex-lovers and cause confusion with jealousy and the false likelihood that he was in high demand.

Most of our conversations were around his past lovers. The German blonde, the Irish redhead, the Greek with long black hair, the mousy brown Polish, the Italian brunette. Oh wait, I was his first Italian brunette, apparently. I knew all their names because he was so proud of each and every one of them. He had been through more nationalities than you'd find at a United Nations Convention and *they were all* crazy, apparently. Self-awareness, where the fuck are you? Because this guy should seriously come with a food warning label 'may contain traces of nuts'.

He began posting random articles on social media I felt were directed at me. Titles like 'Stress causes aging' and 'Drama causes wrinkles and fine lines in older women'. Although he said the articles were not directed at me, when I challenged him on it, he'd say it was reading material for his 'online' friends. I knew they were meant for me, it was his condescending way to gauge if I was reading his posts and taking the bait.

I refused to be Nguyen's friend in the world of cyberspace, so I unfriended him. I did not want to be *just* another girl on his friends list.

"Emmie, why did you unfriend me, are you trying to upset me on purpose?" he asked one night.

"No, Nguyen. I prefer to think of myself as different. I like to think I have class, that's something you can't buy or friend request, it's something I was raised with." I said sarcastically.

"I'm comfortable in my own skin Nguyen, I don't need to seek outside validation online." I abruptly ended our conversation.

I was done with him using social media as a tool to irritate me. Where he once had used it to feed my confidence, he was now using it to tear me down.

Why couldn't he stop and see who was standing in front of him? He could put more attention and effort into having a real relationship with me, rather than playing this bullshit game of make-believe on social media and in his head.

What is this socially accepted biosphere of the twenty-first century? This sewage pipeline, the connecting gateway to falsehood, rapidly filling with fake people and pretend lives. I, god damn it, am a realist! I am a woman of the world. Not some selfie-taking, standing on my head with one leg in the air amongst a field of fucking flowers, kind of girl. I viewed the world standing on two feet, firmly planted on the ground. Social media is so overrated. And so were some of its users. This monster actually has the ability to shamelessly kill people off, kill relationships off, and kill self-respect. Yet society still supports it. It continues to feed people like Nguyen. He was using it as a tool to chase his own pipedream. Our relationship was becoming intensely frustrating.

I would have days where I was completely in love with him, and my insecurities had all but vanished. These were the days we had intelligent conversations, fun outings, great interactions, great joke sharing, and lots of laughter, providing his timetable permitted uninterrupted time together. Nguyen and I were spiritually connected, as he would quite often tell me. In hindsight, was he spiritually connected to something else? His wine perhaps.

Nguyen rang me, "Hello beautiful, I have booked our accommodation for the conference in Canberra."

Nguyen had a Leader's Summit in Canberra and he asked me to go.

"I can't wait!" I said.

"Pick me up from work and we will go straight to the airport from there."

I was so excited. A little getaway with the man of my dreams. I was counting down the days to our trip away.

Nguyen arrived on time.

"Hi honey, how was your day?" I asked eagerly and excited as I got into the car, throwing my carry-on luggage in the back seat.

No response, the air was so tense between us. What was going on? I was so confused we were going to Canberra together and headed for the airport. My carry-on bag filled with lots of sexy sleepwear. What was wrong with him, what was his problem now?

I was actually beginning to feel intimidated by his nonverbal phases. Not a single word. I had chest pains, my anxiety was gripping me, and my heart was beating a hundred miles an hour.

Hello fear, why are you here? Fear, does it rear its little head to protect us? I think it does, because my parents instilled fear into me from a very young age. But in this case, I don't like how fear feels. My father would make me feel intimidated and scared when I had done something 'wrong'. I hadn't done anything wrong to Nguyen, I simply jumped into his car and asked how his day was.

We arrived at the airport and parked the car. We got our luggage from the back seat. We promptly checked in, like robots. I wish I had the courage to speak, but my fear stopped me.

"I'll be right back. I'm just going to the ladies restroom." I said. I saw Nguyen walking towards the airport bar, completely ignoring me.

As soon as I got into a cubicle, I rang my best friend Sharni Kendall. She had better answer, please answer Sharni!

"Hey."

"Sharni! Sharni, I can't do this anymore. I can't go with Nguyen, he's so moody, and he actually *scares* me. I don't understand any of this." I said, choking back tears.

"He isn't even speaking to me. We drove to the airport without exchanging a single word. I want to go home, and I don't want to go to Canberra anymore. He's emotionally draining, I'm so upset Sharni!" I blurted out in less than twenty seconds.

Sharni is my friend who can see situations differently and impartially to me and then shares her opinion in a diplomatic way. No profanities, only simple, pleasant terminology. If anyone could calm me down at times it was her. She was one of my nearest and dearest when it came to speaking the truth. In fact, sometimes the truth hurt, and I would abruptly hang up on her because she was simply too nice in the way she explained things.

"Emmie, just go," she said.

"He's a weirdo and I find it really difficult saying this to you, but once he gets a wine into him, he will be back to his normal social self. You *already* know this. You, girlfriend, have got yourself a Jekyll and Hyde."

My tears had stopped and were replaced with our chuckling. Sharni helped me put things into perspective. I quickly patted my face dry with squares of toilet paper, departed the ladies restroom, and made my way back to Nguyen.

Sharni had met Nguyen a few times when we were out and about together and had summed him up as, "Someone with deeply entrenched issues." I knew deep down that was Sharni's polite way of saying, "That's one fucked up dude."

"Hi beautiful, I ordered you a wine!" Nguyen said, as he put his arms around my waist and drew me closer into him, and kissed me on the cheek. At that very moment, I knew I was safe. The colour red had returned! Sharni was right.

Nguyen was on his second glass, the empty one sitting proudly on the bar.

CHAPTER 4

GROWING UP IN my household, you would undoubtedly find chillies, three gourmet varieties, fresh, gold, and plastic.

Fresh red chillies were used in my mother's cooking.

She would say, "A bit of heat will make you strong."

The gold chilli hanging off my father's gold chain, and the big red plastic one hanging from the rear vision mirror in his car. These red chilli peppers are known as Cornicello or Corno. However, this word had a double meaning. If someone crossed you, some would call them cornuto (another word for bastard) and most likely spit on the ground after they said it.

Red chillies are as important in an Italian household as the fridge magnets with pictures of Saints on them. They were all there for one purpose, protection, to ward off evil and envy. My parents believed envy was a deadly sin and we had to protect ourselves from it.

When my father argued with my mother, he would throw his hands up in the air and yell, "Santo Antonio, Jesu Christo, Mamma Mia!" That was code red and I would run for cover. When he calls for Saint Antonio to help save him, it was bad.

I could gauge the seriousness of their arguments on which saints they cursed and vented to. My parents' arguments consisted of calling Saint Antonio, Saint Giuseppe, Saint

Maria and occasionally if they didn't like what they saw they cursed to Saint Lucia the patron saint of sight.

"Each night before bed you pray to Jesu and you pray to a saint," they'd say to me.

Most conversations between my parents were civilised, however, there were times I thought my mother would unnecessarily push my father's buttons. She really held the balance of power in their relationship and whether my father knew this or not, it came down to one word. Trust. He trusted her. Although at times he would make silly accusations, it was his fears and insecurities, not hers.

Ida Sopracasa is very attractive, and it's her confidence that is the standout attraction. My mother is fearless. I learned at a very young age by observing her that confidence is sexy, and men find this irresistible. They believed anything she said.

"Emanuela, if someone hurts you at school, I come there, and I kill them! Then I spit on them!" she would say.

Needless to say, I would keep the bullying at school to myself and not share this with her. I didn't want my mother 'killing' anyone.

There was never an in-between at home when it came to problem-solving. It was always extreme. I didn't have to worry about this as my parents solved all my problems, as long as I was 'good'.

My father didn't handle suggestions from others well. In fact, he would argue with others if they didn't take his advice on board because he was always right.

"Compare, you don't know what you are talking about! My brother builds the best houses, not the company that the Siciliano on the other side of town has started. We use real bricks!" he'd say.

'Compare' is a term used by Italians if they are a godfather to a family member. My father knew a lot of comparo's so I guess I must have had a few godfathers when I was baptised.

Although my father didn't cook, he did have a big say when it came to which oil my mother used and that was olive oil. It was a sin to use anything else. Olive trees are a sacred symbol of peace, and it's a sin to cut one down. It's bearing fruit which produces the best oil, and Italians don't compromise when it comes to the best of anything.

"Ida, you better not buy vegetable oil, it's not real oil you know. I know it's the way now, and I don't care how much money you save, but you better buy olive oil, my stomach can't tolerate cheap!" he'd say.

He was right, neither of us could tolerate cheap if it wasn't simple and natural my stomach couldn't tolerate it either. My mother would buy tins of olive oil in bulk or sometimes my father would source it homemade. There was nothing quite like it, fresh pure olive oil and my father and I would sit at the table dipping chunks of warm continental bread into it and eating it. Father-daughter time well spent.

My father's favourite day of the year was Palm Sunday. He would go to church and then he would go to the cemetery to place olive tree branches by the tombs of loved ones. Each with a little holy cross made from palm leaves. It was the beginning of the Holy Week and as long as my mother cooked with olive oil it would be a peaceful, holy time for all.

Coffee was another ingredient not to compromise on quality. Freshly roasted, perfectly blended, and sourced only from the best continental deli. When we had visitors come over, the first thing my father would say was, "Ida make coffee!" It was good coffee, the aroma was intoxicating. It was served straight from 'la macchinetta', the Italian coffee percolator. Although served in the tiniest espresso cups, the conversations my parents would have with friends over coffee were at times as intense as the black, golden froth liquid they drank.

My parents were one of the first families amongst little Italy to install an air conditioner and a telephone. No more running across the road to use the public phone box or sweltering the great Australian heat indoors. My father decided to go for the recognition he so deserved and had the telephone installed the same week as the air-conditioning unit. We had visitors coming over for a whole month to look at our new devices so very advanced in technology.

My parents had purchased a fancy hallway table to showcase the telephone. It sat proudly on a white doily. It was strategically placed directly underneath the holographic picture of Jesus, maybe he was there to protect it, or to scare me from ever attempting to use it. It had a fancy Italian pen next to it and a pad of paper. I didn't understand why, who was going to take the messages? I wasn't allowed near the telephone. I wasn't allowed to use the pen either, it was 'too good' to use. I tried to take the pen once, but it was attached to a chain so I couldn't even try it out when my parents weren't looking.

I was always miffed at how my mother accessorised and showcased objects around our home. The lid on the toilet had a fluffy cover and matching floor mat. Even the spare toilet paper roll in the bathroom had a doll cover sitting on top of it. It was a pink and white coloured frilly polyester dress with a dolls head sticking out the top of it, yet I wasn't allowed toys? Each time I went into the bathroom, all I wanted to do was play with the pretty doll and ended up forgetting the real reason I was in there. *Why did I have to sit on the cold terrazzo floor to play with a doll? Why couldn't I play with dolls in my room?* I would think to myself. I wanted my own doll.

I was relieved we had a telephone and we no longer had to hike across the road to speak to my nonna in Italy, crammed in a public phone box. Each time my father called his mother, I was expected to go with him. With the time difference between Australia and Italy it was usually very late at night or first thing in the morning when we called her. I was always conscious of the surrounding homes around the phone box because my father spoke very loudly.

After stuffing what seemed to be a hundred coins in the big black box and dialling thirty odd digits, he would yell down the telephone.

"PRONTO, PRONTO, PRONTO QUESTA (this) È (is) AUSTRALIA!"

God, I hope the neighbours don't come out! I'd think to myself. I was expected to tell my nonna on the other side of the world how happy I was and how great my life was! She would ask me the same question each time in Italian.

"Do you play with kangaroos?" As if they're some domesticated pet over here. At the end of each conversation my father would finish off with "CIAO, CIAO, CIAO!"

Finally, we could yell down the phone line in our own home without an audience. No peeping eyes through white metal venetian blinds across the road anymore.

The air conditioner was placed in the most important room of the house, the kitchen. I never really understood why, because on hot summer nights I was still laying in my bed roasting and unable to sleep. I would have thought a central location in the home would have made more sense, but my mother insisted she felt the heat more than anybody else when she cooked in the 'good kitchen' so my father honoured her wish because what my mother wanted, she got.

I never really understood this because my mother rarely cooked in the good kitchen, she would cook in the second kitchen outside. As to not dirty the one inside, just in case we had visitors. I think she insisted the air conditioner was in the kitchen area so she could show it off to her friends.

Watching her cook would make me sweat, even on cold days. She would run from the outside kitchen inside each time she forgot to take something with her. I would watch her from the inside kitchen window, carrying large pots of pasta and opening the back door at the same time, without breaking into a sweat. If my mother caught me watching her, she would yell at me to go out and help her.

I would obligingly run to help her out, but really, I was the one who was annoyed. We had a brand-new kitchen inside, yet she chose to cook outside. Watching her run in and out preparing for special occasions was ground-breaking.

My mother was taught all about the evil eye as a child back in Italy. Malocchio. The superstition is passed down from generation to generation.

"Ma, I've got a headache." I'd say.

"Get the olive oil out and a plate with water!" she'd instruct me.

After a few special prayers under her breath and a little spell, she would dip her finger into a tiny shot glass of olive oil and let drops fall into the plate of water. If they expanded, you had the 'evil eye' and she would sprinkle salt into the plate to break the spell. The oil on the water disappears, and so would your headache.

"Some bastardo gave you malocchio, but I fixed them. I broke the spell with the salt!" she'd proudly say, pretending to spit on the ground.

She always did manage to break that spell! My headache would magically disappear, my mother the magician. I didn't care what she used, at the end of the day, she always had the ability to make me feel better and make my worries disappear. I'd rather her use a bowl of water and oil than actually have to kill someone to make them vanish that way.

CHAPTER 5

GOOD STUFF GROWS BETWEEN TOMATO PLANTS

Mᵧ COUSIN RENATA Sopracasa was a free-spirited hippie that lived with her mother and older sister. I really had trouble telling the difference between the two. Her sister was more like her mother and her mother was still grieving the loss of her husband who passed away ten years ago.

Renata's father was my fathers' younger brother, and he passed away when she was only seven years old. Zio Dino died in front of Renata of a massive heart attack. I don't think she has ever forgotten that day. She was only a little girl who witnessed her hero die in front of her.

Renata lived up the road from me and she was only one of the few cousins I could visit on my own without a chaperone. We all felt sorry for Renata because she was a little different, a little quirky, tried to be more Aussie than Italian. She tried to escape her heritage and culture through her choice of music and natural therapies.

It was Saturday afternoon, and I had just finished work at Signora Grazia's continental deli.

"Ma, I'm going to see Renata." I said hastily, heading for the back door before she could respond.

"Ask your father first! If you have an accident in his car driving, he will kill you!" she yelled back.

I tiptoed into the lounge room, praying my father was asleep on the sofa. Yes, out cold, fast asleep!

"Ciao ma, back soon." I said bolting for the back door.

Renata's house looked identical to mine. She lived in a modest three bedroom, neat, tidy, basket range brick Italian-style house. Her father had built both our homes. He was a builder and most of the homes in the area looked the same. He used the exact same style bricks for each one, whilst my father ran the business side of things. Their front garden had rosemary bushes, a large bay leaf tree that shielded rows of strawberries from the sun growing beneath, and a lemon tree by the driveway.

As soon as I walked up the driveway, I could smell the sugo (Italian sauce) cooking inside. This was a traditional type of sauce, not out of a store-bought bottle, this kind was special. It was made with love. We were all commissioned to help out on sauce day where my father would help his sister-in-law make her one hundred bottles worth.

"Ciao zia, is Renata home?" I asked my aunt.

My aunt was permanently dressed in black clothing from head to toe, black shoes, black stockings, and black cardigan, even on warm summer days. She was still in mourning. I felt awkward around her, never knowing what to say. Zia always looked slightly confused and would rarely reply when you tried speaking to her. Her eldest daughter Maria looked as old as her mother did. Maria was at the sink washing up dishes from lunch.

I didn't think Maria would ever get married, taking care of her mother and younger sister. God, I did not want to end up like her! Maria was so dedicated to taking care of her mother. I mean, zia wasn't even old! They both looked so ancient. Is this what grief and heartache does to people?

Rumour has it, Maria had her heart broken once. She had met a man who was in Australia visiting from Italy and they fell in love, were engaged, and soon to be married.

Apparently, he left her waiting at the altar. The story goes, he took off and went back home. I mean, she should have found an Aussie, not an import. Imports were always difficult and unpredictable. They would come here looking for love and cash. Life was different in Australia for those who immigrated. We had rules and traditions to follow. It's not like that in Italy anymore, they have evolved with the times. Upon discovering this, they all go back to their homeland. After that, Maria stopped working at Signora Grazia's deli and decided to be housebound, dutifully taking care of her mother and Renata.

Was this the life of Italian unmarried women, living in Australia? Oh God, I did not want to be an unmarried woman. I did not want to be wearing an apron, standing at the sink, washing dishes and cooking sauce.

"Hello, Maria." I said as I went up to kiss her on the cheek.

"Hi bella, Renata's in her room." She said.

I could hear the music coming from Renata's room as I walked up the passage. She was playing Whitesnake and I could hear their song *Here I Go Again*.

As I opened her door with the gigantic poster of a peace sign taped to it, I caught a whiff of something. What was that smell? I walked over to her and sat on the edge of her bed.

Renata was sitting in the corner of her room, multi-coloured velvet patchwork-covered cushions scattered on the floor. Her walls are covered with posters of Def Leppard and the all-girl band Heart. I was forbidden to use sticky tape or apply anything to my bedroom walls, but Renata was different. Her dad had died, therefore giving her exempt rights. It didn't matter if the paint peeled when she pulled off the tape, my father would come around and patch it up.

With a red cigarette lighter in her hand, she was sucking from something that looked similar to a cor anglais. However, this one was made out of glass and was filled with a yellow liquid. Renata wouldn't know what a cor anglais was. She would not know that it's a woodwind instrument and it is similar to an oboe. Renata dropped out of school in year ten and worked at Signora Grazia's deli with me. I worked at the deli each Saturday morning and Thursday afternoons after school.

Renata hated school and would go to pick fights with other kids. The teachers politely *encouraged* her to leave.

Unlike Renata, I was still in school, an all-girls private school. I was not allowed friends visiting let alone friends in my room. It would come as too much of an inconvenience to my parents. My mother would have to re-clean the house if guests were coming over. I was only ever allowed to visit my cousins occasionally, when my father fell asleep on the sofa after lunchtime on a Saturday.

"Renata, I want to talk to you. There's a community meeting coming up soon at the town hall, and our local Member of Parliament will be there. I thought we could go together so I can speak to him. I have an issue I'd like to raise with him. There isn't any lighting around the bank by the laneway, and our mothers and lots of elderly people use that bank. It's really unsafe. It needs proper lighting it's a safety issue especially in winter when it gets dark early." I said, not getting any response as she stared at me with a blank look.

"I want my life to be different. I want to date guys. In fact, I want to date lots of guys, not have to marry the first one I meet." I went on to say.

"I want opportunities. I want an opportunity to live with a guy before marriage. Wouldn't that be the best, getting to know someone really well before signing on the dotted line, and having the choice to walk away if things don't work out, in a civilised manner. What do you think Ren?" I asked.

"Emmie, get your head out of those stupid books! Stop watching Sophia Loren movies, your life isn't one big fantasy," she said in-between long drawn out puffs.

"Get out of your fucking ivory tower. Keep things real," she said.

"Why do you care so much about making things better? Who cares about safety issues around some old bank, our mothers know how to take care of themselves. If someone approached your mum and tried to rob her, she'd probably ask them what part of their skull they'd want to keep, before she bashed them with her designer handbag. I swear, she carries bricks in her bag!"

I began to laugh, she probably would.

"Seriously Emmie, you care too much about things. I don't understand why you are the way you are, but you're always wanting to change things or help others. Let someone else do it, isn't that why we pay taxes. As for your fantasies about men, grow the fuck up, because they love you and leave you, got it!" she said with conviction.

"No one cares about helping others nowadays, it's all too hard for someone like us, don't go causing trouble."

I slid off the bed and plonked myself down on a soft purple velvet op shop cushion. I was starting to feel a little dizzy. I was not like Renata, she was different. She wore black eyeliner that made her sad big green eyes look creepy.

She always had frizzed untamed hair. I don't think she ever brushed it. She would occasionally wear it up, and her face was always pasty white. Her wardrobe consisted of t-shirts with rock band names on them and black jeans.

She was trying to escape her life, while I was trying to find mine. I was different. I was gracious and respectful, as my parents had raised me. I wore nice clothes, and I did not look messy like her. I took pride in my appearance, just like my mother taught me.

My idol was Sophia Loren. Renata's was Axl Rose from Guns N' Roses.

"Renata, I want to leave home when I turn eighteen. I want to find my own way in life. I want to make a difference to this world we live in. I want to help women discover who they are. They shouldn't have to settle for second best. I can't help the way I am, but that's what I want to do." I said, looking for support and some sort of encouragement.

"The only way you'll ever leave home is if you get married, otherwise it'll be in a wooden sealed box," she said, shutting me down.

Renata was right. I had to get married before I could leave home, or my father would kill me. What was my life to become, and what the fuck was Renata smoking?

Renata shoved the glass looking cor anglais towards me and lit it from underneath. She had filled it with an Italian yellow herbal liqueur. I saw the bottle sitting by her bedside table next to her black-haired troll doll, which she relied on for good luck.

"Here, have a puff of this, its Italian marijuana," she said.

With that, I sucked hard. Within minutes, it hit me, and I rolled back on my side in fits of laughter. I could not stop laughing, this stuff Renata gave me was good.

When I arrived back home, I went straight to my room. I locked myself away in my own little quiet space, segregated from the drama that waited on the other side of my bedroom door. It was different from Renata's room. My bedroom was spotlessly clean. I had my desk in one corner with a laminated mat of the world map sitting on top of it. I had a bookshelf filled with books. I had a box hidden under my bed filled with more books. I had a spotted pink and green pot plant sitting by the window seal, a little pink Pixie. In another corner of the room was the object that I feared most, this distressing item known as a 'glory box'. It is the ugliest looking box I had ever laid eyes on. I dreaded my glory box. I was too scared to even open it, thinking the angel of death would jump out and take me. It holds every kitchen utensil, every Italian white hand embroiled sheet set, every handmade multicoloured crocheted doily, every floral towel set and every possible conceivable, impressive, collection of crap stamped with 'made in Italy' my mother had stuffed in there from the day I was born.

My future sat in this one ugly brown box. It was safely fastened with three large elaborate brass latches, and locked with a key. Why was this ugly box in my room? I am convinced my mother had put it there to serve as a reminder of her expectations of me, marriage.

Maybe Renata was right, maybe if I attempted to escape the life my parents had mapped out for me and I were caught, my father would bury me in this box! It was the closest thing I had ever seen resembling a coffin, the heaviest wooden box ever to be made.

I had to forget about my dreams. Renata slapped those ideas right out of my head. My glory box was a constant reminder to me that I had a *predetermined* future. *I'm sorry to all my worldwide sisterhood I can't help any of you. I must help myself first*, I thought. *I can't fight for you I have to fight for my freedom now.*

I looked at my books and saw *Little Women* sitting proudly on the shelf, but I pulled out my favourite book, *The Diary of Anne Frank*. She too was a prisoner trapped in a little room, wanting to change the world, and learned at a very young age all about uncertainty and fear. The only difference was, she was loved, and she wasn't an inconvenience to her parents. She also had met strength and resilience at a very young age.

I felt a lump in my throat, perfectly positioned to stop me from sobbing. If my father heard me crying, he would probably threaten to hit me. Stupid Renata and her laughing juice, it had worn away, just like my enthusiasm and dreams.

CHAPTER 6

FORGIVE ME MARY FOR MY SINS

I LOVED HIGH school. I felt so accepted. Most of the girls there aspired to be hairdressers, but I was one of the few who wanted to go to university. They were more into their appearances while I was more into my books and filling my void with knowledge.

Most of us were from Italian backgrounds. We had Italian as a subject choice at school. We embraced our culture and we were proud to share our stories. We understood them well. We would joke and laugh about our traditions, our parents, and family. We all had the same thing in common, we loved Italian food. We all came in different shapes and sizes. Mainly large.

I was popular at school and I didn't have to hide in the library as I did in primary school. I still visited my favourite room each morning before class so I could read the daily newspaper. I liked to keep myself informed with what was going on in the world. It's important, knowledge is power.

The school library had motivational posters pinned on the walls, my favourite spoke of compromise, "You are all that you have."

I understood this one and didn't think it was as convoluted as some of the others. This one was reflective of my belief that I entered this world alone, and I would exit it alone, and thus solely responsible to take care of the 'in-between'. My 'in-between' was arming myself with knowledge and not limiting that knowledge to what people told me or expected me to believe.

Mr Shaw, the librarian, was most impressed with me wanting to read a newspaper, and would have it waiting ready to hand it to me as soon as I walked through the sliding doors.

"Good morning Mr Shaw."

"Good morning Emanuela, here we go, hot off the press," he'd say waiting to hand me the morning edition.

One morning I was sitting, quietly reading when my friend Silvia Rossi came up to me completely stressing out. Her long woollen tartan skirt was half around her waist, not sitting quite right. Her heavy school bag around her shoulders had swung it out of alignment. The school principal, Sister Josephine would not be impressed if she saw Silvia's skirt.

"Emmie, Emmie, can you please read my English assignment, please Em! I'll buy you a cream cheese and Vegemite roll at recess! Please Em! Mr Milne is going to kill me I have to hand this in today." Silvia said, her stress causing little beads of sweat on her forehead to shine.

"Sure, Silvia I'd be happy to, hand it over." I said.

My trade-off for proof-reading assignments and helping the other girls with homework was getting my hair braided or snacks from the canteen. I mostly preferred getting my hair done. Some of the girls were very talented and creative when it came to hairstyles. My contribution to creative hairstyles consisted of handing them over an elastic hair tie.

The only thing I seemed to be artistically creative at was in the field of forgery. I could copy any signature out there. Regardless of penmanship, or different hand writing styles, I was a master at it. I was forging signatures on notes for girls who wanted to leave school early. Supposedly for doctor's appointments, so they could meet a boy at bus stop eleven and have an early kiss before the others arrived.

I was forging notes for girls who didn't want to go swimming because they had their periods. Once a year we attended the school aquatics day. The sports teacher Mr Peters, would roll his eyes at the abundance of notes handed to him by the students. He knew quite well that we all couldn't possibly share the same menstrual cycles at the same time. He struggled to find girls to compete in the swimming events. This would allow them time to socialise with the boys from the single-sex school up the road instead, who were attending for the same purpose. We would sit in the grandstands at the sports arena, laughing and mixing with the boys and trying not to get caught.

Some of the girls wore eyeliner and mascara. It made their eyes look so pretty. I wanted to feel beautiful too. I also wanted to wear makeup. I would have to ask Renata for some next time I saw her. She had plenty.

I was an A grade student in most of my subjects, English, geography, history and drama. I loved reading, it would take my imagination to great places to escape. I also loved geography as this subject taught me about Australia, my birthplace. I'd have to learn about different regions of Australia if I was ever going to escape from home.

I understood history well. I wished I could go back in time and rewrite my life, where I did not feel like I had to fight for freedom and I grew up in a house that had its own museum and art gallery. Drama, what can I say, it came naturally.

Sister Josephine adored me. Only on one occasion she totally lost it at me and most likely went back to her office to pray to God to save my soul. I saw her walking across the school oval one morning as I was walking to class. Big mistake, we had made eye contact. She yelled at me from across the school oval.

"Emanuela Sopracasa!" she said in her stern tone as she picked up her pace heading in my direction.

I ignored her and looked down, pretending not to hear her and kept walking.

"EMANUELA SOPRACASA!" she was now yelling as she was running towards me with the beige veil on her head waving behind her in the wind. She had caught up.

"Pull your skirt down, tuck your shirt in, wipe that disgusting black colour away from your eyes and get to class immediately young lady! So *unlike* you, Emmie!" she said with genuine disappointment in her voice.

"I expect better than this from you. You, out of all people should know better. You have an example to set to the other girls here, you are head prefect of your year!"

"Sorry, Sister Josephine," I said, standing in front of her rubbing my eye.

Sister Josephine walked off and I heard her mumble, "Deus propitius esto" under her breath. 'God forgive', in Latin.

I was trying to reinvent myself. My heavy woollen skirt felt like it nearly hit the ground, so I would roll it up. My shirt was too big for me, and my tie constantly needed readjusting. I wanted to feel good about myself. I lacked the confidence in my appearance that the other girls showed. Sister Josephine ignored others who wore eyeliner, so why was she criticising me?

My eyes were watering and sore, I could not stop rubbing them. Stupid Renata probably gave me a contaminated eyeliner. I was probably going to get conjunctivitis. With black smudges on my white shirt and face, I made my way to the bathroom.

I liked spending lunchtimes on the lush green oval reading. The lawn beneath me always felt so soft. My school was so pretty. Statues of Mother Mary strategically placed around the campus to offer peace and comfort to her students. Some had her holding baby Jesus, but the best one of all was her standing alone with her arms outstretched, like an independent woman of the world offering eternal freedom to all. I liked praying to Mary, she understood me.

I could hear different conversations the girls were having who were sitting nearby eating their lunch. They were laughing and discussing the boys that they would see each morning and afternoon at the bus stops. I wish I could catch the bus. I was not allowed to. My father drove me to school, each and every day. I hated it. I want to have fun with my friends at the bus stop too. I wanted to meet the boys. I hadn't kissed a boy yet, let alone met any.

Notes were being sent home soon for school camp and I really wanted to go. I wanted the opportunity to stay up late and talk with my friends. I wanted to join in the group activities the teachers had planned, giving me the opportunity to be adventurous for once. I wanted some time away from home. I wanted to experience freedom for a few days. The thought of this excited me. No expectations, only fun.

In the past when the girls went on overnight retreats, Sister Josephine would let me do my schoolwork in her office during the day, so I didn't have to sit in the library alone. I liked Sister Josephine, she had very kind blue eyes, and she was always looking out for me. She had fair skin and I wondered at times what colour hair she had under her veil tightly bobby-pinned to her head. I think she summed up my father quickly at the entrance interview I had during the enrolment process. She would often ask me how life was at home.

"Good," I'd say, I mean what was it meant to be like? My parents fed me and they offered me safety and security. I had my room where I would spend most of my time in. I really didn't know any different, other than not having much of a social life, and not being allowed to have a boyfriend. I guess it wasn't all that bad.

She would come and talk to me at lunchtimes out on the school oval and give me mint flavoured lollies she carried around in her pocket. I think she felt sorry for me, or maybe she could smell the occasional cigarette on my breath? I wasn't sure, but I welcomed her lollies and her kindness. We'd have conversations where she'd tell me I had potential, and I wasn't like the other students at the school. She'd say I was smart, articulate, and my high standard of schoolwork made her very proud. She said I was a good role model for others. She spoke Italian quite well for an Aussie nun. She's had conversations with my father in the past about my education and how I should be planning for university after high school, but my father didn't see a need for that. My parents had different expectations. Italian girls were taught to cook, clean and raise a family, not to be career orientated.

My father didn't want me learning about economics and world politics. He wanted me to learn *home* economics where I was taught how to sew and cook. I wasn't good at sewing. I failed that part of the subject. I think super gluing the hem to my skirt instead of using an actual sewing machine must have done it. I didn't know how to thread the bobbin to the machine, so I took my skirt assignment home and used super glue instead. When the teacher asked me to iron my skirt in class for the final presentation, the hot iron stuck to the glued fabric and it was an instant fail. She said I had the potential for "problem-solving" skills, but not in her sewing class.

The day had arrived and I summed up the courage to ask my father if I could go to school camp. It was time to leave for school. My father and I rarely spoke in the car, and I always felt like an inconvenience when he was driving me.

"Papa, school camp is coming up. It's two nights away, it's in the hills in an old seminary, and all the teachers will be there. I really want to go." I said with a tone of desperation in my voice.

I mean why would he say *no*, right? I was at an *all-girls* school.

I sensed the tension in the air immediately. I began to feel like this was a bad idea, going straight to the head of the dining table. I should have veered via my mother first. What was I thinking?

"No!" he said, direct and straight to the point.

"Perché?" (Why?) I asked in Italian.

Oh no. I should have kept my mouth shut and resorted to plan B, my mother. She held the balance of power. It was too late now! I'd broken the cardinal rule, don't ask your father why! His answer was final.

"Emanuela, I say NO and I mean NO. You are at school to learn, not to play," he said in broken English.

What the hell! Play? Who the fuck *plays* at school, I was seventeen years old for God sakes? I smoked behind the sports shed at lunchtime with some of the girls. I had my driver's license and I was still driven by my father to school. I hated him!

I no longer cared. I never asked him for anything and all I wanted to do is go to school camp. It was only two nights away from home. I hated being so accommodating to my parents. I never caused them grief. I never rocked the boat as Renata did and she got what she wanted. She grew dope in her mother's vegetable garden amongst the tomatoes.

All the other girls at school go to the Italian club disco on Sunday nights to socialise and have fun. Their parents picked them up and dropped them off, they didn't seem to be an inconvenience to them. But not me, I was sitting in my room reading. They were allowed to catch the bus to school. They were allowed to go to the local church feasts. I went once, with my mother, how embarrassing. I was so angry. I hated my books. I hated my family, I hated being good all the time. I hated rules, but most of all I hated me. I wished I was dead! *Lord of the Flies* was going to be my number one favourite book from now on because my life sucked!

We arrived at the front gate. Mother Mary stood there with her arms outstretched like she was waiting for me. I felt like her eyes were looking down at me. I got out of the car and I got my bag out of the boot. I straightened my tartan skirt, fixed my tie, and I looked up at Mother Mary, trying not to blink. I could feel my tears starting to rise. I stared directly at her and thought *I hate you too.*

I walked to class with the biggest lump in my throat to stop me from crying, because I knew if I began, I would not be able to stop. I hated myself for thinking I hated Mother Mary when I didn't. I didn't want Sister Josephine seeing me upset and asking me if I was okay. Deep down she already knew. She would let me sit in her office with her while all my friends were on school camp and that sucked too.

CHAPTER 7

ONE DOOR CLOSES ANOTHER OPENS

THERE WAS A funeral across the road from the deli at St Patricks Catholic Church. Signora Grazia was buzzing around the front cleaning the windows, wiping them down with scrunched up newspapers and methylated spirits. She was 70 years old but running around like a 40-year-old wondering who it was that had passed away. She said it would have to be someone 'rich' to be buried on a Saturday. Apparently, it costs more.

I was saucing the lasagnas, getting them ready to put out in the fridge. Where was Renata? I hated doing this on my own, red sauce splattering all over me.

"RENATA," I yelled out with no response.

I hoped my cousin Rosie was coming in today. She is very similar to me, extremely smart. Or was I? Rosie has similar hair to mine, long and wavy, and big brown eyes. She dresses conservatively, unlike Renata. Rosie's mother is my mother's younger sister. Perhaps our intelligence came from our mother's bloodline.

Rosie Santino was at university. She was one of the lucky ones. Her parents supported her on-going education. She was studying science in the field of genetic research. We'd often have discussions around genetics and how our ancestry was complex. How your genes are passed down from generation to generation, but we can choose at any point to say, "I am not my genes." Some say that this is not possible, but like Rosie said, "We don't have to behave like our parents."

I agreed with Rosie, we would have philosophical discussions around the environmental factors that influence behaviours. We were all born with different characteristics and genetic profiles. Our genes play a role in determining behaviour. However, little did I know that in the future my resilience would have an end date, like the boxes of food in the deli. I saw my dominance as task orientated, and not bossing people around, as my father did to me. But perhaps I had empathy and compassion for others like him. Maybe my father wasn't taught how to value himself as a child. Maybe I was more like him that I cared to consider.

I love Rosie, she is very independent and down to earth for an Italian female. She was allowed to attend a unisex school because her parents lived directly across the street from one. Her mother would sit in the front lounge room of their home and watch Rosie in class in-between her soapies on the television.

She was supposed to be coming in with Dave today. Dave Smith was Aussie number two at Rosie's high school. I felt sorry for Dave, he always looked hungry, and his father passed away when he was young. Maybe I should set him up with Renata?

"Hey, Emmie!" Rosie said as she walked through the front door brushing away the plastic coloured fly strips from her face.

"THANK GOD Rosie, I am dying here!" I said excitedly while I noticed Dave standing behind her.

"Hello, Dave." I said sounding annoyed.

He was standing there shyly in blue jeans, a brown checked shirt, and white sneakers. His blue eyes had the same look Renata's did. His brown hair short and tidy, he looked like he'd stepped out of the barbershop. Rosie stepped over the boxes of tuna in olive oil and walked over to exchange pleasantries with Signora Grazia.

"Would you like me to make you a panini roll, Dave?" I asked.

"Yes please, Emmie," he said in a polite, quiet voice.

"What would you like in it?" I asked.

"Can I please have chicken, lettuce, and mayonnaise?" he had the nerve to ask.

I was getting annoyed now, was this guy serious? First, he is super polite and far too quiet, his voice barely audible. Now on the rare occasion he speaks to me, he wants what? Mayonnaise? What the fuck is mayonnaise?

"Um Dave, we don't have mayonnaise here, we have chargrilled eggplant in oil, sundried tomatoes in oil, chargrilled capsicum in oil, olives and anchovies in oil. I will make you a panini with mortadella and provolone cheese okay?" I said with attitude and tone.

"Thank you, Emmie. I am sure I will love whatever you make me," he said grinning.

I swear he tries to push my buttons, I thought while preparing his bread roll.

Dave was *so* annoying. The only time Italians ate lettuce was when it is served finely shredded in a prawn cocktail at weddings or with their meat in the red sauce at dinner as a side dish. And mayonnaise, really? Where the fuck was Renata? This is her type of guy! She likes working with blank canvases.

"Emmie," Rosie calls out as she is headed for the front door. "I'm coming over to your place later I want to talk to you, Ciao." And with that, they both left. Dave, panini in hand wrapped in a white paper napkin and Rosie with her hand up in the air to signal a goodbye. I had people waiting to be served, coming into the deli from the funeral across the road and the tiny shop began to fill up quickly.

I was turning eighteen next month. Maybe Rosie was coming over to talk about what type of cake her mum was going to bake me, for my birthday party. My aunt was the best cook, and desserts were her specialty. I never had a birthday party before. This was no ordinary party like other eighteen-year old's have, this one would consist of old people socialising in the 'second kitchen' outside. There would be me with my only two cousins. One no doubt, would be smoking pot behind the garage while Rosie and I would be drinking bourbon on the front lawn, out of prying eyes.

No party balloons or school friends at this gathering. It would be simple with masses of Italian food and homemade wine. The conversations were centred on when I was going to find a boyfriend, now I had turned eighteen. Perhaps one would fall out of the sky and land on my lap. I could hear the conversations playing out in my head already.

"You can't bring home a Greek boy, they eat lamb, and they're not Catholic! You will be buried in a different part of the cemetery from him when you die!" My father no doubt would say. I wondered if my father knew it was the Greeks who settled in Naples. He seemed to ignore this historical fact.

When I arrived home from work, I went to my room to change and it wasn't long after Rosie arrived.

"Hello, zia." I heard Rosie say.

"ROSIE!" I heard my mother say.

"Emmie, vieni Rosie è qui." She yelled out for me to come into the kitchen because Rosie had arrived.

"Hey, want to go out the front?" I asked Rosie.

I had a cigarette tucked in my shirt pocket which I took from my father's packet when he wasn't around. We began smoking at a young age, I guess it was our way of rebelling, sneaking around to have one when the opportunity allowed. Maybe that's why we were both short, smoking had stunted our growth, just like our cultural expectations.

We went to the front garden of my house out of my mother's sight. Standing under the fig tree protectively covered with white bird netting.

"Emmie, I have something to tell you," she hesitated. "Dave likes you." She said, as I was attempting to light up my cigarette.

"Seriously, Rosie," I said, as I took my first drag, annoyed at the mere suggestion of this.

"Emmie give him a go. Your father leaves for Italy again soon, this is your chance. We can work around your mother, and he's a decent guy!"

"Emmie, I won't be around for much longer. I graduate next month from university and I've accepted a job in Melbourne." Rosie said with reservation. I knew that very moment she hadn't told her parents. God help us all.

"Don't pass up on this opportunity, go out with him, go see a movie, go out on a date," she said taking a drag on the cigarette.

My thought bubble went into overdrive. I would no longer have anyone to talk to, and I was losing my cousin, more like my sister, my best friend! I'd only be left with Renata. This was all too much for me to take in, the cigarette started to make me feel dizzy. Dave? Oh God. Dave was older than me. He had five brothers, he dressed like a nerd, and he was an Aussie boy. There was something odd about Dave and I could not put my finger on it. It was his eyes, they looked sad. But, *should* I consider Dave? I am about to turn eighteen and I am about to graduate from high school. *Did I intentionally push opportunities away because I am fearful of disappointment?* I thought. Dave *is* an opportunity. Maybe I shouldn't be pushing him away. I would have to think about this one.

I woke up one morning hearing my dad going completely troppo. What was it now? Why couldn't I have one decent sleep in? I had only finished exams the day before and it was the last week of school next week. It was a Saturday morning for goodness sakes.

My father came storming through the front door. Wait, the front door? Hang on, this must be serious! The front door was never used unless you were getting married or dead. I saw him holding a bunch of flowers, an enormous bunch in fact. He was accusing my mother of having an affair because these flowers had been delivered to Ms Sopracasa. My father had been watering the garden out the front when the delivery man pulled up in a van and handed them to him.

Was my mother having an affair? Who could blame her if she was. My father stormed past me in the hallway as I was standing in my bedroom doorway.

I followed behind him into the kitchen where my mother was standing at the sink filling the coffee percolator. He was shouting at her as he put the flowers down on the table, demanding she tell him who had sent her the flowers. She looked totally surprised, clueless at what all the commotion was about. No one sent flowers to our home.

"You're stupido, maybe they are for you and not me," she bit back.

Here we go, I was thinking, as their voices continued to escalate.

There was a little white card poking out the top of the perfectly, and beautifully, arranged posy. Pink and white roses sprayed with white baby's breath and a bright pink satin bow tied around the clear cellophane paper holding this delicate arrangement perfectly in place.

I grabbed the card out and opened it, hoping to shed some light so they would both shut up.

It read, "Emmie will you have dinner with me? I promise not to order anything with mayonnaise. Dave."

I stupidly had read the note out loud. As soon as I finished reading the room went deadly silent and my father turned, he stood and stared at me. His traditional death stare, an instant dose of fear. I was fucked.

CHAPTER 8

EXPECTATIONS VERSUS PERCEPTIONS

DAVE SMITH LOVED pasta. He loved it so much he takes his time eating it. It was frustrating to watch at times. As I was about to delve into dessert, he was still on his mains.

I can't eat any slower, I thought to myself. *God, I wish he would chew a little faster!*

Italians ate very quickly. We ate on the run, no sooner was the food on the plate, the plates were in the sink ready to wash and put away.

I guess he was raised to appreciate and savour things, mostly because his mother couldn't afford much. He grew up in a strong Catholic household with five brothers and a single parent. His mother was extremely hard working and she always put her boys before herself. She spent most of her time cleaning the local doctor's surgery and stacking shelves at night at the supermarket across town. She would do household chores and cook for the boys in-between her jobs each day.

Dave went to the same high school as Rosie. Dave is four years older than me. I liked Dave, apart from his nerdy clothing and outdated style, but otherwise he seemed okay.

Dave grew up not too far from where I lived, in a little house on a big block of land. Maybe his mother needed the outdoor space for the boys to run around as children. The lawns were kept neat, she was house proud. I would see her mow them. I remember always seeing the clothesline spinning around in the breeze, loaded with washing. I used to walk past Dave's house some Sundays on my way to church. I assumed Dave's mother didn't have much time on her hands for herself. She was too busy trying to make ends meet.

My mother was ecstatic I was dating Dave. I guess this was all a part of her big plan. She could finally empty my room out, throw me out with my horrendous glory box, and palm me off to someone else so she could give up cleaning at the local hospital.

You see, my mother was working five days a week so she could save for my wedding. It had to be *the* wedding with all the frills and spills. Amongst the Italian communities, it was all about image and who held *the* best wedding of the year. There were standards that had to be maintained and upheld, expectations were sky high. At times, I honestly believed she did not care who I married as long as she got me out of her home and could convince my father in the process in doing so. Then other times she had standards as to who would make a better suitor.

"Emmie, I really like you, I think you're different than all the other Italian girls I knew at school," Dave said whilst wiping away the pasta sauce from the corner of his mouth.

"Different? How so?" I asked.

"You're very pretty and you have lovely, exotic eyes." He said in a polite voice.

"Gee, thanks, Dave. So, it's just my looks you're attracted to, were the other girls at your school ugly?" I asked.

"NO! It's not *just* your looks. It's your fiery temper and attitude, it's a sign of how passionate you are. You're an intelligent, kind-hearted person, and although you have strict parents and a sheltered upbringing, you still manage to find ways to express yourself. Most of all, you're not afraid to speak your mind, and that takes guts in today's society. I like how your green eyes turn a shade brighter when you're angry, especially when I come into the deli and ask for mayo." He finished off, and we both laughed.

Well, Mother Mary! I think Dave might be on his way to winning me over. I was surprised Dave saw me in this way. I wasn't like the other girls? I wasn't at university, and I worked in a deli helping little old Italians navigate their way around the aisles of pasta and arborio rice. I read books and occupied my time with cooking and trying new recipes, how was that attractive? I had found other ways to fill the voids in my life. I wasn't allowed to party like other girls, I felt like I was sitting idle for the time being until I found my purpose in life.

My father was due back home from Italy in six months. Time was ticking.

Dave worked as an accountant. He liked his job and he was very good with numbers and figures. I had only recently finished school. I was planning on going to university, but I had not decided on any course as yet. It was a toss-up between journalism and law. I still had a little time to choose and I was researching my options.

"Emmie," my mother called out one afternoon after I had arrived home from work. She never calls me by my shortened name. She had called me into the kitchen.

"When's Dave going to ask you to marry him?" she asked in broken English. She was sitting at the dining table as judge, jury and executioner, folding the washing.

Here we go, I thought to myself. I had only been dating the guy for a few months.

"I don't know, I think I might go to university. I don't know if I want to get married at my age," I said as I sat down opposite her, looking for words of encouragement. This was my future she had planned, not hers. I wanted her support and encouragement, not her absent-mindedness when it came to my goals and dreams.

"Emmie," she began to say in her sarcastic tone.

"If you want to leave his house, you will need to get married. No university, no travel, no fun. If you want those things you can do all of that and *more* with your husband." She said as she was tapping her finger on the table.

I looked at her, perhaps with my father's innate death stare. I stood up, turned away, left out the back door, and walked to Renata's house.

I had to eventually explain to Dave that my family had expectations, especially now that he was coming over and having dinner most nights with my mother and I. She was tricking him. She was slowly sucking him in like a tarantula luring its prey into its sticky web.

I would watch her each time she refilled his plate, I could see her mind ticking, "A way to a man's heart is through his stomach."

"Mangia (eat) Dave," she'd say sticking golden crumbed cotoletta (veal schnitzel) on his plate made especially for him. She would even make his gravy and that was as uncommon as mayonnaise!

You see, I had failed to explain to Dave, once he set foot into my parents' home that was it. The deal had been signed, sealed, and delivered.

I liked Dave he was funny, quirky, smart, and confident in a weird kind of way. Perhaps, I even loved Dave. My heart was starting to grow. I began to think of our future together, and what that might look like. I could see us living in a little house somewhere local, maybe a baby or two in the next few years, who knew?

Dave came over most evenings. We would sit together and watch television. We would sneak in a kiss when my mother left the room.

One night was special and took he me completely by surprise. Dave and I had been dating for four months and it was our anniversary.

"Emmie," he said when my mother left the room.

"I have something for you." He pulled out a small package from his coat pocket. I wondered why he hadn't removed his coat when he walked in.

Dave handed me a small flat book it was called, *Everything Men Think They Know About Women*. I opened the book and it was filled with blank pages. I looked at him with an annoyed frown. Dave leaned over and turned a few more pages and there it was. He had written in blue ink.

"Emanuela Sopracasa, I love you so much with all my heart, will you help me fill these blank pages in this book and teach me how to be a better person for you. Emmie, will you marry me?"

"YES!" I said.

My mother came running in like she had a secret spy camera in the lounge room and knew he had popped the question. We were all hugging. I didn't have to teach Dave to be a better person, he was already the best.

Word spread very quickly, from one side of the world to the other. My father had found out the very next evening, by someone living in Australia, who had told someone else who lives in Italy, who eventually rang someone they knew in the local village where my father was staying.

I heard my mother on the phone to him, excitingly informing him a suitor had been found and I was getting married. They were planning my wedding already. The timeline had been set. We were getting engaged in November and married the following September.

Less than fifteen months from meeting one another. I was so happy, I loved Dave. He was my best friend and he accepted me for who I was. He didn't care that my parents were loud and screamed when they had simple conversations. He accepted all of us as we were.

The impending wedding was the talk of the town amongst little Italy. Visitors would come by to meet this stranger by the name of Dave Smith, the Aussie man I was to marry. My mother spent her days frantically cleaning and waiting on curious visitors who popped in. I would spend my weekends washing and drying espresso cups. No sooner would they empty, more people walked through the door and I would have to offer a refill. My mother would tell her friends all about *the* wedding. What the flowers would look like, the cake, the cars, and the menu.

I didn't have much of a say in the planning or how I envisaged my wedding to look like. Other than the colour of my bridesmaid dresses that was more or less it. I really didn't care. I had to pick my battles, and this was not one of them. I was finally going to be a Smith and my life was going to be so much different now. Who cared about some over the top Italian wedding? Once I signed on the dotted line, my life would be free of expectations and I would embrace my independence like a born-again Evangelist. No more 'F' for fear and finally 'F' for FREE! I could finally come and go as I pleased. I did not have to plan and plot anymore to ask a simple request that would always lead me to disappointment.

I was going to raise my future children by not guilting them into doing things. I was not going to have the same expectations from them my parents had of me. They would not have a predetermined future and have anything to fear from life, but to embrace it instead. They would be born free.

They would be our little mixed bags of Italian sugar-coated almonds and Australian liquorice allsorts. The Smith family were going to be a little team and more importantly 'F' for Family! Always there for one another and no one, was going to tell me how to raise my babies.

CHAPTER 9

VULNERABILITY, WHAT WAS this? I was a successful, mature woman. I was hardworking, I gave back to the community, fighting for the rights of others and social injustices. Nguyen had the same work ethics that I did. We were both very committed to things we felt strongly about. I had spent years assisting women to progress in their lives. I met women from domestic violence situations, with mental health issues and some who faced homelessness. Listening to their stories gave me a better understanding of what each one faced and what their requirements were, to assist them in changing their poor circumstances. I would research options and connect them with the right agencies to bring forward transformation. We would develop plans together that would enable them to successfully transition on to better things.

I really appreciated sharing these stories with Nguyen. He *seemed* to have a very good understanding of these sorts of situations. Nguyen was an extremely generous man, if he could fund the build of a home to offer shelter to the under-privileged, he probably would. Then most likely posting it on social media for the likes.

Nguyen had asked me to move in with him. We had been living together for eight weeks. Nguyen was an outstanding cook. He would have dinner prepared most nights.

I was halfway through my meal. He had prepared the most perfectly seared salmon with sautéed asparagus and homemade hollandaise sauce.

"Hey beautiful, I have something for you," Nguyen said over dinner.

He got up from the dining table and walked to our room. He returned with a little white box. He handed it to me, proudly standing there waiting for me to open it. Staring into my eyes, I opened it eagerly. I lifted the top lid, and looked up at him. He had beautifully dark intense eyes.

When I looked down at my gift, I saw the most striking pair of earrings sparkling like magical stones, the television light behind me bouncing off of them. Diamond encrusted emerald earrings. The finest little diamonds surrounding these beautiful green stones. I felt like I had stopped breathing for a moment, his generosity leaving me in awe. He would put so much thought into buying gifts for me.

"I had to buy you these, they match your eyes. You have the most beautiful, seductive, captivating green eyes I have ever seen on a woman, you have so much class and sophistication." He said, as he sat back down to finish his meal.

Why did I feel guilty he was spending so much money on me? He was always buying me things. He is an impulsive spender. I could not possibly match this type of gift giving. Most of my work involved unpaid time, volunteering at women's shelters and running campaigns to introduce change to policies that affect the underprivileged. What was my guilt here to teach me I wondered?

I began to share my day with him over dinner.

"I had a woman come into the office today. She was mentally challenged. She had been homeless in the past. I had difficulty explaining to her the correct process for rental assistance. She became agitated very quickly. I had to ask her to leave, I felt really bad for her," I said.

"She scared me. I had to make a few calls, asking others for their advice. They suggested I meet with her at a café somewhere, in a public place. I hadn't thought about this before. I'm worried because her current lease runs out in ten days. I want to help her keep off the streets." I said.

"It's your approach," Nguyen said.

"You come across as too controlling. You want to control situations that have not even occurred yet," he said sharply, taking a sip of his wine.

What? I was confused, I was too controlling. Me? Here sat a man opposite me who had given me an incredible gift, who proclaimed to love me and wanted to support me. Yet in one swift move, struck his samurai sword and cut me off at the knees. I could see my little emerald earrings sparkling in the open box by my plate, so natural and untarnished.

"I guess you're right Nguyen, I didn't look at it in that way. I guess she isn't homeless *yet*." I said sombrely.

I went back to finishing my dinner, although I had now lost my appetite. I wished I could share my day and thoughts with him without it becoming about *me* and my flaws. Why couldn't he see the positive in me instead of looking for the negative? I was trying my best.

I thought of Dave. He would have encouraged me to help her and find suitable accommodation. He saw me as proactive, and not controlling. He would have looked at the situation totally different to Nguyen. He would have made positive suggestions. I missed Dave and our conversations.

Nguyen looked quite pleased with himself. Just like the perfectly cooked salmon he prepared, he fed me lack of self-worth and lack of self-respect. Then the heartburn hit.

This was not the first time Nguyen had dismembered me. I had to be very careful not to upset him. His moods changed very quickly and when he became depressed, this influenced his sleep patterns. Maybe he was tired. Nguyen was the most generous man I had ever met, and yet I struggled with this side of him. I felt like I did not deserve his generosity. He would make me breakfast in bed, or if I fell asleep on the sofa watching television, he would cover me with a blanket so I wouldn't get cold. He would plan days for us to stay in bed watching movies. He was a beautiful man when he remained focused.

I saw Nguyen as a unique individual, not as a human rights lawyer. I told him very early on a person's occupation does not define who they are as an individual. He has his job and I have mine, but I wasn't with him because he was a lawyer, I was with him because I loved him and because of his kindness towards me. These qualities made him the person I loved. He could be sitting homeless on a park bench for all I cared, I would still love him. In fact, I'd sit next to him and share my sandwich.

Apparently, it was *his* perceptions of me that made him feel not good enough. He would tell me he felt this way, but I didn't listen to him. To me he was all and more. I had saved up and I was going to buy him a park bench for Christmas and have a little plaque attached to it inscribed with, 'We are who we are and I love you exactly the way you are. Emmie and Nguyen'.

Nguyen's outbursts at times were intimidating, and I avoided these as best as I could. I did most of the housework, and Nguyen did most of the cooking. He loved cooking and used it to express his creativity. He would make the best Chinese hand-pulled noodles in beef broth and Mongolian beef in a slow cooker. He would take my palate on little adventures, discovering different cultural flavours and sometimes explosive parties, involving different sauces, herbs, and spices.

The good in him seemed to outweigh the bad. I mean who could blame him if he came home in a mood and smashed a plate on the kitchen floor? He wasn't very good at communicating his feelings towards me other than sex and the occasional, "I love you."

He said the plate slipped from his hand as he was taking it out of the dishwasher. But I could have sworn he threw it and it smashed into the corner of the kitchen cupboard. I *saw* him do it. I was probably wrong, he was right, it must have slipped. He was tired that day, I shouldn't have asked him to empty the dishwasher, it was my fault. That was *my* job, not his.

Nguyen's lovemaking was as intense as his moods. His romantic approach included having Champagne, red wine or alcohol in general by the bed. He would take sips from his glass during our lovemaking. He was the most passionate lover I've ever had. I thought it was such a romantic gesture to have a bottle of my favourite wine by the bed ready to go. That's where we would share some of our best conversations after. We would discuss issues Nguyen said needed addressing. According to Nguyen, I had a psychological problem because I couldn't urinate in his presence. I thought of the time I walked in on him using the bathroom.

"Sorry, I didn't realise you were using the bathroom," I said, as he was standing at the basin shaving.

"I'll use the other bathroom." I said.

"Emmie, you can use this one, don't be stupid, you're here now," he said.

"I'd rather use the other one, thanks." I said as I walked out.

Later that evening after we had made love, Nguyen proceeded to tell me he once knew someone who couldn't urinate in front of him and how mixed up she was. He said I had to sort myself out. He said I had problems that needed addressing and using the bathroom in front of him was one of them.

That led me to think about my newly obtained health condition. I had never experienced urinary tract infections in my life and now that I was with Nguyen, I had one every couple of months. Could it be possible he was sleeping around? Maybe he was right, maybe I had to overcome my shyness and use the bathroom when he was in there. Maybe it is all in my head. I loved how this man had my best interests at heart.

Our lovemaking was as dominating as our eyes and simply euphoric bliss. It didn't matter what I was wearing, it could be the finest silk nightie to one of his t-shirts, and no sooner would I jump into bed it would be taken right off. Nguyen said we had a spiritual connection like no other he had ever experienced. Sometimes we would lie there entwined, his legs wrapped around my waist with him inside of me in complete stillness and oneness. Our souls completely liberated and we did not require the physical rhythm to experience this. In fact, sex with Nguyen could be best described as a drug high, you never knew where it would take you.

He didn't like the sense of being alone, so falling asleep together with our arms around one another made us both feel safe. Nguyen quite often experienced dark thoughts and this suited our lovemaking well, his impulsiveness, and risk-taking drove me crazy.

I loved this man so much. *I will never leave you Nguyen,* I would think to myself lying next to him at night. Things really aren't *that* bad.

I began to think of the past discussions we had around if we tried for a baby.

"I want a baby, Emmie," he came home and said one night. He had caught me completely off guard.

"I don't know if I want one at this stage in my life, Nguyen, I'd like to travel and not be tied down to motherhood all over again. Our kids are young adults now," I said.

The following week it was a completely different story. I told Nguyen I was thinking that I would like to try for a baby, that I had changed my mind after thinking more about what he had suggested.

"If you fall pregnant, I'll pay for you to have an abortion," he said.

"What!" I said horrified.

"I'm not ready to have a baby with you and if I did, I would be taking care of it not you," he said.

I was lying in bed starting to feel totally lost remembering past conversations, churning in my mind. I felt like I was going crazy, my head was spinning so fast it felt like I had smoked hydroponic pot that had been doused in toxic pesticides.

I was raised to respect others. I was raised to be patient and good things would come my way, and you do not walk away from situations, especially those involving people you love. You are there to serve a purpose, and most of all 'be good'. Fuck, so really, I was raised to value others, even if they mistreated me. Raised to have little self-respect and wait out the storm, no matter how long that may take, otherwise guilt would set upon me and eat me to death.

My life is fucked. My subconscious mind was taking over my feelings and my sleep. At that point, like a bolt from the universe, I heard myself say, "*Stop being a victim, Emmie!*" Sounding just like Nguyen.

His favourite saying, rooted in my subconscious. My mind screamed, "*Shut the fuck up! You never-ending roller coaster! Some nights I just want OFF!*"

Beyond the controlling power of my mind, I had visions of my upbringing and my perceptions of it not being normal. I was wrong. In reality it offered me safety and security, not confusion or rejection. The faith instilled in me back then, had now provided me with the clarity to realise my current situation was not normal. I was spiritually enlightened growing up. Nguyen often spoke of our spiritual connection. He'd say when you are spiritually connected to someone it goes beyond an emotional level. Our souls felt liberated and did not require any physical stimulation and we were connected by a universal source of energy which formed a merging between the both of us.

I began to realise Nguyen was full of shit. Portraying himself as '*spiritually enlightened*', telling me we had a soul connection. He was ego driven, lacked honesty and forgiveness. We weren't spiritually bound to one another. I was caught up in a world of fake bullshit this man had spun, not only to me, but to the ignorant world of social media, and anyone else who fed off his deceits. Here I was, lying by his side with his arms wrapped tightly around me. Was I going crazy? I felt like I was.

I was so confused. I was living with him, and he still had to schedule me in around his other commitments. We weren't a team. I was an accessory, like my mother's handbag collection. I didn't have a voice and when I did, I was deemed as too difficult. He didn't love me as he didn't know how to love. He once told me an ex-girlfriend had sent him a thank you card, possibly thanking him for being out of her life and teaching her about toxic relationships.

I had warning signs that I chose to ignore. He projected his drama onto me. Because of his insecurities, I became the problem, I became his drama. He didn't want me helping Dave and he didn't want me to see my friends or my children. He was jealous of my relationships. He was jealous of my success and achievements. He was the one that was scared and insecure, not me. He lacked strength and resilience.

The Italian in me was back. I had to find a way out of there, and I was taking those exquisitely beautiful fucking emerald earrings with me. He was right about one thing they did match my eyes.

CHAPTER 10

T HE BIG DAY had arrived. I had woken to a beautiful summer morning, the sun shining bright. The front door to my parents' home was wide open ready for the festivities to begin. The kitchen table had been set and laid with the most elaborate handmade crocheted tablecloth my mother could set her hands on. I could see my reflection on the silver trays that held the crystal liqueur glasses. These were ready to be filled with various colours and flavours, with the bottles laid out beside them. Trays of Italian biscotti and different coloured sugared almonds ready for the visitors to come by. They would offer their congratulations before I made my way to the church.

I spotted the Baci chocolates, silver little boob shaped balls with blue writing, these little morsels are the crème della crème of Italian chocolates. I took one, slowly peeled back the foil not to damage the little note inside that each chocolate came with. These are like delicate Italian fortune cookies, reminding me of the biscuit variety found at the Chinese takeaway. I popped the decadent little boob in my mouth. My note read, 'The person you love the most stands before you, stop searching'. *Hmm,* I thought *how appropriate.*

Rosie and Renata were my bridesmaids. Rosie flew in from Melbourne to be with me and to help me get ready for the wedding. They were due to arrive any minute, makeup and hairspray in tow to begin the day. It was 6 o'clock.

"Buongiorno, good morning!" They had arrived.

"Where's the dress, Em?" Renata eagerly asked, busting to see it. My mother insisting it was the year's best-kept secret, no one was to see my wedding dress until I walked up the church aisle. According to her, it was bad luck for anyone to see this as she didn't want anyone giving me the 'evil eye'. Things had to run smoothly for her on her day.

We were all standing side by side in my mother's bedroom looking up at my wedding dress and veil hanging from the curtain rod allowing it to drape without creasing. We were all amazed how the weight of the dress had not brought down the curtain rod. The sunlight peeping through the window made my dress look like the white light one would see if they went into cardiac arrest. I felt like I was having an out of body experience, staring at my dress. The white light leading the way for the dearly departed to a better place of peace for all eternity.

"That's one mad arse looking dress." Renata piped up.

"How the fuck are you going to get into that one?"

"No idea, Ren," I said.

She was right. I was staring at this white iceberg that had the ability to take down more than the Titanic. It could take me down with one wrong step. The lace heavily defined the outside layer of the dress and the silk underlay weighed a tonne. The tiny beads sparkled so brightly, and the sleeves looked as heavy as the bodice. With the help of my frantic mother and my two favourite cousins, I managed to step into my dress, carefully and precisely.

"Rosie, I need to go to the bathroom!" I said in a moment of sheer panic, once all the buttons had been secured at the back. It took three people to do them up.

In one fast swoop, my mother hurried all the visitors into the 'good room', shutting the frosted glass doors to rope off an area for me to walk to the bathroom without anyone seeing.

Like a production line in a factory, I had Rosie, Renata and my mother yelling at us not to let the dress touch the floor. I felt like the last marshmallow shoved in some kid's mouth at an eating competition. With no more room to move, I had finally managed to fit into the bathroom.

The cars had arrived. With the volume dial set on high, I grabbed my father, farewelled the guests, the loudness, the theatrics, and my childhood home. I waved arrivederci, see you later!

When we arrived at the church, my father stood proudly by my side. As I approached the church doors, the sun reflected upon the heavy copper fixtures inscribed with Latin. They were opened for us to enter. *Ava Maria* began to play, and I knew this was my cue.

Let's get this show on the road. People began to stand and turned to look at me, the church was full. The choir sang as I made my way to Dave, where my father shook his hand and then took his seat next to my mother.

The ceremony was a traditional Catholic mass. Half Italian, half English, it seemed to go on forever. Translation after translation, I caught Father Vincent briefly checking his watch while the photographer tried to capture our every move.

As Dave and I read our vows, I reflected upon his words, "Love is patient, love is kind. It does not envy, it does not boast, it is not proud. It does not dishonour others, it is not self-seeking, it is not easily angered, it keeps no record of wrongs. Love does not delight in evil but rejoices with the truth. It always protects, always trusts, always hopes, always perseveres." (1 Corinthians 13:4-7) Dave lifted my veil and kissed me.

I glanced over at Rosie with my eyes a little teary, knowing I had better not cry and spoil my makeup. Like drinking wine out of the Holy Grail, my journey with Dave was on its way and Holy Communion had been offered to all.

"I now pronounce you Mr and Mrs Smith," Father Vincent happily proclaimed. We both made our way, hand in hand, out to the front of the church.

Sprayed in paper confetti and our cheeks covered in various shades of fuchsia pink lipstick kisses, Dave and I made our way to family photos at the local park.

"You look so beautiful, Emmie," Dave said.

This was our very first moment alone as husband and wife.

"How are you Mrs Smith?" he asked.

"I could really use a cold drink," I said.

The warm afternoon sun was bearing down on us. As the day went on my makeup began to feel as heavy as my dress. I wanted the formalities over and done with. The photographer was instructing us on different poses for our photos in the park. We posed under trees, next to rose bushes, and next to the wedding cars. The bridal party were all worn-out. Rosie and Renata helped me with my dress, lifting the veil and train each time I had to walk somewhere.

The wedding reception was held in traditional Italian style. There were over two hundred people. The room was filled with a sea of different coloured box hats worn by the women, perfectly colour matched to their husbands' silk ties. It took us over forty minutes to greet each guest as they walked into the venue. The Italians took up most of the venue space, with around forty Aussies scattered amongst them.

The wedding cake was a tier of ten sponges lavishly cemented together with white mock cream. It surrounded a fountain spurting out green water matching the green bridal party attire.

Free flowing alcohol and the degustation of food was endless. Hospitality staff ran around filling glasses and replacing empty plates with the next course throughout the evening. With the speeches completed, I could not wait to get to our hotel room.

"Emmie, so what do you think it will be like having sex with Dave?" Renata asked me, as she slid over into the empty seat next to me on the main bridal table.

"I guess probably the same as last week." I said to her.

"WHAT THE FUCK, EM!" Renata was shocked, her green eyes wide open, as she brushed away stray hair from her face.

"Well Renata, it just happened. We were at our house finalising a few things, waiting for furniture to be delivered and we decided to try out our new mattress," I said giggling.

"It was amazing, there's no special recipe when it comes to making love to someone who holds a piece of your heart in his hand each day, it comes very easily and naturally. It's more than sex when you truly love someone," I said.

"If Dave can get through all these bloody pearl buttons on the back of my dress tonight without going completely mad, then we might get another crack at it." We laughed while filling our glasses with more Champagne.

I watched Dave making his way around the room, socialising in his black tuxedo. He looked so handsome. He was meeting and greeting the two hundred plus random guests neither of us knew. I really had no idea who they were. Here we were, little Italy in this one room and my fearless Aussie husband, politely thanking all the guests for attending and helping to make our day special.

The live band in the background announcing it was time for the newlyweds to leave, and for all invited participants to form the farewell arch to see us off in our wedding car. Dave had not only won the hearts of all in the room, but mine as well.

Dave had decided to book us into a hotel for our first night as husband and wife. He knew exactly how to shut my mother up and shut down her expectations simultaneously. She had insisted we sleep in her bed at her home on our wedding night, and she and my father would sleep in the spare room. I refused to have a 'make the bed' ceremony (an Italian tradition for newlyweds). She had Italian sheets she wanted to use and show off to her friends, which came straight out of the horrendous glory box. Like that's what I'd really want to be doing on my wedding night. This was one battle she was not going to win. Bless Dave for booking a hotel. Bless him for coming to my rescue, and fuck her Italian sheets. This was MY life now.

We made our way down the human arch like entering a righteous passage where I would find delicious refuge in the arms of the man I loved.

"Emmie, I will see you tomorrow at your parent's house for the next day celebration, we can talk then." Rosie said, putting her arms around me and kissing me on the cheek.

"Go live your life, Em. Start saying no to this bullshit, to this antiquated tradition shoved down our throats. Break free Em, you're an adult now." Rosie whispered in my ear.

We had made it, finally Rosie and I were free.

CHAPTER 11

MARRIED LIFE TO Dave was fantastic. We lived in a little cream brick two-bedroom home in the suburbs. It had a pretty garden with rows of yellow and white daisy bushes out the front, and the most beautiful silver birch tree I had ever seen. We had a white bamboo love heart hanging by our front door. Our neighbours were very welcoming to us as we were the youngest couple in the street. When we moved in, we had our surrounding neighbours come over to welcome us. They brought us fresh peaches, strawberries, and quince fruit all from their gardens. I would turn them into jam and share my little jars with them all, as a thank you.

Dave was teaching me how to face the fears my parents had left me with. He said the electrical safety switch would kick in if I ever touched the power point with wet hands. He said I would not be electrocuted and die. Dave had the best sense of humour, always making me laugh. He taught me how to drive at night-time. My parents put the fear of God into me when it came to taking the car out at night. They convinced me that if I drove at night my car was sure to break down and some lunatic would come and kill me. Control and manipulation seemed to go hand in hand with them. Dave's little exercise to teach me how to drive at dusk took around a month. We would drive around the back streets in two cars with him driving behind me. We would set up routes to follow, around the block, then around the area. I would feel so safe knowing Dave was right behind me, and then he sent me off on my own. He pushed me out of the nest. I had no choice but to fly solo.

"Em, can you please go pick up the pizza I ordered?" he asked.

"It's 9 o'clock, it's dark!" I said sounding horrified.

"Em, remember what I taught you. Fear is in your head nothing has happened and might not even happen. We'll have children one day that I'm sure will need picking up and dropping off at nights," he said.

Children I thought, *our children*. With that word ringing through my head, I grabbed the keys he was dangling in the air. I walked out the front door to the car with confidence and ease. My future children will have a confident mother, not a fearful one. I had to set an example. I certainly wasn't going to instill this bullshit type of fear into my children!

Within less than six months I had grown into an independent young woman. I had cut my long hair to shoulder length and streaked it blonde. I changed my sense of clothing style. I began to look more like my cousin Renata, a free spirit. I wore thongs, tight jeans with tie-dye t-shirts, and I no longer cared what people thought. I had finally reinvented my sense of style and my sense of self and I didn't need anyone's approval.

My parents would pop around to visit when Dave was away, I think they realised very quickly they had met their match with their new son-in-law. He was so supportive of me and he had a way of stopping negative conversations between me and my parents even before they began. He recognised where a conversation was heading by the tone, as he didn't speak Italian. He was never rude to them he would simply steer the conversation into different directions.

"What have you done to your hair?" my father asked furiously, sitting at the kitchen table.

I hadn't seen him so angry for years. His face was red hot with anger. He hadn't seen my new hairstyle yet. I had been avoiding them and was waiting for when Dave could come with me to visit them together. They had decided to pop in as they hadn't seen me for a few days.

"And put some shoes on," he added.

"SHHH, don't say anything!" my mother said elbowing him in his arm.

"Yes, Emanuela, why aren't you wearing any shoes?" my mother agreed.

I got up and walked into my tiny kitchen to make them a coffee, ignoring the conversation and not entering into it. I was fussing about in the kitchen, trying to avoid eye contact with them both. I could sense my father seething from the other room. Young Italian women did not cut their hair, only older wiser women with ten kids could do this.

"Emanuela, what did you do to your hair and why aren't you wearing any shoes?" he pursued.

"I'm married now papa, if I want to cut my hair I will." I said, still feeling fearful that I had stood up for myself.

What was my problem? Wasn't marriage my magic cure to make this all go away, my fear of my parents and their controlling ways?

"Dave doesn't care if I cut my hair, it's MY hair." I said from the kitchen.

"You might be married, but you are still my daughter and I will always have a say," he said.

I felt like crying. Dave was always away working, and I needed him here. I wanted them to leave now.

This was my home I had nothing to fear, I told myself. Dave and I had sex in the next room for goodness sakes, I was an adult now. *Breathe Em.*

I served them their coffee. My mother grabs her black leather Dolce handbag. She took out a diamante hair clip.

"Emanuela, let me pin back your fringe, your hair will look much nicer with this," she said.

I couldn't believe my mother still had a backup plan in her handbag after all these years. I sat there with my fringe clipped back looking like a ten-year-old.

"Now you look beautiful!" she said.

My mother got up and ventured into my bedroom, snooping around. I got up to follow her.

"Emanuela, why don't you put the nice sheets on your bed? I don't like the green and black you have on there." She said.

"You have beautiful Italian sheets, what will people think if they see this? Your aunties would be ashamed, you'll embarrass me," she said.

I stood right by her side and we were both staring at the quilt cover I had chosen, my arms crossed. I leaned over to her so my father couldn't hear my voice travelling into the next room.

"That's the latest designer quit cover, I saved a whole month for it, and it's my bed. I don't care what people say or think, I'm not embarrassed, and this is my home."

With that, I turned and went back into the next room to finish my coffee.

I loved my parents, I knew they meant well, but they didn't understand times had changed and people change too. They migrated to Australia as young adults and they still held their traditions close to their hearts.

I was no longer a little girl who was expected to be on good behaviour, I was out on parole. I was not an inconvenience to Dave, and he was my life partner. We were a team, we loved each other very much, and we accepted one another. My parents no longer had the ability to stuff expectations down my throat. I felt for them because they only wanted the best for me, but Italian traditions were evolving, even here in Australia. The face of multiculturalism was changing. I hadn't felt a lump in my throat since the day I walked out the front door of their home to make my way to the church to marry Dave. This was my life now. I visualised a sign saying, 'KEEP OUT' just like my mother had in her 'good room' at her home.

I enrolled in night school. When Dave returned from his interstate trip, he helped me select courses, so I could study and eventually leave working at the deli. He was encouraging me to find a real job and meet new people. The community high school wasn't far from home.

I really enjoyed learning. It kept me occupied when Dave was away. I was studying information technology and finance. I would attend for three nights a week.

I also made new friends. I met Dimitri Panaganis and Dina Williams. Dimitri was Greek and hilarious. We would joke with one another saying we were there to rebel in high school as adults because we were denied the opportunity as teenagers. We both came from similar cultural backgrounds where rebelling was not allowed. Our parents wouldn't have coped with the inconvenience. He wore the latest streetwear, emulating his teen years at adult night school.

Dina was a hip, fearless, newly married Aussie chick who spoke with her hands and was good at putting others in their place, including her husband Darren. We all gelled together so well, multiculturalism at its best.

"Ella." Dimitri would call me.

"It's Emmie Smith." I would snap back with attitude.

"Don't pretend to be an Aussie, with a nose like that, you won't get away with it." Dimitri teased.

We would both laugh.

Dimitri was my age. He had graduated with a teaching degree but was undertaking some extra courses while he was waiting for a placement. Dimitri reminded me of the boys at bus stop eleven in high school that the girls would often speak of. One of the cool boys, dressed in oversized shirts, and skinny jeans, but with an edge to it. Dimitri and I would go and grab a bite to eat some nights after class when Dave was away. Dave was so accepting of my new friends. He would always encourage me to join in and hang out with them. When he was home, we would all catch up and go to the local pub on a Thursday evening for happy hour. Those times were few and far between, he had to work away a fair bit.

"Ella, you ready for a yiros?" he'd ask, as I was innocently peeping into empty classrooms.

"Sure, why not," I said grinning.

Dimitri helped me with my information technology assignments. Greeks thought they were so good with solving and working their way around technical issues.

Dimitri and I would walk up and down the empty hallways of the high school after classes had finished. It felt strange and eerie with no students around, only the cleaners dusting and fluffing about, late at night. He too was helping me face my fears. Even as an adult in an empty high school I began to feel safe and independent with my new found friend.

CHAPTER 12

HIP HIP HOORAY

I WAS APPROACHING my twenty-first birthday and Dave was planning a surprise. We had been married two years at this stage, and it was the best two years of my entire life. I was so excited. If it's going to be anything like our first wedding anniversary, I knew it would be phenomenal.

That was a night I'll never forget. Dave had gone out and bought me a black silk beaded lace dress. He laid it out on our bed for me to wear. We were picked up by a limousine and taken to the best five-star restaurant in town. I recall the waiter used a little silver dustpan and a tiny brush to come to wipe away my crumbs on the fine white linen tablecloth.

We took our taste buds on a trip down fine dining. The finest duck liver pâté served with little pieces of homemade baguette. Roast lamb served with buttered baby potatoes and heirloom carrots, and the most divine pistachio panna cotta finished off with petits fours all perfectly matched with an assortment of wines. I was so excited that as soon as we arrived home, I raced to ring my mother to tell her all about it, knowing she'd most likely be in bed asleep. I was busting to share my amazing night with her.

I knew Dave had sent out the invitations because I heard Dimitri whispering to Dina in class about what they should buy me.

"SHH, she's coming!" I heard him say, stuffing a catalogue in his back jeans pocket.

"For the record, I like Estee Lauder." I said.

I was really getting into makeup in fact I was really enjoying wearing it. I had discovered I had a real talent for applying it. I even impressed Renata.

"You look so different now," Renata would say.

"Married life agrees with me, Ren." I would beam.

"Ella, how did you go with your assignment? Dimitri asked. "Dina and I have handed ours up."

"Yes, not too bad, I'm very pleased with mine. Thanks for helping me." I said.

We took our seats in class. The exact same spots each week, so we could hand one another notes while the lecturer was teaching, like naughty school children.

The next morning, Dave was due to go away again for work and I could hear him on the phone plotting and planning my birthday celebrations.

"I said I want the hall to be decorated with pink, purple, and white balloons, not black, red, and gold!" Quickly turning into a whisper as he saw me walk into the kitchen. *God, I miss Dave when he goes away, I wish he was around more* I thought, grabbing a juice from the fridge and walking out of the kitchen so he could finish his phone call.

Although I missed Dave when he was away, it forced me to become so much more independent. I was now making most of my own decisions, not having to seek permission from anyone. If I chose to go out and have a coffee with a friend or seek retail therapy I would. My fears had all but disappeared. I slept at home alone when he wasn't there. At first, my mother insisted she would stay over, but I didn't want her to. I wasn't afraid of the occasional noise I'd hear outside. Dave bought me a cordless phone that I kept right by my bed.

"If you're really worried Em, dial triple zero," he'd say each time he had to go away.

I would come home from night school and make myself comfortable and chat on the phone to Dimitri for hours. Dina and Renata would come over and visit. We would have 'makeup nights' where we would sit at the kitchen table with it covered in eyeshadows, lipsticks, and pencils, busily experimenting with colours. *I love my new life I am so grateful.* I would tell myself.

"I'll do your make up for your birthday, Emmie," Renata piped up.

"Only if it's a normal attempt and you don't make me look like a Goth." I said. We all laughed drinking our Lambrusco, trying not to poke our eyes out, the sweet red bubbly wine affecting our senses.

My birthday had finally arrived. My mother tried frantically to help out with the food preparations, insisting she made her homemade lasagna and trays of crumbed veal schnitzels. Rosie's mother had made her famous potato croquet and arancini balls, hundreds of them. They had been working around the clock cooking.

Rosie arrived from Melbourne that morning. I missed her so much, and I couldn't wait to party tonight with her.

I had so much to do, but Dave insisted he took care of things at the venue. He was making so many trips there and back with the help of his brothers setting up for the party.

"Em, time to go," Dave said. "Let's go celebrate and have some fun."

My birthday party was like no other. As soon as I walked into the hall, it reminded me of an Aussie wedding reception. Wall to wall paper streamers in pink and white, helium balloons held down by little pink paperweights, a big banquet table with rows and rows of food platters. Eskies filled with ice cold bottles of beer and wine. Dimitri was DJ for the night, he had set his gear up in the corner of the room with his multicoloured strobe lights flashing onto the walls and ceiling.

"Dave this is beautiful, I love it so much, thank you." I said.

I was so happy. With Dave tightly holding my hand, we walked in together to greet our guests.

"Emmie!" I didn't know who to turn to first. Both side of my cheeks quickly filling up with different lipstick shades, I was feeling very blessed.

My mother and father were proudly standing watching me, I walked up and greeted them. They handed me a little box and I opened it. I saw a gold key on a chain. No ordinary key, but the most beautifully designed old-world key with a long chain. Italian gold. The chain once belonging to my Nonna Emanuela, my father's mother. I kissed them both and my father proudly put it around my neck.

"Auguri per mille anni," he said, wishing me well for a thousand years.

Dave attended to the needs of our guests. Socialising and making them feel welcomed. My handsome man, knowing exactly how to be a good host. I saw him thanking my mother and aunt for cooking and helping out. Dina was playing matchmaker for Renata and was eyeing off potential Aussie men. Dave and his friends were sitting at one end of the room, laughing and making jokes. Renata was trying to get their attention.

"Go make new friends Renata." I said.

"They don't bite. GO! Dina will introduce you. Darren is sitting there with them." Dina's husband had become a good mate of Dave's.

I was finally able to spend some quality time with my favourite cousin.

"Rosie when are you moving back home?" I asked.

"It won't happen, not anytime soon. I don't want my parents marrying me off to some Italian guy. I'm taking my time, and I'm lucky the research centre at the hospital keep extending my contract. So, for now, I'm safe." Rosie said.

Who could blame her? She was lucky, her mother was afraid of flying and she got car sick on long drives. Her parents did not visit very often.

I introduced Rosie to most of my new friends as the night wore on. I had filled her in about them all when we spoke over the phone previously. It was nice for her to finally put faces to names. I had wondered if she might like Dimitri. I hadn't gotten around to introducing them yet. She had already asked me who the DJ was so perhaps she was interested, but Dimitri was too busy spinning his tunes. Rosie was single and I thought I should return the favour since she introduced me to Dave.

Dimitri saw us looking over at him, our eyes locking, he started to play the song *Venus* by Shocking Blue. He ran over to me and grabbed me by my arm and started twirling me around on the dance floor. Renata and Dina were both laughing. I couldn't keep up with him. I pushed him away, laughing, making my way back to Rosie.

"I think it's time I repay the favour Rosie, since you introduced me to Dave all those years ago." I said, trying to catch my breath.

"What do you think of Dimitri? He is teaching maths at St Joseph's junior school." I asked excitedly.

"I caught him eyeing you off before, why don't you go out for a coffee with him before you head home next week? I could set it up for you?" I suggested sheepishly, eagerly waiting for her response.

"He's a really nice guy and he's very funny. He rides this ridiculous red pushbike everywhere. I swear he'll get mowed down by a car one day." I said laughing.

I was watching Dimitri, as he had made his way back to his equipment. He stood in his corner spinning the record player like a true professional with his earphones on.

He was playing Blondie, and I saw Renata and Dina dancing with their new male friends. The boys were holding cans of beer in their hands, laughing while the girls danced around them.

"I'm not suggesting a long distance romance. It would be nice if you forged a new friendship with someone, maybe even catching up with him on your return visit home. Is it possible?" I asked.

"He keeps looking at you!" I said, looking over at Dimitri.

"Em, he's not looking at me, he's checking you out. He likes *you*," Rosie said, sounding concerned.

I laughed. I was beginning to feel anxious.

"Rosie, seriously, I highly doubt that. We're friends, we all hang out together, including Dave." I said as I was tilting my head towards Dave. Why would I look at any other man? I was twenty-one years old.

I remembered when Dave used to tell me not to be naïve. I am vulnerable because I had a sheltered upbringing. He would often say that I was someone who only saw the good in others and wouldn't recognise the bad. He worried because I still had a lot to learn about people and life. He was trying to teach me how to say 'no' without feeling guilty. My newly found independence came with responsibilities and life had a way of teaching us lessons. He would say that I should rely on my instincts to make smart choices and not be influenced by what others think or say. He said people will try and take advantage of me because I had a very infectious personality and I was forgiving and kind hearted. He would say not to trust everyone I met as they could be opportunists.

At that very moment, I knew I had a lot of growing up to do. I still acted like a little girl at a big birthday party, excited by the music, balloons, and cake.

Rosie and Dave are so much wiser, and more experienced at life. They are both insightful and both working in professional fields. I had only recently left one home for another, I hadn't moved beyond cooking and cleaning, the only difference is I slept with my husband.

Rosie was right, I knew Dimitri adored me. I could sense it. We had chemistry between us, but I was not interested in him in that way. I appreciated our friendship, I would be there for him offering advice on girls, and we would hang out occasionally eating yiros.

"Emmie, I know you love Dave, and you're both completely devoted to one another, but you're still so young. He's your first love, the one and only man you've been intimate with. I guarantee, you'll meet many more guys who wish they could have you in their lives, or simply have you in their beds. Someone else's intentions may not be the same as yours." Rosie said.

"Be smart enough to acquaint yourself with people before you let them into your life, because the lessons they inflict could potentially be heartbreaking and life-changing. Some might see you as a challenge. I'm sure you'll meet men who are nuts for a good challenge or simply nuts in the head. There are lots of unpleasant people out there." Rosie said lovingly with her hand on my shoulder.

I realised at that point Dimitri had to go. I was going to miss him. I didn't need further complications in my life. I also thought to myself how these sorts of conversations with Rosie made me nervous.

Heartbreak I thought to myself, what's heartbreak? I'd only ever read about heartbreak in Jackie Collins novels. I had learnt a lot about acceptance, but not heartbreak.

The lights went out and I heard, "HAPPY BIRTHDAY TO YOU, HAPPY BIRTHDAY TO YOU, HAPPY BIRTHDAY DEAR EMMIE…"

CHAPTER 13

D AVE AND I had been married for nearly three years, and I had people asking me for two and a half of those years when I was going to produce a little Italian-Aussie scrambled egg. I desperately wanted a baby, my own little baby girl. I felt ready. I was reading different types of books now, more in line with *Organic Homemade Baby Food* and *How to Remedy Reflux Naturally.*

"Dave I really want a baby, I want to raise our little family, I want a baby, Dave." I was hounding Dave each time he was home and not away working.

"I'm always home alone, it's been three years now. I'm not waiting any longer," I demanded.

"Em, I'd really like to save a little more money," Dave replied.

"NO, DAVE, I want a baby!" I fired back.

"Why is it always about money with you?"

I mean, people had a lot less than we did and they still had children. Dave had limiting beliefs centred on finances. His brothers were all successful, unmarried and very wealthy. I guess Dave had these beliefs because he watched his mother struggle, but we had to draw the line somewhere. Most of our arguments now centred on how quickly I could undress him and have sex with him before he left for work. It was the same topic over and over, I WANT A BABY.

Dave was still working away, and I was still entertaining myself. I would spend my weekends making pasta with my mother and stocking up the freezer. Gnocchi, fusilli, linguine, I had my own little continental deli at home. I mostly ate alone, or on occasions, I would invite Renata and Dina to come over. I accepted the fact Dave worked away and I kept my feelings to myself. Dave was trying to start his own accounting firm, which involved him travelling interstate. I had completed two years of night school. I was still working at the continental deli.

Was I becoming like my cousin Maria, only a married version? I was grateful for my newly found independence. I wanted to share this with the man of my dreams, but he was rarely home.

I had made Dave's favourite dinner tonight, chicken tortellini alla Emmie. Fresh mushrooms, chicken, cream, lots of parmesan cheese, avocado, freshly cracked black pepper, shallots, exactly how he likes it. I had the night planned. I had music playing, a little bit of Wilson Pickett singing in the background. I was wearing my sexy pyjama shorts and a see-through top. I was going to be dishing up more than Dave was expecting tonight. I was ovulating and this was my chance. *Let's get the ball rolling,* I thought, bring on my baby girl.

I was ready to serve up dinner, expecting to hear his car pull up in the driveway. The phone rang.

"Em, I'm going to be really late, I won't be home for dinner." It was Dave. Without even a response, I hung up.

Disappointed and upset, I went into the kitchen, turned off the stove, turned off the lights, and went to bed. Tomorrow would be a better day, I told myself.

Dina is my best friend, my-slap-me-in-the-face type of girl. If anyone had the ability to knock sense into me, it was her. She had my permission to do so when she felt the need was necessary. She was now working at the deli with me. Renata had left work and moved on with her life. Dina and I had big future plans to ultimately find work together and discover our true calling in life. For now, however, we had both decided our true calling was to become mothers.

Dina and Darren married the same time as Dave and I. Although she's an Aussie, she seemed more Italian than me. She spoke with her hands. I laughed each time she did and it frustrated her.

"Will you please listen to me, Em," she'd say, frustrated whilst waving her hands around in the air.

"Not if you keep your hand action going, you remind me of my mother, Dina," I'd say smiling.

That morning at work I was feeling deflated.

"I'm over slicing ham, I'm over saucing trays of pasta, and I am really over smelling like olive oil," I said to Dina.

We were both working at the slicers.

"What should I bring to Renata's?" Dina asked.

We were all invited to Renata's house for dinner the following night. Renata's mother and sister were in Italy visiting family and she was home alone. We would all be sleeping over. Renata had a rumpus room at the back of her mother's house that had a bedroom and a bathroom attached to it. Darren and Dave got on really well together. Both beer drinkers, it allowed the girls to stick to our Lambrusco and catch up for chat sessions.

"I'll make tiramisu for dessert," I said.

"Why don't you make your homemade sausage rolls? I've been craving those."

"You're not pregnant, are you Em?" she asked.

"Pfft, you need to have sex Dina, in order to fall pregnant. It's not the Immaculate Conception here." We both laughed.

I was really looking forward to all of us catching up. I was sick of sitting at home alone on a Saturday night. The few friends that I did have, were all married and off doing things with their partners. Renata was off living her life. She had discovered painting and was travelling to various art shows interstate, catching up and staying with Rosie in Melbourne, living it up. We would occasionally go to international film festivals together and watch movies with weird story lines whilst trying to read the subtitles at the same time. Getting my head around some of her film suggestions were challenging at times.

"That's some weird sex shit, Renata!" I'd lean over and whisper in her ear during the watching of a French film.

"Maybe you should give it a go and you might get what you wish for." She whispered back.

I was a homebody, cooking, cleaning and bored. I wanted a baby, not kinky sex.

My conversations with Dina at work were mainly centred around food, and anything else on how to keep our men happy.

"Dina, what are you cooking Darren for dinner tonight?" I asked in-between serving customers and stuffing panini bread rolls with small goods and cheese.

"I found this great recipe I want to try, it's in the latest Woman's Weekly," she said.

"It's battered Chinese honey chicken."

"You actually paid for a magazine, how did you afford that?"

"I didn't, I was at the doctor's surgery, and I saw it and ripped it out. I coughed like a nut job so no one could hear the ripping sound." She said as we both laughed.

We couldn't afford to treat ourselves with life's simple pleasures like magazines. We were paying nineteen per cent interest rates on our home loans, welcome to the nineties. I had to budget, we all did. Dina understood this well. Times were tough, we were focused on having a baby, and we had to save in order to allow us time off work. We had to cover medical and living expenses. We wanted to stay at the local private hospital when the time came.

Dina and I would get excited about finding new recipes and cooking them for our husbands, waiting in anticipation with each mouthful they took for their critique. Did we pass, did we fail, and was it a ten out of ten?

"Dina, see you at Ren's house, and don't forget my sausage rolls," I said as I hugged her goodbye.

The next evening when we all arrived at Renata's we could smell the Middle East from her driveway. We all looked at one another.

"I reckon we're going to be in for a treat tonight," Dave said, smiling, holding onto the esky filled to the brim with wine and beer.

"You got to love these Aussie blokes," Renata said as she came out to greet us, standing on tippy toes kissing both Dave and Darren.

"Seriously, there's no way an Italian guy would bring his own alcohol when someone invites them over for dinner." She was right, my father would be horrified. If you invite someone over as the host, you supply endless food and drinks.

Renata, bless her, had prepared a Moroccan inspired meal. Lamb shanks cooked with fennel seeds, star anise, saffron, cardamom, cumin, and fresh chillies. Alongside the fluffiest couscous to soak up the sauce. Renata was a very good cook, it ran in the family. She was walking from the kitchen in her flowing burgundy skirt and a black velvet top.

We sat outside on rugs laid out on the lawn. Renata placed the food in the centre of the rugs like a picnic. The food was delicious and plentiful. The stars were out, and Renata had pink light globes hanging from the clothesline, the power cord running from the back of the house. Dave had helped her connect it all up. It was the perfect autumn night, too cool for mosquitoes and warm enough to still be outdoors. Dina and I were sitting side by side cross-legged slowly leaning toward one another. After each glass of Lambrusco, we would lean a little heavier, and the wine was going down quite easily.

"Look at Dave and Darren. Laughing and teasing Renata about her artwork," Dina said.

Renata was showing the boys her charcoal drawings of male nudes she did during art class.

"Ren, how do we sign up to volunteer our time as a live model for one on your classes?" Darren piped up.

Renata eyeing Darren in disgust, "Not in this lifetime buddy, you're lucky to have Dina!" And we all laughed.

She was right in a way, our husbands were both very lucky to have us as their wives.

If we could peek into our future, Dina and I would probably say, "They had it too bloody good." Unfortunately, Dina and I were setting the bar quite high for ourselves, without even realising it. I mean, what did we know?

As the night went on, so did the wine and beer, and out came Renata's favourite friend, her glass cor anglais.

"So, what are you going to fill it up with this time?" Dave asked.

"Rum, for all the Aussies here tonight," she said as she opened the bottle and poured it in her glass pipe.

Guns N' Roses played in the background.

"Dave, I love you," I said.

"You love everyone when you've had too much to drink," he said with a big grin.

He was right. Lambrusco acted as a love drug for me and as a truth serum for Dina. When I was intoxicated, I would tell everybody how much I loved them.

Dina was busily telling Darren all the things she did and didn't like about him. I was staring at Dave with big love-struck eyes, amongst the puffs of smoke Renata was producing and smothering us with.

"I think I better put this one to bed," Dave said, as he was gently lifting me up off the rug. I could hear *Sweet Child O' Mine* playing.

CHAPTER 14

SOUP IS REAL ITALIAN MEDICINE

I HAD BEEN unwell for six weeks. My mother promised me her Italian wedding soup. It was like penicillin. After having only one bowl you would instantly feel better. It would take all morning to make, starting it at dawn so it would be ready by lunchtime. She would make her own stock which had baby mince meatballs, shredded spinach, and shredded chicken from the broth floating in it. It was simply delicious, and I needed this medicine. I had a virus in my system, it seemed like I had it forever.

"Emanuela, I told you to wear shoes, you are sick because you don't wear shoes or dry your hair after you wash it." My mother said, as she was ladling more soup into my bowl.

"Ma, people catch things seriously, it's not because of my bare feet or wet hair," I said in-between slurps.

"Go see Doctor Rogers," she said.

I don't like doctors and I avoid going at all costs. But Doctor Rogers had been our family doctor since I was a little girl and she was so nice and very understanding. In fact, Dave's mum cleaned her surgery.

I woke up feeling a little better. I had to go to work, we needed the money, and I didn't want Dave telling me I didn't contribute to the household expenses. He was constantly on about money and finances. It would go straight over my head. I was too focused on other things. He suggested we should get a dog so I would get off his case about the whole baby matter. I wasn't interested. This caused more arguments as I found the very idea annoying.

I managed to get myself to the deli.

"How are you feeling Em, any better?" Dina asked.

"A little, my mother has been coming around with soup." I said.

"I don't understand the only thing that doesn't make me feel so sick is peanut butter. I think it must line my stomach or something, it must set like cement," I said to Dina almost laughing.

"What are you on about?" Dina asked.

"Well, I get hungry and then when I eat, I feel unwell again, it's only soup and peanut butter that seems to stay down. I heard there's a new virus out and about that really lingers on for weeks. God, that smell of oil! I think I'm going to throw up!" I said, as I ran to the back door.

When I came back Dina was eyeing me up and down.

"Em, are you sure it's a virus? I mean you couldn't be pregnant, could you? Why don't you go buy a pregnancy test from the chemist? It's been weeks now, and when you begin to feel better you get knocked back down again."

"I've still been getting my period. I've been spotting, and it's still as regular as clockwork, every twenty-eight days," I said, sounding disappointed.

"I don't want to buy any more pregnancy tests from the chemist because they all come back with the same result."

"Go home," said Dina.

"You look tired. I've got you covered here."

I always had such high expectations each time I would buy a pregnancy test from the chemist. *I'm not doing it to myself anymore* I thought as I untied my apron and hung it up by the back door as I walked out.

Dave returned home that evening to find me lying on the sofa with my jar of peanut butter beside me and a spoon sticking out of it.

"Emmie, wake-up," Dave said shaking me.

"Let me help you to bed, are you feeling any better?" he asked.

"NO!" I snapped, as I rolled over and went back to sleep.

Eight weeks had passed, and I finally gave in. Dave was away again, and I booked myself in to see Doctor Rogers.

"Emmie, how can I help you?" she asked.

"I've been sick now for a number of weeks. I have this virus and I can't shake it, plus my ankles feel weird and they look all puffy. I've tried resting and eating well, but the only thing that helps settle my stomach is peanut butter. I have it on toast or in ice cream or straight out of the jar."

Doctor Rogers took my blood pressure, it was slightly elevated. She listened to my chest, and she felt my ankles and feet and then proceeded to take blood from my arm.

"Just to make sure all is well, we will send this blood sample off to check for any nasties."

Nasties? I thought to myself. What does she mean by that? Why do doctors talk like this? I'm an adult, not a child.

She then handed me a white stick.

"Now Emmie, can you please go down the hall to the bathroom and urinate on the stick for me. This side up once you take the cap off, not for long, enough for the sponge to become wet." She instructed.

She spoke to me like a little girl, with the same jar of lollies sitting on her desk from twenty years ago.

Yeah right, like I'm ever going to be pregnant, I thought. I took the stick and made my way down the corridor.

I handed back the stick to Doctor Rogers. She placed it down and waited. I could see from where I was sitting, two bright red lines popped up. *See negative*, I thought.

"Emmie, did you know you are pregnant?"

"NO! That's impossible!" I said.

"Dave and I have only had sex once in the last eight weeks! He's been away working."

Doctor Rogers laughed so hard her office chair tilted forward. "Emmie, it only takes the *one* time to get pregnant," she said.

I explained to her I was still spotting lightly each month and I thought this was my period.

"This can be normal for some women, don't worry about it we will get Trish at reception to book you in with an obstetrician. Come back and see me next week, I want to check your blood pressure and go over your blood test results." She said, while she gave me a big hug and kiss on the cheek.

"Congratulations, Emmie."

Oh my God, I had a little peanut growing inside of me! I thought it must have been that night at Renata's. *I'M GOING TO BE A MOTHER!*

I drove straight home. I wasn't going to tell Dave yet. He would be back soon and I would surprise him then. I'd pick him up from the airport.

I called Dina at the deli to tell her the news. I called Rosie who had Renata visiting her and told them both. All three of them with the same response, screaming down the phone line.

"EMMIE, YOU'RE GOING TO HAVE A BABY!" They were all so happy for me. I was so excited, but I wasn't telling our parents. I wanted Dave home to do this. I couldn't deal with telling them yet. This was their first grandchild on both sides.

The next morning, I drove to the airport to pick Dave up, no taxi ride home this time.

"Hey Emmie, are you okay, what are you doing here?" he asked, looking very surprised when he saw me waiting.

"Parking is expensive here. I could have taken a taxi." He said, as he was leading me to the exit sign above the glass sliding doors. *Expensive*, I thought. Wait until he finds out what I'm carrying.

"Dave, I'm pregnant!" I was busting to tell him. I stood there, waiting for a big hug and kiss.

"What?" he stopped to ask.

"I'm pregnant, and we're going to be parents!" I said.

He must have been in shock, because he didn't say much after that. We drove home exchanging small talk about his latest trip. When we arrived home, I reapproached the subject of my growing belly.

"Dave, what's wrong? Seriously, can you please say something?" I snapped. I was tired and annoyed. I had been throwing up every morning. I had no one to take care of me, and I felt like shit!

"I'm worried about finances and how will we manage, you won't be able to work."

My eyes must have lit up the room because I was about to detonate like the atomic bomb did when the US dropped it on Japan. Dave sensed it and stopped before he could finish his sentence. I was standing there ready for battle, but then I stopped. No one in this world was going to harm my little peanut. I wasn't going to introduce her to stress yet. I was responsible for my body and I had to protect this little person growing inside of me. I had to remain calm.

"We're going to be parents. You're going to be a father. Think about that Dave, you didn't have a father growing up. Think about the person you want to be to this little peanut growing inside of me. Regardless of the monetary value you seem to place on our future, think about this moment and the other ways we can spoil our daughter, with love." I said calmly.

"How do you know it's going to be a girl?" he asked, rubbing my belly.

"I just do, call it mother's instincts." I said, as I kissed him.

"Now I need your help Dave, we have to decide when we're going to tell our parents."

"Let's wait." he said.

My baby girl had graduated from little peanut to little buzzard bee in no time at all. She had begun to kick and move about. The feeling was exhilarating. There was no other way to describe it. Dave would make me toast smeared with peanut butter and a cup of chamomile tea each night before bed. That seemed to keep my little bee happy, allowing us to happily doze off together.

I stopped throwing up and my belly started to grow. Sex became amazing. My breasts were huge, I was always ready to go and so was Dave. Having cut back on his interstate trips, he was spending more time at home and in the bedroom. It was like we were making up for lost time.

With Renata's help, my dress sense changed from tight jeans to flowing dresses. She helped me hide my belly. My little bee was still our secret and I was not ready to share this with my parents yet. I wasn't ready to hear about the impending baptism and future traditions and expectations when my child hadn't even arrived. I was happy being in the moment, focusing on my little bee, Dave, and my jar of peanut butter. I was in heaven!

CHAPTER 15

THE GOSPEL ACCORDING TO DAVE

DINA WAS COMING over to have scones with jam and cream with our hot chocolates. Her pregnancy cravings were sweet like mine. Dina had found out she was expecting three months after me. We needed our sweet fix before going baby shopping together.

I was busily taking the scones out of the hot oven and wrapping them up in a tea towel when I heard her walk through the front door. Thanks to my mother and her Italian superstitions pregnant women had to try everything that was offered to them, otherwise their child would be born with a birthmark. Anything of an indulgent, decadent sweet nature I had to try. I tried alright. I had gained twenty kilos. I had three weeks left before I could meet bee, I still had lots to do, and I could barely walk.

"Hello fatty, how are you feeling?" Dina asked.

"Really emotional. There are moments I want to cry and then I feel happy again. I can't stand Dave touching me and if he tries again tonight, I'll snap his hand right off!" I said angrily.

"I can't stand having sex anymore, and my back is killing me. I want bee out now. I can't even roll over in bed. Dave had the nerve to suggest calling Father Vincent to see if he could come over to pay me a visit. He thinks I'm possessed because of my mood swings. He thinks if I take Holy Communion that may help me."

"What did you say to him about that?" Dina asked, sheepishly smiling as she smeared homemade strawberry jam on her scone.

"That I was going to scratch his fucking eyes out if he did!" I said, and we both laughed.

When Dave arrived home that evening, I showed him our newly made purchases I had selected with Dina. I bought little fluffy booties, little one-piece jumpsuits, cardigans, and fluffy blankets. The nursery was set. We had painted bee's room in pastel yellow and white. Everything colour coordinated beautifully.

"How much did all this cost?" Dave asked. Before I could answer I felt like someone had stabbed me in my lower back, quick, sharp, and intensely fierce blows.

"I don't feel very well Dave," I said, as I felt the most excruciating pain ever. I looked at the clock, it was 7 o'clock.

I looked at the clock, 9 o'clock the following evening. 26 long hours later, lying in a pool of sweat and exhausted. I had finally pushed Miss Chloe Beatrix Smith out and she had made her spectacular entrance.

"Hello world, watch out, it's me Chloe!" she screamed.

"I told you we were having a girl," I said, looking at Dave. He was protectively holding Chloe tightly wrapped up in a flannel baby wrap.

The very next morning the stream of visitors began to roll in. I really thought the hospital I was staying at was going to put a ban in place, for noise pollution. Italians aren't very good at hiding emotions, even happy ones.

"MAMMA MIA! What a bea-u-t-i-ful baby!" they would all yell. "SHH, please," I'd gently say.

"Emanuela, make sure you keep the baby warm, make sure she has socks on, make sure you breastfeed, make sure you get enough rest," and on it went, my mother, the first time nonna.

Dave was amazing, keeping a protective barrier between Chloe and the visitors, using himself as a human shield between her bassinet and them. My aunties had decorated her tiny cradle with rosary beads for protection. When her grandparents visited, poor little Chloe was passed around and kissed like a religious artefact. My little screamer, she had not stopped since she introduced herself to the world, and girl, was she loud.

Rosie took some time out from her work to stay with me for a few weeks. I really enjoyed having her around. She understood exactly how to help, by keeping me calm when my mother would visit.

"Emanuela, if Chloe screams dip her ciuccio (pacifier) in some scotch whiskey, it helps your father sleep at night." My mother said, as she heard Chloe scream.

"Are you crazy? That's child abuse. I won't be dipping her pacifier in anything. She's hungry, that's why she's screaming!" I said, as I saw Rosie laughing quietly to herself.

"In Italy when babies couldn't sleep, our nonna's would pick red flowers, the type with black seeds in the middle. They would boil them and give a little of the liquid to the baby." My mother said.

"Oh my God Rosie, is she talking about red poppies?" I asked.

"I think she is." Rosie said laughing.

"What the fuck Rosie, this is all too much for me to take in. Seriously, I can do without her home remedies," I said laughing, shaking my head from side to side.

"My little darling Chloe, I'm here to protect you and guide you as best I can," I would whisper in her tiny ear trying to settle her.

"You're a happy little girl, you're smart and a future leader. The world is yours, fearless little bimba" (Infant).

After a few weeks of Chloe being at home she began to settle. I had a very strict routine, and it ran like clockwork. Visiting hours were according to my rules, not everyone else's, and so was their advice on parenthood. Grandparents' visiting was restricted so Chloe could sleep and feeding time was done in a quiet room with music softly playing. I had created a calm environment with scented lavender candles burning and I would lightly spray diluted organic lavender oil in and around her crib.

Dina, Renata and when Rosie was home had free passes. They could come and go as they pleased. I welcomed their visits and adult conversations.

When Dina came to visit, I would rub her fat belly as she was ready to pop.

"Does labour hurt?" she asked.

I couldn't stop laughing. I was laughing so much I felt like I had Renata's Italian laughing juice in me.

"YES, it fucking hurts! Imagine pushing out a three-kilo watermelon from your rear end." I said, laughing.

"Stop, stop I don't want to hear anymore," Dina said, covering her ears.

"I had grand visions for a natural birth until the four-teenth-hour hit and then I started to scream like a mad woman having a psychotic episode. My contractions were three minutes apart and Chloe was not budging. I begged for pain relief and I tore Dave's t-shirt in the process. The nurse couldn't stick that needle in me quickly enough," I said.

"And it continued for another twelve hours!"

"Great! Look at what women endure, hey?" Dina said, as she took another look at Chloe, fast asleep.

The day had arrived, Dina had given birth. I was dressing Chloe ready to take her to meet her new little friend Holly. I had my own little stash of oversized bows attached to headbands. Chloe didn't have any hair and began to look a little like a boy. She had a beautiful moon face, but a completely bald head, not one single strand. The pink headband she wore made her look like a little girl.

"That lucky thing popped Holly out in five drug-free hours," I said to Dave as he walked into Chloe's room.

"So, no torn clothing or scratch marks on Darren's arms then? No skin DNA under Dina's fingernails?" Dave said in his sarcastic tone.

The hospital was the same one I had Chloe in. We had both consistently budgeted enabling us to have our babies there.

We congratulated Dina and Darren, the room was quiet and stress-free, the six of us, the newly appointed soul sisters meeting for the first time. Holly was simply stunning, masses of dark hair and sleeping contently. Dina and I were looking at them both.

"So, I guess we got what we signed up for right?" she whispered to me.

"I guess so, I'm so happy, aren't you?" I asked.

"Yes, absolutely. We're finally mums." She said.

When we arrived home, I began cooking dinner. Chloe was fast asleep. Dave was working in the lounge room, his books and financial statements spread out on the floor. I hated when he spread his work out like this because I knew I would be in for 'the talk'.

"Dave dinner is ready," I called out.

We sat down to eat, perfectly cooked grilled swordfish with organic chargrilled vegetables. Dave looked down at his plate. "How much did this cost?" he asked. *Here we go.*

"You'll need to go back to work soon Em, the interest rates on the mortgage are so high and you keep spending on food, do we need to eat like this?" he asked, pushing his plate towards me.

"Yes, we need to eat. What are you talking about, me going back to work? Chloe is only three months old. I'm not ready to go back, I don't want to work in a deli anymore, and you've never complained about the food I've served you in the past!" I huffed.

"Find yourself a real job, you'll have to start paying super-annuation and contribute to the finances." He said.

I could feel my tears welling up in my eyes and then I felt a lump in my throat and the tears stopped.

"Sure, I'll start looking tomorrow." I said.

That night I pulled a few seat cushions off the sofa and laid them down in Chloe's room where I would sleep by her crib. I wasn't going to sleep with Dave tonight. I was angry with him.

My father would hand over his pay cheque to my mother. She would pay all the bills and put food on the table. She would give my father a weekly allowance. My father trusted my mother to spend their money how she saw fit and he never once questioned her over their finances. There was no 'ours' or 'joint' with the finances in this household, Dave controlled these. He gave me an allowance that I would purchase food with. He paid the bills, he paid for our home, and he would remind me of this often. He would also remind me how I didn't contribute, and I began to feel very guilty. I took care of our baby and our home and I loved doing this, I thought I was contributing?

I didn't have a university degree and I wasn't bringing in a wage like he was. I had to find a job and it wasn't going to be in some stupid little shop. I looked over at Chloe's crib, she was fast asleep with her little arms above her head tightly snug with her little yellow and white frilled quilt covering her.

I had waited four years for my little bee because we had to factor in the financial impact children would have on us. I wasn't ready to hand her over for others to take care of her just yet. I accepted I had to return to work, although I didn't care that I had no money to spend on myself, I managed to make do with what I had. I never complained to Dave.

I realised my mother wasn't happy with my clothing options, she would always sneak money into my bag when I went to visit her. "Go buy yourself something nice to wear," she'd say. But I never did, instead I would purchase things for the household or for Chloe.

I felt so guilty that I wasn't contributing like Dave wanted me to. I was beginning to feel like a failure, and I felt like I had to put a plan in place. I would start researching childcare centres and job opportunities, but I cared about Chloe and she was my first priority. I could forego the nice things I once had, and I cared about how Dave began to make me feel. I was consumed by the pressures of this partnership and was conveyed as an unintelligent individual. Sometimes I felt he was too ashamed to introduce me to his clients. On the occasions he took me to work dinners, they would have discussions about world politics and the stock market. They never thought to include me in these types of conversations, and the other wives were always rude to me. I felt like some alien from another planet, the Italian girl who had a baby and whose education stopped at attending a community night school.

As I was trying to get comfortable on two cushions that kept moving beneath me, I thought of Dimitri.

"Don't pretend to be someone that you're not, don't turn your back on your culture. It's in your blood Ella, be proud, not ashamed." His words were turning in my head. God, I missed him.

I was smart, I was driven, and I had my bee to set an example to. Fuck Dave's work colleagues who liked to eat my food but failed to include me in any conversations. Fuck them all. Dimitri was right!

Chloe started to stir. Feed time again.

CHAPTER 16

FORTUNE COOKIES ARE MISLEADING

I OPENED THE door of my cottage to find Jess standing there holding a little white box and a bottle of my favourite French Champagne.

"Hi! What's all this?" I asked, surprised.

"I told you yesterday I was coming over today, we are going to celebrate. I have Champagne and two raspberry tarts to start the party rolling," Jess said, making her way to my kitchen.

"What are we celebrating?" I asked, as I was following behind her dragging my feet.

Jess turned around, "You, my dear, have dodged a bullet, one, so big in fact. You dodged the bullet with a silver lining, Nguyen!" She said, with a big grin on her face.

Jess and I sat ourselves down, raspberry tarts and glasses of cold Champagne ready to go. She always looked so pretty. The local beauty therapist perfectly waxed, polished and manicured, and had now become my psychologist.

"I need to tell you some home truths about Nguyen," Jess began.

"I've known him for years, I know his ex-wife, his ex-girl-friends, his friends, and his family," Jess said.

I settled myself comfortably in my chair. I was in for a long afternoon conversation and counselling session.

"Emmie, Nguyen is a non-emotional person. He doesn't understand when someone is upset or needs support, as he can't process emotions. He sees them as a difficulty or an inconvenience but really, he lacks empathy or compassion for others. He doesn't understand the concept of emotional value. When the other person begins to express their emotions, he decides the relationship is no longer viable. He labels that person dramatic, controlling, dominating, needy, or even crazy, to justify his inabilities to connect with people on an emotional level." Jess explained.

"I thought he was my partner for life. He said things that made me feel like I was the only woman in his world. But then he had replaced me very quickly. I wasn't expecting to have my emotions scrunched up into a little ball and thrown into the trash." I said.

"I understand Em. He uses social media as a tool to initiate contact with women. It's easier to spin his web behind a screen and not face to face, as it requires less effort. I mean, if you met this guy for a first date without any prior contact, you would sum him up pretty quickly and most likely run for the hills! He likes to 'smooth talk' before the first date. I bet he swept you off your feet, right?" Jess asked.

"He did, he liked the photo you posted of us both when we went to the concert in the park. It went from there." I said.

"Geez, that was ages ago, and let me guess, he called you beautiful right?" Jess asked.

I was shocked, I thought I was going to choke on my raspberry tart and started to cough a little.

"YES!" I said, "How did you know?" I asked.

"Because he says they're all beautiful in the beginning, Em." Jess said, and I began to cry.

"Honey, most of his relationships expire after two years, including his marriage. As soon it becomes too difficult for him, he will start to make excuses, and sometimes the other person will feel like they are going crazy because they're at a loss or feel like a failure. He will idolise her and then back away, leaving them confused and hurt. Like he did with Amanda, and to this day she still blames herself. She walks around thinking she's the failure, and can't move beyond the pain, how fucking sad is that?" Jess said.

"Then there was Kate. He dated her for a year, and he told everyone she had mental health issues. She's actually a really nice person. Last I heard she was still nursing in a city clinic somewhere. All she wanted was closure because he had already moved on to Amanda. Kate wasn't crazy she only wanted a face to face explanation, which under normal mature relationship breakups you would most likely get. That's the normal, respectful thing to do, you'd think. But Nguyen doesn't operate like that, he doesn't know how to." Jess said.

I was slowly emptying my box of tissues, in-between sips of Champagne and sobs.

"You need to stop believing it was you and find some belief in yourself."

"I love you too much to see you like this, but I haven't finished yet!" Jess continued, topping up my glass.

"I get it Jess. I can see now he was an attention seeker, using social media as a tool." I said.

"I understand how he builds you up and puts you on a pedestal, but then his rejection destroys your self-esteem and makes you feel like no one is ever going to love you like that again. But it wasn't love. It was never going to be love, he didn't love you. He spent money on nice things, but they meant nothing to him. He didn't find joy in giving them to you or from anything you gave him." She said.

"I'm really angry at myself because I put thought into the things I gave him, and the things I did for him, I did that out of love. He actually told me off once for leaving the price tag attached to a shirt I bought him, I left it on in case he wanted to return it." I said.

Jess pulled out her phone and found a photo of Nguyen and Amanda online.

"LOOK!" she pointed.

"SEE! That fucking necklace that you have around your neck is the *EXACT* same one Amanda is wearing in this photo!" she said.

"He bought her that for her birthday. When he dumped Amanda, he had just finished having sex with her, then he left her, devastated. He told her she was too needy and clingy. I'm now guessing he dumped her because he had you in his sights."

"I still feel like I have fucked up in some way," I said, in-between sobs. "I feel like I wasn't easy to get along with. I feel like I should have tried harder."

"He doesn't deserve you or any other decent loving woman. I know it's horrible to hear. But you have to stop wasting your time trying to figure out why you weren't good enough, why doesn't he love you. You are feeding your insecurities." Jess said with conviction.

"He will always be looking for greener pastures, never satisfied in his life, and if it was you marrying him, he would ultimately leave you and you wouldn't be able to stop him. Stop blaming yourself and trying to be what others want you to be, that's not love, that's being a people pleaser." She said.

"Don't mourn him, Emmie. Be angry for yourself, but be sorry for him because he will never have that real deep connection that genuine people have. You are a survivor. You deserve to be in a real relationship where you can grow and change and it's accepted, not dismissed. Turn your attention to the person who deserves it most, YOU."

Jess was right. I already knew all of this deep down. I had been caught up in some pipedream, a stupid excuse to let some bastard treat me badly. But she was also right about me being a people pleaser. I'm in my forties and I still struggle with saying no.

"Things weren't always bad between us, Jess. We had fun times and we shared lots of laughs too. I blame myself because I was supporting Dave, supporting my kids, and trying to be there for Nguyen. I was burning the candle at both ends and I wasn't coping. I wasn't exactly nice all the time either, I could be mean to him too. I was intentionally pushing him away because of my fear of getting hurt. I did apologise and try to explain that the pressure was getting too much, but I never got a real shot at explaining this to him." I said wiping my tears.

"Explain? EXPLAIN! What the fuck, Em? If he loved you, he would support and listen to you, that's what relationships are about. It's called under-stand-ing..." she over expanded the word angrily.

"You wouldn't have insecurities if he made you feel secure in the first place."

"He saw you as an option and not a priority. He feels vulnerable on his own so he seeks a new lover to transition to. Do you really think he didn't have her on the scene for a while? You don't ask someone to marry you after a few weeks, Em? Did you ever think your fear actually may have saved you on this one occasion?"

Jess was right, Nguyen couldn't stand me supporting Dave. I explained to him that being married to someone for twenty plus years was hard to turn your back on. *He* was still paying his ex-wife's parking fines ten years later. I wouldn't dare interfere with his relationship between him and the mother of his children, so what gave him the right to have a say with my relationship with Dave, the father of my children? It felt like he wanted me to choose. I was controlled and blamed for various reasons. If I didn't know any better, I'd think he was egocentric.

I thought about my parents, raising me to be respectful, and to be 'good'. I had visions of high school coming back to me, of my life growing up, and of my marriage. I *am* a people pleaser, and I tend to go with the flow for the people I love and I'd do anything for them. Is this a bad thing? No, but without boundaries I risk getting caught up in a pipedream, it can be unhealthy. I had to make changes to my life primarily to prevent this happening to me again. I had to recognise the signs sooner and remove anyone who were ever to take advantage of my emotional state again!

"I'm a leader in my life, I take action, I know the old me would have said, "Fuck you," but he had this power over me." I said.

"Do you remember when you stormed into John Heddle's office, and you had your folder of statistics and evidence on social media bullying, and what was going on at that school?" Jess asked.

"Yes!" I replied. John Heddle was the school principal of the elite private school our children attended.

"You said to Heddle, "*Your* school fosters bullying, it has a longstanding culture of harassment. As the school principal, you turn a blind eye to the students who come from backgrounds of wealth and fail to support the students who are being bullied and targeted." And he stood up from behind his desk, took your folder, slammed it down, and told you to leave immediately. In fact, you said he yelled at you." Jess said with a smile on her face.

I began to laugh, "That fucker did yell at me! He was furious! I told him I was going to go to the Minister for

Education because he was failing to address the effects of online bullying that target kids like ours. And we, as parents were stupid enough to pay exorbitant fees for our children to attend his privileged, pretentious school. I told him he could kiss my well-educated, well-rounded arse goodbye because I was pulling my son out of his un-Christian like community."

Jess and I were in hysterics. I did go to the Minister for Education. I did report the school for failing to address such issues, and I did enrol my son into another school. I caused such a stir I had parents congratulating me at the local shops because their child had experienced cyber-bullying too and it went unaddressed. These kids were too frightened to speak up. Over two hundred parents signed my petition to introduce change to the school policy addressing cyber-bullying and online safety.

"How did that make you feel Em?" Jess asked.

"Fucking awesome!" I said.

"That's the Emmie we all love and want back." Jess said.

She was right. I had to find my resilience. Even our self-beliefs have expiry dates. I thought Nguyen was a blessing when I first met him, but instead he turned out to be a lesson.

Of course, I loved Nguyen. What we had may not have been real to him, but it was to me. It was very wrong what he did to me. Did he care? Most likely not. How did he think I would feel after hearing his happy announcement? In true style, I didn't react and I walked away with class and dignity, unlike Nguyen. I was simply too good for him.

Fuck you, Nguyen Xin.

"Cheers, girlfriend!" We both drank to that.

CHAPTER 17

BIG GIRLS DON'T CRY

I LOVED MY job. I was so blessed my role allowed me to factor in work-life balance. Finding a job wasn't hard it just took a little longer than I had planned. I was determined to prove a point to Dave. I wasn't going to sit at home crying and feeling sorry for myself. I wanted a job that was going to feed my desire to want to work each day. I was working for a politician in a community liaison role.

I had met my boss at a rally. I had been attending lots of political rallies. I had become very active in my local community. I guess I inherited this from my father, "Keep the bastards honest," he'd say. Something I felt very passionate about was the farming industry and the introduction of genetically modified foods and crops. Society had to take a stand against industries trying to change the components of fresh produce. Who cares if an apple wasn't as red and shiny as it should be, or carrots weren't long and straight?

My boss was a local Member of Parliament and was supporting genetically modification to canola crops. He was speaking on behalf of the farmers who supported it. I was a part of a campaign team that organised rallies to push the government to have GM foods and crops regulated. I mean, who was approving and passing all of this? Food safety regulations were limited and the law around this was loose. This allowed for organisations to abuse their power and ultimately fail the consumers who were unaware of what they were buying or eating. There were no mandatory labelling identifying such foods.

I would take Chloe with me. She would sit in her stroller embracing her surroundings and participating in the chanting around her shaking her wooden maraca. Someone had to lead the way and get the point across to stop messing with our food we were feeding to our children. Renata had designed me some t-shirts and screen printed one for Chloe to wear. It read 'I'm lucky, my mama knows what she feeds me'.

The day I was offered my job, Ryan Hadwell MP and I were on the top steps of Parliament House. I knew who he was, and I had very little time for him. He was a short little arrogant man. He knew who I was too. He had caught me on many occasions sticking flyers around the outside of his office walls. 'GM-FREE', 'KEEP OUR CROPS HONEST', they would read with pictures of yellow corn and canola flowers on them.

As soon as my boss had finished speaking and addressing the crowd of people, it was my turn.

"Minister Hadwell promotes GM foods and is trying to block regulations to this. He leads people to believe that there is nothing wrong with genetically modified foods. He's trying to sell us the benefits, however I am here to inform you about the opposing argument. He tells us crops would grow better under harsher climates, will require less water, more resistant to insect attack, and grow quicker. There will be less money for farmers to outlay, therefore greater profits. But what about the farmer who lives in the next paddock and who is trying to keep his crops organic? This would be impossible for that to occur if you have someone next door spraying their crops. Think about the long-term impact this has." I said.

"What happened to transparency and labelling the foods we buy so we can make informed choices for our families and our children? What about soy, cotton, canola farmers. Keep things real, let's keep our foods real." I said.

"The regulations around GM crops are the responsibility of Federal and State Governments, Minister Hadwell is a representative of our State. And what a sorry State we live in if he blocks the regulations to GM foods. Who will undertake the risks associated with GM produced foods? What government body will oversee these processes, gene technology, and the cultivation of these crops?" The crowd were cheering and clapping, some were heckling the Minister.

"Miss Smith, you've really stirred up the crowd, you're a very passionate individual who never seems to give up." He leaned over and said to me.

"It's MRS Smith. And NO! I don't give up. Sir, YOU have a lot to learn about the importance of food! You should be setting up community gardens in our area, teaching children responsibility and educating them through growing their own foods. Promoting healthy eating, look at the bigger picture." I said, without stopping to take a breath.

"Will you work for me, *Mrs* Smith? Are you prepared to develop such plans? I am looking for a community liaison person, someone who has the drive and determination to make this work."

"You're supporting genetically modified crops, are you deranged?" I asked.

Ryan laughed, his belly started wobbling.

"I want to listen to my constituents, or I might actually lose the next election. You're going to help me win, Mrs Smith. I want you to help me understand both sides of the argument. My advisors could use a little help too, they're advocating for the agricultural industry, you're advocating for families and communities. We could potentially make a nice little working party together. I need to look at the wider community and its needs." He said.

I was completely surprised. I didn't see myself working for the opposition, but what if I could actually make a significant change through Ryan Hadwell? This was an opportunity I knew I had to seize. I had to get my foot in the door, even if it was via the back entrance.

"There are some days my assistant will need to come into work with me," I said, as I looked down at Chloe.

"Name your terms, Mrs Smith. Come see me after this rally, if I make it out of here alive thanks to you." He said.

"It's Emmie," I said, as I extended my hand to shake his.

Working full time had its challenges. Some days I felt like crying and I did, mostly because I was exhausted. I had to leave Chloe with my parents or at the local childcare centre. I felt like I was missing out watching her grow up. Her vocabulary was growing, and she understood my mother speaking to her in Italian. "Mangia, bella," (Eat, lovely) my mother would say to Chloe, indicating for her to eat and she would take another chunk of continental bread and put it to her little mouth. Chloe was coming home with ribbons and clips in her hair and having a great time. She was well fed and happy. My mother had even taught her an Italian song, *Ciao Buongiorno*. Chloe preferring this, instead of me singing *Twinkle Twinkle Little Star*.

Dave was extremely happy also. I was finally contributing to the household expenses. He didn't care if I attended my political rallies as long as he had a hot meal each night to come home to. *He* worked full-time. Implementing community gardens wasn't as easy as I had anticipated.

I had proposals to write up and meetings to attend. I had presentations to prepare for Ryan when he attended local community groups. I then had Chloe who needed me most.

This new balancing act taught me all about exceptional organisational skills, because without these I would drown. However, my guilt was consuming me.

I was excited. I finally had a day off and Dina and I were taking the girls into the city for a little retail therapy.

Dina was a stay at home mum, she was thriving taking care of Holly and planning her next addition. Dave and I had decided on one child, he said we couldn't possibly afford any more. I guess deep down I did want another baby eventually, I secretly wanted three. I had always wished for a brother or a sister. Dave had five brothers, and it made me a little sad to think of Chloe growing up without a sibling. I was an advocate for others, however I seemed to let myself down the most. I wished I had the nerve to be honest with Dave about my maternal desires, but I didn't want to disappoint or let him down. He had our future all planned and paid for.

"Emmie you look tired, you look like you could use a coffee," Dina said. We had been walking around with our bags attached to our strollers, both girls happily sitting in them sipping on their drink bottles.

"Let's go try the new coffee shop that's opened up around the corner, we can sit in there and feed the girls lunch," I said.

It was too loud in the food court beneath the department store.

Dina and I were walking side by side, Chloe and Holly occasionally holding one another's hands from their strollers, making our way to the elevators.

"Ella! ELLA!" I heard as I turned around.

Dimitri? Was it him? I was looking, but I could only see the lunchtime crowd streaming into the food court.

"ELLA," I saw Dimitri running towards me.

He still looked the same after all of these years. Still the same smile, and the same butterflies in my stomach.

He put his arms tightly around me, and for a moment, the world stopped spinning.

"Dina!" he said, as he turned and kissed her on the cheek.

I looked around and I saw a tall woman awkwardly standing behind him. I heard Dimitri had recently married.

"Dina, Ella, this is my wife Constantina." He said, pushing her towards me. I leaned up and politely kissed her on the cheek.

Constantina looked more like a Con, I thought to myself. She was taller than Dimitri. She had a very masculine look, harsh and chiselled. She seemed pleasant enough. She bent down to greet the girls in their strollers while introducing herself to Dina, engaging in a conversation.

"I heard you had a baby, Ella. I thought you would have named her after your mother," he said.

"I'm not a traditionalist Dimitri, you know that." I said, sounding a little annoyed.

"You are, more than you'd like to think." He said.

"She's gorgeous, Ella, she has the biggest green eyes like yours. I hope you're going to teach her Italian." He said.

He moved me away from the stroller and closer to the crowds of people, out of hearing range.

"I know why you cut me out of your life. I accepted that, but just know we will be together again. We'll always be in each other's lives. Something will eventually bring us back together. All we have is time and plenty of it, it's just not the right time *now*." He said. I felt my face heating up.

I caught Constantina glancing over at me. He guided my arm back to the stroller.

"I've seen you in the newspapers, still advocating, trying to make a difference to this world. Don't let yourself down in the process Ella. You should be priority number one, that's going to be your biggest fight." He said.

"Look after her, Dina. She forgets she's important too and doesn't have to save the world." He said.

He bent down to look at Chloe and stroked her arm.

"You, little miss, look like your mummy."

He stood up and hugged Dina goodbye, he turned to me and kissed me. He took Constantina by the hand, and they walked off. He turned to look back at me, and I knew it wasn't goodbye at all. The universe had sent me a little reminder that he was always going to be there for me no matter what, and I smiled. I knew I would see him again.

"What did he say to you? What was that all about, you know he's always liked you right?" Dina asked.

"MAMA I want ikey!" Chloe said, pointing to the ice-cream stand in the food court. *Perfectly timed*, I thought, avoiding answering Dina's questions.

"Yes, my darling, mama will buy you ice cream." I replied.

CHAPTER 18

INTELLIGENCE IS A CURSE

MONEY WAS GREAT for Dave and I, our finances were very healthy. Ryan Hadwell MP had won the latest State election, therefore rolling over my contract for another three years. He said I was the smartest asset he had on his dynamic little team. "Tax-funded money well spent," he'd say, each time I presented him with a work-related report.

I was earning a pretty decent wage, for a *woman*. I had moved on from the community liaison role to political researcher. My financial contribution to my marriage assisted our little family to move into a bigger home with a tennis court and a swimming pool. "Great for entertaining," Dave said, as we signed on the dotted line when we bought it.

He had his latest fast car and various other toys he enjoyed playing with. Going away for him now consisted of fishing charters with mates and five-star accommodation, no more interstate business trips. He had purchased a nice little office in the city that he worked from. I now welcomed my alone time at home, Chloe and I would entertain ourselves. We would go out to lunch, high teas or to the movies, and I would take her to see the latest kids live shows. We would bake cakes together and make different coloured play dough and macaroni necklaces.

I was feeling very blessed, in fact as soon as I woke each day, I would thank the universe for its generosity. Chloe was about to begin school. I was fortunate to have Dina and Renata on standby when I needed help taking her to and from kindergarten, when I had to work. Things were running smoothly, it was like Dave and I had rediscovered our love for one another. We were in the throes of planning Chloe's birthday party. We had arranged a baby zoo to visit and pony rides for all her little friends. We had a large front yard that was surrounded by beautiful black fencing and gates, the ideal spot.

I was looking forward to seeing Rosie again. I had finally accepted she would never return home, she had met Karl and they moved in together. Karl worked as a radiologist. Her parents still had no idea they were living together. Karl would stay at a mate's place if her parents ever visited. They found it hard accepting he was German and not Italian. In fact, they preferred saying he was an Aussie. Rosie had really crossed the line with this one. In their eyes, he was an outcast. Karl was a Lutheran. They were both flying in for the party. Rosie and Renata were Chloe's godmothers.

"Mama, when is the zoo coming?" Chloe asked, as she jumped on the bed, missing Dave's head.

"Time to get up Dave," I said nudging him.

"Soon darling, let's go get you some breakfast first," I said as I climbed out of bed.

"You have a big day ahead, are you excited?" I asked her.

"Y-E-S!" she screeched.

The party area had been set up. Renata came over the night before to help. She decorated the entertaining area in rainbow coloured streamers and balloons. She had made the paper streamers and lanterns with Chloe. Renata was running children's art classes. The catering had all been taken care of, this was arriving all prepared in time for the guests to eat. I had no time to make or bake anything these days so paying someone else to do all the hard work was the best option.

I heard the intercom buzz, it was Renata. I pushed the button to open the gates to let her in.

"HAPPY BIRTHDAY CHLOE!" she said, as she made her way inside running up to kiss and hug her.

Chloe was so excited. She was having a birthday party with her friends, and was growing up so fast.

These sorts of parties stressed me out a lot. We always seemed to be entertaining these days. I was over the large crowds of people, the food preparation and the excessive consumption of alcohol.

Chloe took off outside to wait for the pony to arrive.

"Feel like a glass of Champagne?" I asked Renata.

I popped open a bottle of our favourite French bubbly. *Gone are the days of Lambrusco,* I thought to myself as I was pouring it into crystal glasses.

"We should wait until Rosie arrives," Renata said.

I walked over to the fridge and opened the door. I showed Renata the side shelves that were filled with bottles of French Champagne. She laughed.

The day seemed to fly. Caterers soon arrived, and the kitchen benches quickly filled with trays of food, ready for the guests. I was excited for Chloe, she was running around with her friends without a care in the world. I could hear her laughter from outside. It was moments like these that my stress disappeared, hearing little children laughing and embracing the moment.

Rosie was outside exchanging pleasantries with the Italian relatives, introducing Karl and explaining the war was in fact over. It was safe to accept the new German into the family. She was listening sympathetically to them. They were explaining what life had been like for them as children growing up during the Second World War in Italy. The trauma they all experienced because of the German army invading their village and the pain and memories they still carried with them today.

I stood by the sliding doors eavesdropping and listening to their conversations.

"Rosie, the German army cut all the electricity to the village, we were too scared to even burn candles at night in fear they would see us." I heard my mother say in Italian.

"Rosie, it was terrible for us. I was only a little girl your zia had to go out and pick apples and then carry a big basket full on her head and walk through the village alone. She was stopped by two German soldiers. Imagine the fear, Rosie." I heard my aunt say to her.

"Yes, Rosie bella, all I remember is big black shiny boots up to their knees. I would never make eye contact with those bastardo brutto" (ugly bastards). I heard my mother say.

"That bastard Mussolini was in bed with the Germans, then Italy changed sides on October 13, 1943." My father said. *Bless him*, I thought, he always remembered significant dates.

I wonder what Karl would think if he understood Italian, as I continued to listen. I didn't want him to feel awkward. I could hear Rosie trying to explain strategies in Italian on how to change the pain and suffering they were feeling with optimistic thinking. These had been very dark times for our parents.

I was laughing to myself. She was so smart in her field of work, but not so smart when it came to smoothing over, and sweet talking her way around Italians. She wasn't going to find any scientific formula to navigate her way out of this one. We simply did not marry non-Catholics, and her well-meaning suggestions meant very little to them. If you're not armed with a good supply of food or sympathy, you're as good as gone to an Italian. They didn't want positive healing they wanted their opportunity to speak and someone to listen.

"Rosie, can you please come and help me inside," I called out to her. I began to laugh, I had my Champagne in hand, and poured her a glass.

"Rosie, why don't you let your parents stick with their story about Karl, so what if it's exaggerated? Haven't you learnt anything from your upbringing?" I asked.

"Let them tell people he's a good Catholic Aussie doctor. Don't take things like this to heart. You already know it's all about other people's perceptions with our parents. There's always going to be competition amongst them. It's not something you can control or change. Accept them for who they are, they have limiting beliefs. Big deal. They exaggerate most things!"

"I agree, but it's disrespectful to Karl, he wants to fit in so badly and I shouldn't have left him out there on his own." She said eyeing off the side glass doors.

I began to laugh, "He's a grown man, he will be fine. He's German," I replied.

"Rosie, stop denying yourself the opportunity for happiness, you have a beautiful man who loves you. Here, have a glass of Champagne," I said handing her one.

"He's already fitting in, he's sitting outside with them, isn't he?" I asked.

"You have the opportunity to marry for love and not for convenience if you choose to do so. Our parents were restricted to who was available in their village at the time, imagine that? I'm sure they had dreams and aspirations like we do, but unlike us, they lacked the opportunities. Marriage is a universal happening, if you and Karl choose to live together instead then do so. That's your business."

"When did you become so mature?" she asked.

"Mature!" I said sounding surprised.

"Learning from experiences makes you wiser. Through positive and negative experiences, you become a more insightful and judicious individual. Life dishes out more than we can handle at times and I've had my fair share. How you handle situations is based on the different circumstances that you have encountered throughout your lifetime. I guess I've matured learning through past events and how well I've moved on from those. Remember what we used to say as teenagers about our parents' behaviours?"

"Yes, we can choose not to be our genes or adopt our parents' behaviours," she said.

"That's right. But not only that, we can choose not to think like them and find ways on how to deal with their traditions and expectations. It doesn't stop when you find a life partner or have kids like we once hoped, we can't run from it, but we can find ways around it."

Rosie was listening intently, looking at me like she had discovered a new gene mutation. I could see her mind thinking.

"I guess in reality I don't care what they say about my relationship with Karl, you're right it's really not a big deal. I love him, we have a great set up in Melbourne, and they'll eventually accept him," she said.

"They already have, Rosie, because we'd all know about it if they hadn't!" I said.

"Has Karl used the R-word on you yet when you've been stressed?" I asked smiling.

"YES!" she replied.

"And…?" I asked.

"I told him to GO TO HELL and to never use that word again!" she said.

I was in hysterics. I was laughing so hard.

"See, he fits in beautifully then! You gave him an out and he chose to stay! He's not going anywhere you've got yourself a keeper." I said.

"I still remember the day Dave told me to *relax* and I went crazy. From that day on he has never repeated the R word and he still stuck around. Never tell an Italian to relax!"

"Here, try my stuffed mushrooms," I added, handing her some on a plate as she popped one in her mouth.

"Oh my God, these are delicious," she said grabbing a second one.

"I thought you said you didn't make anything, you had it all catered for." She said.

"I had only said that so my mother wouldn't stress out, it put pressure on her because she had to cook for the party. I told her what she wanted to hear. I could think of more constructive ways of spending my time, other than helping her cook. She's getting old. She should be resting, and not cooking for others." I said.

The party continued well into the night. The guests had left, Chloe was bathed and in bed. It was the adults turn now. The Champagne bottle numbers were down in the fridge, we had gone through nearly a dozen between all of us. I was looking at Chloe's gifts, a table full of 'stuff', the latest toys that her uncles had spoilt her with. Rosie and Renata had given Chloe the most exquisite little heart-shaped charm on an Italian gold chain. It had her initials engraved on the back with the number five on it. Chloe was safe. She was surrounded by intelligent, strong, fearless women. Little bee held the world in the palm of her hands.

Chloe's education started off with a bang. She had settled beautifully into her new school. She had decided she wanted to play the violin. She was thriving. She had signed up to play school sport as well, and her social calendar was filling up fast.

I had always wished she had a sibling and now my wish had come true. I knew I was pregnant even without taking a pregnancy test. I wasn't feeling sick like I had with Chloe, I was feeling great. I didn't even book in to see Doctor Rogers, I sat and waited… for thirteen weeks. It was easy to hide. I hadn't gained weight and I wasn't craving sweets. In fact, I wasn't hungry at all. Perhaps I had lost my appetite, knowing Dave was going to hit the roof when he found out. I knew I should have had a scan at twelve weeks, but I was postponing the inevitable. I knew the exact night we had conceived our latest little addition and that was the night of Chloe's fifth birthday party.

"Dave, can you please schedule a morning off next week?" I asked at dinner time.

"I need you to come to an appointment with me."

"What kind of an appointment, is it at Chloe's school?" he asked.

"No, Dave it's at the hospital. Doctor Rogers has booked me in for an ultrasound. I'm pregnant. In fact, I'm nearly sixteen weeks."

"What? You've known all this time without telling me, you kept this from me?" He was seething.

"I wasn't ready to tell you for this exact reason, predicting your reaction. Your insecurities over our finances depress me. It's always about the future with you. I'm in my twenties for fuck sakes, enough already!" I hadn't yelled at Dave like this before, I was shocked and I thought he was too, it must be my pregnancy hormones. I could feel my face and my chest heating up.

Chloe had come out from her room with her quarter size violin in one hand and the bow in the other.

I was furious. I was sick and tired of planning for the future when I was missing living in the present. Everything had to be planned with Dave, including his sperm. He must have had more Champagne that night than he could handle. I was beginning to feel very controlled by him. I was beginning to feel sick and it wasn't the pregnancy. It was a feeling I had that life was about to throw different lessons my way, and I wasn't sure I was ready. I was scared. I stood up.

"Are you sure you're not Italian because it seems to be all about image to you and what others think! Nice car, nice home, means nothing Dave if you can't fill it with a family." I said.

"Chloe, you're going to be a big sister." I said, as I took her instrument and led her by the hand to her room.

"Are you excited?" I asked.

She looked as stunned as her father. I left Dave sitting alone at the dining table.

CHAPTER 19

XAVIER JULIUS WAS born on Christmas Day. It was the best Christmas I ever had. I was in labour for a total of four hours, no pain relief, no dramas, with only a few simple pushes and out he popped.

By dinner time, I was sitting up in the hospital bed eating slices of Christmas turkey served with cranberry sauce. Xavier was the complete opposite to his sister. He had lots of hair, dark eyes, and most importantly he was quiet. There were no crowds of people lined up at the maternity ward door waiting to meet him, only Chloe and Dave.

I left the hospital the very next day. My mother helped me at home for a few days after, but I already had everything under control. I had pre-prepared meals in the freezer, baby clothes washed, neatly folded, and disposable nappies stacked up in his bedroom cupboard. I didn't want my mother sensing matrimonial woes between her only daughter and son-in-law, I mean, what would people think?

I had spent most of my pregnancy arguing with Dave over money and how we would make ends meet. Our finances weren't in a state of disrepute, in fact, they were still quite healthy. It was Dave's thoughts that had grown into an invasive weed. I was annoyed at supporting him and reassuring him all would be fine. I already had one child and I was preparing for our second. It was his fears and insecurities, not mine that were causing problems between us. He couldn't see we were already 'wealthy'. We were fortunate enough to have one beautiful, happy healthy well-adjusted child that we loved very much, with another on the way. Life wasn't really all that bad, but it's what he was choosing to make of it. He was too busy trying to acquire more. I wasn't too happy with my character of late either, because I viewed our wealth differently to how he believed it to be. Although I was perceived as stupid, I had moved beyond the 'uneducated fool' I had once felt like. His story needed editing, or I would begin to write my own.

I had lost my job. Politics doesn't wait for someone to come back from maternity leave. In fact, it wasn't even an option that had been offered to me and I had been replaced quite quickly. Note to myself, this was an area I had to tackle when I got back on my feet. The working conditions for women were unsatisfactory and inadequate. I had no right to return to my previous employment.

"Emmie, if you need a reference, I would be most happy to provide you with one," Ryan said, when he handed me my last pay cheque. *Thanks,* I thought to myself as I walked out the door. On the pin-up board I left behind hundreds of photos of the community gardens I helped establish. I had served my purpose well.

XJ was the baby of my dreams. My little marshmallow, so quiet, cuddly, and cosy, I loved him so much. I would feed him, and he would happily lie next to me. His big sister would come in and pat him on his head and gently kiss him. He spent most of his time eating and sleeping. When he was awake, he would observe Chloe playing nearby.

"XJ, do you want to play with me?" Chloe would ask as she shoved a doll in his face waving it about.

"CHLOE! Gentle please, remember what I've told you XJ is still little, you have to be gentle with him."

He was unlike his sister. Not a single peep out of my boy, it was extraordinary. I would often check to see if he was still breathing when he was asleep. I could have ten kids if they were guaranteed to be like XJ. Rosie should write her latest thesis about this, two siblings out of the same gene pool with completely opposite traits, from conception.

"Mama, I'm going to play a song for XJ on my violin," Chloe said, as she came home from school.

She had become quite the little violinist. Nothing was too hard for Chloe and she loved a challenge. Students at her school were envious of her. She was the life of the party, the Pied Piper who has an infectious personality. She suited carrying a violin case reminding me of a 1950's gangster. *XJ might need someone like her in his life,* I thought to myself.

I began visiting a local women's community group and I would bring XJ with me. I would walk past the centre on my way to take Chloe to school. It was a centre for disadvantaged women and single mothers. It's where they could drop in with their children for a coffee and chat with a social worker. It was federally funded and overseen by the local council.

I walked in one day, looking for a place that might like the books I wanted to donate. Dave suggested I begin borrowing books from the library instead of buying them, saving on costs. I also had lots of balls of wool and knitting needles belonging to my mother, who now preferred to buy her grandchildren cardigans instead of knitting them.

The social workers welcomed donations like these. I set up cane baskets I had purchased myself around the coffee room filled with my donations. It felt good giving back to the community. I had committed to going in once a week to refill the baskets with wool as my contribution to the organisation.

XJ was growing up fast and I was itching to get back to work. I was sick of the dramas at home, the same topic regurgitated over and over.

It wasn't long before the social workers became my friends. Although I wasn't a single parent, they welcomed my time and contributions.

Sharni Kendall was one of the new social workers at the women's centre. I found her quietness, insightfulness, and humility cute. Sharni was gay. I hadn't really met any gay women before in the mid-nineties. She was Malaysian, arty looking, thin, short, dark hair, and wore glasses with brightly coloured frames. We connected from day one, although she disputed this.

"Who's that chick? She has the eyes I had always wished for," I heard Sharni ask the other social worker.

"She looks a bit mean though. I'm a bit apprehensive to approach her."

I made my way to Sharni, trying not to laugh out loud. I hadn't realised I came across as hostile. I preferred to think of myself as confident, well organised, and focused.

"Hi. I'm Emmie, and that's my son Xavier Julius, XJ for short," as I pointed towards him.

"Pleased to meet you." I said, as I offered to shake Sharni's hand.

Sharni smiled. "Want a coffee, Emmie?"

"I would love one." I said.

Sharni and I became best friends quickly. She was a quiet achiever and extremely humble. We shared meaningful stories where I would confide in her about my life, my fears, and my dreams. She would respectfully listen, and I did the same for her. She held no judgment towards me or the types of conversations I'd have with her. She was always there for me day or night. I would quite often tell her she would make the perfect male partner and we would laugh. She understood my sense of humour well. She was always trying to entice me to eat unusual food stepping outside of my comfort zone. We would spend time together at the centre, where we would brainstorm.

Changes had to be made to improve the working conditions for women.

"Why is it that a man can contribute into his superannuation fund, but women can't because they're a stay at home mum? They've had a break in their employment. They're not earning a wage. They're not being paid to cook and clean. Marriage shouldn't imply if you have a husband then he's your future financial security. That mindset needs to change. I bet the women who come here never saw themselves divorced or separated, we don't have crystal balls." I said.

"You've got balls, Emmie," Sharni said.

"Someone has to these days, women are being screwed over," I said.

"How are we going to do this?" I asked her, taking a scrapbook out of the back of XJ's stroller, ready to scribe ideas with a blue crayon.

"We need to focus on creating independent financial security for women, but we need to change the way they think also. We have to begin with empowering women. Drop the fear, and help build their confidence, so they don't return to bad relationships because of money." I said.

"We could run some great workshops here at the centre, they already see this as a safe space, and we could network with local businesses. Finding women who work in financial institutions who are prepared to donate some of their time and skills to speak to them?" I suggested.

"I stopped working to have a child, if I were single how could I afford to pay for my rent or apply for a bank loan?

Some women are from non-English speaking backgrounds. They wouldn't even know where to begin with their rights and entitlements, they're even more vulnerable." I said.

"Emmie, I absolutely love your passion and motivation. I will apply for a Federal Government grant for the centre so I can employ someone like you. I want you to work with me, Em." She said.

"Absolutely, I can't wait!" I said.

CHAPTER 20

DAVE AND I both made a point to support small businesses run by women in our local community. Some had children who attended the same school as Chloe. I had my reservations about it suiting and meeting XJ's needs. I was worried. Chloe had become a leader at school. The principal once described her at assembly as, "Someone others should strive to be like."

XJ attended work with me at the centre. All the women there would pinch his little cheeks and bring him treats. He would happily sit with us sipping chamomile tea and eating organic sugar-free homemade biscuits. He saw first-hand some of the struggle's women encountered in their lives.

XJ was my little shadow. He would help me with the cooking, hanging out the washing, doing the grocery shopping, while Chloe would be tinkering outdoors with her father.

"Dad I want to build a car, why can't we build a car together?" she asked Dave.

"We can build a car. You can build anything you want. You can become an aerospace engineer and build a rocket and fly to the moon and back if that's what you want to do." Dave would say.

Dave was such a fantastic dad, but I wished he would include XJ in his together time with Chloe. I felt at times XJ lacked a male role model. He was beginning to walk around the house chanting, "We want better pay and we want it now!"

His colouring in consisted of helping the women at the centre make posters for rallies.

"I'M A SUPERHERO MUMMY," he'd say, wrapping a poster around his back and running around the room.

"Mummy, can I play with Sam today?" he asked.

"Sure honey, we can go visit Sam." *I could use a coffee and a chat with Jess,* I thought to myself. I was feeling dejected about Dave and his illusions over our finances. I was doubtful over my relationship with him. I was sad and constantly tired. If I looked closer, I would find depression.

Jess Thompson was the local beauty therapist. Chloe and I would get our nails painted there and sometimes XJ joined us. Jess was so bubbly, a mother herself, she seemed to put the needs of her clients before her young family. Jess had a little boy the same age as XJ, Sam. Sam and XJ will be starting school together in the next few weeks. Jess and I had become really good friends. We would catch up for drinks at the local hotel and sometimes stay out late dancing.

"Jess, I'm struggling with my life, I've been feeling down, and I haven't been feeling well either," I said, watching the boys playing out the back of Jess's place as we drank our coffee.

"It's no wonder you're feeling the way you do, you're always fighting for others. Start putting yourself first, you're pretty low down on your own list of priorities. I don't know how you do it or understand why?" Jess asked.

"Someone has to and I want women to be taken seriously in this day and age." I said.

"I feel like at times Dave doesn't value my opinions. I feel like Chloe was the novelty and XJ is the reality with him because he's changed ever since I had him. He puts more pressure on himself with the finances and that has a flow-on effect to me. He behaves like a child himself sometimes. He has this fear of missing out whenever I spend time with the kids. I've stopped asking him to join in with us, because he's no longer fun to be around. He drinks when he's stressed and that upsets me. My priorities changed when I had my kids, I no longer feel the need to party and drink at happy hour. He's an adult and I wish he would start acting like one. I wish this stupid lump would go away too, I have this constant lump in my throat," I said, putting my hand around my neck.

"Go see your doctor Emmie! Take a step back for a second, fight for change at your own pace. You're already making a difference, you just can't see it. Give yourself a break," she said.

I looked at XJ and Sam kicking the soccer ball around on the back-yard lawn. I should listen to Jess.

I told Jess I found a note written by Chloe left under my pillow, which read, "Mama don't cry, please be happy, I love you."

How could I be happy? My life was not about me. From birth it hadn't been about me. People saw me as a 'good girl'.

"Emmie, you're such a good girl fighting for the rights of others."

"Emmie you're such a good girl, helping those less fortunate," my father would say.

"Emmie you're such a good girl, taking care of your family, cooking, cleaning, working fulltime," my aunts would say.

"Emmie you're such a good girl, this family needs someone like you as a role model," Renata would say.

What the fuck constitutes a bad girl then? I would think to myself, because this 'good girl' shit was killing me. I could no longer control this lump I had growing in my throat, whether

I cried or not it was permanently there now. I didn't want to be a good girl, because I wasn't taken seriously. I wanted to be a bad girl, and cutting my hair short and streaking it blonde this time wasn't going to get me noticed.

"Ma, I'm not happy. I'm not feeling well, and I fight a lot with Dave," I said on my weekly visit. "It's not really a healthy environment for the children."

"Leave him!" she said.

WHAT THE FUCK?

"What did you say, Ma?"

"I said, leave Dave. If you're not happy, leave. It's the fashion now, Zia Carmela's daughter is getting a divorce. Leave, think about you and your children. Come back home, Emanuela. Your father and I will look after you all. You will never have to work again." She said.

"I wished I had left your father, that bastardo, I had to stay. I couldn't drive a car like you, I had no family here. I was alone, until your zia came over by plane, not on a ship like me. I was on that boat for three months!"

"Your father gave me NO life, Emanuela, it was hard for me! He threw away my sewing machine because I liked to sew! He's a bastardo brutto!" she said, calling my father 'an ugly bastard'.

There we had it! Because someone else's daughter was getting divorced, it was okay and acceptable. Because *someone else* had told her so, it had become fashionable. There was no way in hell I would ever move back home. I began to feel sick. My life wasn't a designer handbag she had in her wardrobe. I wasn't an accessory. I had feelings and two young children to think about. My life couldn't be compared to what was or wasn't in fashion. It consisted of fucking hard work, to be taken seriously. Trying to establish myself as an individual in my life and in the workforce, I was struggling.

My relationship with Dave was beginning to look easier by the minute. I needed the support of my friends, not my parents. My parents didn't understand nurturing or love unless it involved a full stomach of food and it was still all about my mother.

"Mangia Emanuela," my mother said as she filled my plate up with fennel, pork sausages, and salad.

"You're too thin!" she exclaimed.

I had lost my appetite for months now, my weight shed very quickly. My hair was also shedding. I wasn't feeling well at all.

I rang Dina when I arrived home.

"Dina, I need you, please come over now."

"Give me thirty minutes, I'll be right over," she said.

When Dina arrived, I was curled up on the sofa crying, the children were in Chloe's room playing. I was a complete mess.

"What the fuck is going on?" Dina asked, hugging me.

I bawled on Dina's shoulder.

"I'm not coping with Dave. It's the same thing each day. I don't feel good enough, I'm not contributing, and I'm not making enough money. I'm so tired, I don't feel well, and he's away with his friends. I'm sick of fighting, not only with him but for my life and for others. I feel like I'm in a pressure cooker, I feel really depressed." I said, sobbing uncontrollably.

"I'm taking you to Doctor Rogers. I'll get Renata over here to watch the kids."

Dina drove me to Doctor Rogers that afternoon. She drew blood, to rule out any 'nasties', putting down my dramatic weight loss, hair shedding and fatigue to anemia.

"Are you taking your iron tablets?" she asked.

"Of course," I replied.

"Come back in three days for your results," she said.

On day two Trish the receptionist at Doctor Rogers' surgery called me.

"Emanuela, can you please come in this afternoon to see Doctor Rogers, she'd like to go over your blood test results with you."

Boy, was Doctor Rogers wrong. The 'nasties' showed up alright. "Emanuela, you have Graves' disease. That lump in your throat is your thyroid gland. We have to get you into an endocrinologist as soon as possible."

I wished I could be honest with Doctor Rogers and tell her my lump in my throat was my inability to speak my thoughts from childhood. I imagined and created the lump to stop my tears. It was my way of coping. It was MY life in my throat, the life I felt like I had been denied from birth. As an adult, my marriage was a continuation of my belief of worthlessness. I felt like my life was one big mess, although I pretend it wasn't. That's what my lump represented to me. It may be called a thyroid gland and potentially must be removed, but I would create another one because it's mine, I own it.

I always felt I had to be polite to doctors because they knew what was best for me, but not this time. I already knew what the best thing for me was, compassion.

CHAPTER 21

HOW DO I LOVE THEE?

DOCTOR JEFFERIES HAD finally decided my thyroid gland had to go. I had been seeing him for two years and I was still struggling with my health. I'm surprised he didn't rip my thyroid gland out with his bare hands at our first appointment. We had a love-hate relationship. Apparently, he loved his job as an endocrinologist, as well as pushing my buttons. I hated his sense of humour.

"Good morning Mrs Smith, welcome," he said as he shook my hand and then Dave's.

According to Doctor Rogers, Doctor Jefferies was the best in his field, he came highly recommended.

"Please sit," he said, as he pointed to two leather bucket seats by his desk.

On one side of his office wall he had his University degrees proudly displayed in heavy wooden frames. On the other side he had photographs taken while overseas. He wore a funny coloured bow tie and I could see his quirky navy coloured socks peeking from his ankles. They had bright yellow giraffes on them.

"Emanuela Smith, what an unusual name. Where did that originate from?" he asked, looking at my file.

"Which part, Emanuela or Smith?" I asked.

I saw Dave stiffen in his seat next to me.

"Emanuela, of course."

"Oh, that part. It's Italian." I said.

"So, you were born in Italy?" he asked.

"No, I'm an Aussie girl born and bred here in Australia." I replied sharply.

I wondered if this clown asks all his patients with culturally diverse names where they originated from. I was here seeking medical treatment, not to take him on a cultural tour of Italy.

"I see you have been quite unwell. Looking at your test results, you haven't been able to work for quite some time. Where do you work?" he asked inquisitively.

"I work for a women's centre," I said.

"You're not one of *those* feminists, are you?" he asked with a smirk.

I looked at Dave sitting next to me, he was so uncomfortable he looked stiff as a board.

"Well that all depends, Doctor Jefferies, are you one of *those* misogynists?" I asked.

He sat upright, shuffling my medical record, and my test results looking awkward. I sat there with a smile on my face, I think from that moment on Doctor Jefferies and I understood one another quite well, we quickly went on to develop mutual respect.

Although I was on medication to help my thyroid hormone levels, I still struggled. I was experiencing heart palpitations in the middle of the night when I was fast asleep. I would wake up feeling like I couldn't breathe, like I was having a heart attack. My hands would shake uncontrollably, my weight was still all over the place. One month I was thin, the next month I was bloated. My mother was convinced it was due to not eating right. It wasn't, it was hereditary, and both my maternal grandmother and mother had a thyroid condition. My mother's condition was controlled with medication, mine couldn't be. She didn't understand this.

I had conceited defeat. My lump had to go. I was booked in for a thyroidectomy at a private hospital. I had my stay in hospital all planned and ready to go. I had stocked up the freezer with meals. I had all the washing and ironing done. Dave's shirts were all hanging up in his wardrobe, the kid's school uniforms cleaned, and back up ones ready in case they were needed. I had arranged for Jess and Dina to take it in turns to take the kids to and from school. I had thought of everything. Dave didn't have to worry about a thing it had all been taken care of. I had all the instructions up on the fridge door. Chloe was old enough to help and so was XJ. They were a little team each having set chores they did each week.

I wasn't planning on taking too much time off work either. My goal was to be back after two weeks if all went according to plan. Sharni had purchased a juicer and was making me smoothies at work. She said she wanted me back one hundred and ten per cent. I didn't enjoy being sick, it forced me to stop and allowed me too much thinking time. That was a dangerous combination for me. I preferred to keep busy.

"Emmie, drink this." Sharni had made me my daily dose of beetroot, ginger, carrot, spinach, and celery.

"You know celery doesn't contain any real nutritional value?" I said to her as I sipped it through my straw.

"Just drink it!" she said.

"I'll check on the kids when you're in the hospital. Try not to worry Em, they'll be fine. I don't understand why you had to do everything beforehand though, Dave's more than capable, you know that right? I think you don't give the guy enough credit sometimes."

"Yes, I know, but taking care of my family and the people that I love comes naturally to me. I love doing it, if I can make life a little easier and less stressful for others then I will." I said.

"But what about you, when are you going to put yourself first? You're not Dave's mum, Em, you're his wife, don't become confused with selfless and selfish. If you continue to give at this rate, you'll keep crashing and burning. Don't confuse love with dependence. You're an all or nothing kind of girl aren't you!" she said and we both smiled.

I automatically thought of Renata, thinking of the times when she'd tell me my life wasn't based on a novel and to keep things real.

Sharni was right, I already knew all of this, and I had enough self-help books at home to start my own library, or bonfire. How do I change? How do I put myself first? What does that even mean? I'd have to ask Dina. We chose to set the bar high years ago. *Keep our men happy,* I thought. Pfft.

That night when I went home and had everyone settled, I rang Dina. I had thought long and hard all day about what Sharni had said. She was right, I wanted to better myself. I mean how hard could that be?

"Dina, how do you love yourself first, and what's your purpose in life?"

Dina laughed. She laughed so hard she snorted.

"What are you on, seriously have you been sniffing glue tonight?" she asked still laughing.

"No!" I said, beginning to laugh.

"You know Em, you have a big heart. This whole 'you need to love yourself before you can love anyone else' is misleading because we weren't *raised* to love ourselves. Regardless of cultural background, it was a generational thing for us both. If Dave came home one night and said to you he would cook dinner and get the kids ready for bed while you relaxed in a warm bath, you would feel so appreciated and loved, right?

And you would love him right back tenfold. But like me, you do it all because it's easier, and you don't want to cause an argument because *he's* tired or *he's* worked all day. We have created our own safe zones, and in the process created our own thought patterns. Love is a gift, not a competition. Whether he chose to do what you asked or not, you should still love yourself enough to say okay, I need help here, I'm going to look at hiring a cleaner." Dina said.

"Baby steps Em, don't be so hard on yourself, don't lose yourself in the process. If Dave doesn't want to cook dinner and neither do you, order a pizza! Seriously, who cares anymore, our kids are growing up fast, it won't kill them to eat takeaway now and then. Tell them it's served with love. Isn't that what we were raised to do?" she said sarcastically.

"We all have mental days, but we manage to get through. Tomorrow is a new day."

"Thank you, Dina, you always know the right things to say to snap me out of my insecurities. Who needs all those self-help books when I have a friend like you," I said.

I hung up and went into my bedroom. I began to pack my bag for my hospital stay. I pulled my nightie out of my dresser drawer and a little piece of paper fell to the floor. It was the same one I had taken from the Baci chocolate on my wedding day. I had a habit of keeping these. I picked it up, 'The person you love the most stands before you, stop searching'. All these years later I finally understood its meaning.

The universe had sent me a little reminder. I already loved myself, I liked the person I saw in the mirror each day. It was self-awareness I needed to work on. I had to stop caring what people thought, I had to show myself compassion. If I'm kind to others, I should be kind to me too. Self-care was another one. I should be making my own smoothies and take better care of myself and not feel guilty for it.

I went into my bathroom, locked the door behind me and ran myself a warm bath. I could hear Dave asking the kids where I was as I sunk into the warm water with a big smile on my face. *He's not going to cope well with change,* I thought to myself.

CHAPTER 22

M Y SCAR WASN'T too visible along my neckline. I was so impressed by Doctor Jefferies surgical handiwork I gave him a designer bow tie with little pizza slices on it as a thank you. It was to remind him, I had given him my permission, and in return, he was given the privilege of slitting an Italian's throat for all the right reasons.

Scars come in varying degrees. Some wear them proudly, others would rather hide them. Some you can't see at all and run deep, some heal rapidly and disappear. No one can determine in life how long their scar will remain, but we do have the ability how we choose to look at it. I had scars on my tummy from my twenty-kilo pregnancy weight gain with Chloe. I still wore my bikini when I went to the beach, I didn't care. Dave called it my life map, the little white lines that remind him of bee and her mark she left on me. Dave had scars that ran deep, you couldn't see those types.

Dave and I had decided it was time for couple's therapy. Dave had started drinking heavily. He didn't know how to deal with stress and would turn to alcohol seeking answers. It was frustrating to watch. The Aussie culture openly accepts big drinkers, in fact it's more socially unacceptable if you don't drink. I decided to undertake my own social experiment and stopped drinking alcohol for six months. It was interesting to see people's reactions each time we went out. One sees and hears more clearly when sober.

"Em, have a drink, come on have one!" Dave's friends would say, whilst shoving a glass of wine under my nose.

"No, I'm good. Thanks for asking though."

I could hear them ask Dave if I was unwell or if I was on a diet?

It was like watching a television game show where the participant wins money for guessing the right answer.

I chose to stop drinking alcohol because I no longer wanted to find myself in a situation, I was unable to control. The more you drink, the more you put yourself in a high-risk state. I was able to enjoy a drink or two. I was a happy, fun loving drunk. Dave, on the other hand, had become an angry drunk, and I was scarred. My scar ran right across my heart, not my throat. He had long-standing issues buried deep inside of him and when he drank, these surfaced. I found his behaviour intimidating. I didn't like the role modelling he was projecting in front of our children. We both knew two intoxicated people were not a good mix. I still had enough personal integrity to manage a poor situation. I made the right choice for me. I wished Dave could see this, as he was slowly breaking my heart.

We fought. Each time we were asked to an event I no longer wanted to go. I knew my night wasn't going to be fun and it would be even worse once we got home. I'd rather he went out on his own and I would pretend to be asleep when he came to bed. This had become the norm for us. If he came home and I was awake we would begin to argue, him picking on me.

"Emmie, why do you spend so much on the kids, I hate it when you do this!" he would raise his voice.

"Why isn't the milk kept on the top shelf in the fridge? Why do you keep it at the bottom of the fridge door? It goes off there, you never listen to me!"

"Emmie, why didn't you leave me any leftovers from dinner, and why are you ignoring me when I speak to you!"

The arguments were always the same after pub nights.

"You just think about yourself and the kids," he'd say.

WHY don't you eat at the pub? Why do I have to think about you in your drunken state, you're old enough to feed yourself?

I had accepted a normal Friday night now consisted of doors slamming and me crying. No lump to stop my tears anymore. I hadn't gotten around to creating a new one yet.

I hated Fridays. I would put the kids to bed early or they would stay over at friend's places to avoid seeing their parents argue like this.

"Dave, why don't we go out to dinner this Friday night?" I'd suggest.

"It's pub night!" Had become the standard answer.

Our relationship began to go from bad to worse and I had already predicted Dave wasn't going to deal with change well. The fact that I had gone out and set up my own bank account kind of sealed the deal. I wanted to start saving in case I had to leave.

I was really worried about him. He began working long hours, and I became accustomed to being home alone again. History had a way of repeating itself. I had to tell him the women's centre was soon to close its doors. There was no more funding to keep it open. I would have to start looking for a job. I had around six months left there. This would completely stress him out. His older brother once told me Dave hated seeing his mother struggle financially and the pressure that she was put under had scarred him. Dave's scar ran across his forehead because he could not process the financial burden of daily life for families.

Our relationship was in dire straits and that was when we decided to see a therapist. I saw her flyer up on a community board at the local shopping centre. She was practicing out of Doctor Rogers' surgery. That was mistake number one, always go by a recommendation and not some flyer tacked to a pin-up board.

I was excited, booking in time. We had an appointment with Jane Clark, a marriage counsellor and I had high hopes that she could offer me strategies on how Dave and I could work on our marriage together. Or so I thought. I loved Dave and our family was so important, this therapy was a lifeline for us. It was something I had to chip away to get him to agree to come with me at first.

Dave was so supportive of me and my political ideologies. We understood one another well. He respected my opinions and he loved me very much. Dave was suffering, his scar was huge, and I wanted to help him through this. It's what you do when you love someone with all your heart.

Dave would often tell me he would never leave me. I was his world, and our family was everything to him. He said if he didn't have us then his life wasn't worth living. He couldn't face the prospect without us. We were like roast chicken served with roast potatoes. A family favourite, we were like comfort food to one another. In hindsight, both of our cultures had impacted on our marriage. It was my turn to help him now just like he had helped me overcome my fear of driving at night.

"Emmie and Dave Smith," I heard our names called out, as we were sitting in the waiting room.

I turned around and saw a very young-looking woman with her hair tied in piggy tails held with pink ribbons. I looked at Dave and looked back at this little girl who had called our names.

"Emmie and Dave Smith?" she called again.

We both stood up and walked towards her.

"Hi, I'm Jane, please follow me."

Dave and I sat down in a tiny room with three chairs and a white coffee table in the middle, hosting a pad and pen and three glasses of water.

Jane wore a grey tunic with a white t-shirt underneath and red canvas sneakers.

"How can I help you both?" she asked, as she plonked herself in a chair and grabbed her stationary.

"Dave and I have been married for fifteen years and we've had problems for quite some time now, especially with his drinking." I began to say. "It's had a huge impact on our relationship. I don't know how to help him overcome some of his insecurities over money."

I began to mention our children when she interrupted me.

"Wow! That's a long time to be with one person. I've been with my partner now for five years and we have one child, but we're not married. I don't believe in marriage, but we split our finances, I don't know if that's a good thing or not! I earn more than him." She said and she began to laugh.

"O-kay," I said trying to get her back on track.

"Although Dave and I share our finances, I've decided to open my own bank account so I can be held accountable for my spending, as our arguments were predominantly around my lack of contribution to the household expenses." I continued on.

"Well my partner and I share the grocery shopping and we take it in turns to look after our daughter and we take it in turns to take her to childcare..."

I was starting to shift in my vinyl seat and Dave sensed my anger rise, he quickly intervened.

"Jane, can we please address *our* issues? Emmie and I would like to leave our first session with real strategies we can begin to use at home."

"Yes, but what I am saying is that my partner and I share the household chores and …"

"My partner and I met at yoga class, we connected instantly, and you should both try yoga…"

"My partner and I cook together, we share everything…"

I had totally lost interest, completely zoned out, I was sitting there, deflated. This session was costing us a lot of money. I had some ignorant Pollyanna in her grey tunic with her piggy tails swinging side by side when she spoke. She advised us how to split childcare costs and share the grocery bill. She went on to say how much she loved her partner and how fantastic her life was. Dave and I were educated individuals with real adult problems, and I was resentful that this inexperienced little cupcake in front of me, was making comparisons with my issues to her fluffy fairy floss life.

I wanted a real commitment from Dave to continue with couple's therapy and I was the one who was now put off. Jane had scarred me, right across my wrists, because I was ready to slit them, hearing her jargon.

"I'm sorry Dave that session didn't quite go according to plan." I said as we left.

"You have nothing to apologise for Em, I love you." He said, holding my hand as we walked out of the surgery together.

"I love you too, Dave."

CHAPTER 23

THE WOMEN'S CENTRE had been turned into a community crèche to deal with the demands of our ever-growing population. Now, when Chloe and I walked past the old building, we saw the future generation playing in sandpits and plastic cubby houses. There was laughter, tears, runny noses, screeching and children running and playing outdoors. One's life can be compared to infrastructure. Requiring a frame to build a home, needing bones to support a body, and enabling a brain to allow for change, improvement, and growth.

Sharni and I were lucky enough to still be working together for the State Minister for Women. When it had been decided there was no more funding available for the ongoing services of the women's centre, Sharni and I arranged a campaign to try and save it.

The campaign took months to plan, we had set ourselves a timeframe and we achieved it. We had recruited over forty people to help. We met each Sunday evening for over a month before the deadline. We would have a shared dinner, and then we would print off posters and flyers. The target had been established and a State election was looming. Everyone helped including Chloe and XJ. On the night of the execution, we poster bombed our surrounding areas. Meeting late into the night, we targeted every major intersection and streetlight poles. We were all dressed in black, we looked like a group of criminals planning and undertaking the world's greatest bank heist.

The very next day, people woke up and got into their cars to drive to work. The posters were seen by many and generated calls to local talkback radio stations. Callers were asking why the State Government had decided to close its doors on a service devoted entirely to women.

"Where would women go now to seek assistance?"

"Why hasn't the public been consulted on the closure of such centres and further lack of services?" These were the many questions asked by the public. Mission accomplished, the media were now involved, and conversations had commenced.

A decision had to be made. The pressure placed on the State Government lead to the announcement of the community crèche. It would replace the centre, providing childcare for disadvantaged or single women at a lower cost. The centre's services were being outsourced and overseen by the Minister for Women, where staff would be working out of her office, tendering with outside organisations.

Sharni and I had both been offered positions to work for her. Kate Thomas MP attended one of our 'save the centre' rallies. We welcomed her support and she welcomed our knowledge, passion, and tenacity.

Kate was a force not to be reckoned with and we were the driving force nudging her from behind. She was tall, a brunette, and gorgeous, but came with a flashing sign above her head 'looks can be deceiving'. I liked Kate, she was fearless.

The perception was changing, and the word spread fast, we wanted equality and progression. With the birth of social media, it was so easy to share with the world at a simple click. There were no rules around it, there was little forward planning with the use of social media. This new toy of the millennium was causing grief. Privacy had been thrown out the door together with legal and ethical issues. The nineties were well and truly over, we were in the middle of the new age.

Social networking sparked a revolution, a new breed of problems appeared. Menacing online behaviour surfaced with a new nationality of trolls being born. Social isolation surfaced, and it quickly interfered with daily life, to the point of driving some relationships further apart or disintegrating altogether. Social media had become a platform for promiscuity. Gone were the days of posting a letter.

At a simple click, we had lost the ability to gauge what people had to say at face value, and life had been open to misinterpretation. It had become the norm to see people glued to their phones rather than have face to face social interaction with others. We were now 'sharing' and 'updating' online. If you weren't online, you weren't connected to the 'real' world. Post it! Want to be a manipulator? Post it! Want to be an arsehole? Post it!

Social media wasn't all negative, it had many advantages. Some had found their voice and their confidence, a different kind, one that involved a keyboard. However, for someone like me, it had its drawbacks, and it left a scar.

Sexual harassment and discrimination weren't only restricted to workplaces. This type of behaviour was becoming more common on the internet too.

Domestic violence was something not openly or easily discussed. What went on behind closed doors stayed there. However, people were sharing their dirty laundry and it made me physically ill. No one was taking it seriously.

"Oh, shut the fuck up bitch and go get a real job."

"I'd like to stick something in her mouth and it ain't no roly-poly."

"I keep my sheila quiet with the back of my cricket bat."

"Come suck on my icy pole."

Charming comments, I saw reading an online post about International Women's Day.

We held weekly meetings at work and addressing domestic violence had become my number one item at the top of the agenda.

"I would like to see more discussions held around the safety of women and more awareness of how to identify and address domestic violence situations. I feel the police don't place enough emphasis on addressing these sorts of jobs. It's doesn't seem to be a high priority for them. I don't feel they take these types of jobs seriously." I said at a meeting.

"Emmie, that's a pretty ambiguous statement to make. How do you know they aren't taking it seriously enough?" Kate asked.

"Because I have spoken to some of the women involved when I was at the local hospital recently refilling the information pamphlets. I met one woman in the emergency department, she thought her wrist had been broken. Her partner assaulted her, and the police officer offered her a ride to the ER and left." I said.

"She was waiting to be seen by the doctor, her best friend arrived to support her and told me this was a regular occurrence, and the police were aware. They felt sorry for her and would offer her a ride each time, to the hospital, after they had a 'chat' to her partner about keeping off the sauce. She won't leave him, she doesn't want to leave her dog behind, and can't afford to rent alone. She's too ashamed to tell her immediate family because she already feels like a failure. She had been assaulted, Kate. But mostly she's scared. Where's her support outside of her friends?" I asked.

Sharni made a great suggestion to Kate and proposed her and I visit the emergency department waiting rooms once a week together for a month to gauge if women were in fact there seeking treatment directly linked to domestic violence. We began recording this to ultimately write up a proposal for Kate to recommend a change to police call-outs and the reporting system involving with these types of incidences. I agreed, we needed to have face to face conversations with these women.

"How are things at home Em, how's Dave?" Sharni asked in the car, as we were making our way to our hospital visits.

"He's okay, we're fine when he's not drinking." I replied.

"How are you?" she asked.

"Good," I replied with a half-smile on my face.

"Rubbish! You look like you've lost your spark."

'*Spark*', I thought. Where the fuck was my spark? I had lost more than my spark. Dave and I hadn't had sex in months. I was numb inside. Our arguments had escalated from raised voices to personal insults, to pushing and shoving. I was not one to share my laundry, clean, dirty, or otherwise with anyone. I had my new friend who looked out for me, his name was depression. He was a black shadow of a man who wore a black trench coat and a black hat. He would speak to me after each altercation I had with Dave. He had replaced happiness.

"Let's go grab a coffee at that new café next door to the hospital. I've heard they have the best fair-trade Jamaican Blue Mountain coffee there!"

"YEAH! There's a little of your spark right there, let's go!" she said.

Faking it felt good and this wasn't only restricted to the bedroom, I'd become good at faking interest publicly these days.

The café was packed with people. Sharni and I lined up, and the smell of freshly roasted, ground coffee beans was exhilarating, bringing back childhood memories.

"So, I see you've upgraded from instant to freshly ground," I heard someone behind me say, their hands placed on my hips.

"Dimitri, I have never drunk instant in my life!" I replied, turning around. I knew that voice anywhere.

My heart was pounding. Dimitri kissed me on the cheek, pushed my hair to one side, and then planted a little kiss on my neck.

"Dimitri, this is my friend Sharni. Dimitri and I go back a long way. He's this annoying Greek who seems to follow me around in life and I can't seem to get rid of him!" I said, laughing nervously at Sharni.

"Pleased to meet you, Dimitri," Sharni said.

"Yasou," Dimitri said, as he tilted his head upwards at Sharni.

"You look fantastic Ella, I see you are now working for Kate Thomas," he said.

"How do you know?" I asked.

"It's online. I'm following you, Ella."

"You mean you're stalking me. Are you still teaching?" I asked.

"Yes, and I'm also DJ-ing at the new club in the city. Here, take these. First drinks on me El, I know I will see you there soon." He said handing me a wad of free drink cards.

"You're so full of yourself aren't you Dimitri? I haven't got time to go out clubbing," I said blushing.

"Make time," he said, as he grabbed me tight and kissed me hard on the cheek.

"Sharni it was a pleasure meeting you." In true Dimitri style, like a whirlwind he bypassed the line, shook some guy's hand, took his coffee, walked straight past, winked, and walked out.

When Sharni and I got to the front of the line two coffees were waiting for us, under the name of Ella, courtesy of "DJ."

"Who was that guy Emmie, and why does he call you Ella?" Sharni asked.

"He's my harmless pain in the arse reminder from the universe not to forget who I truly am. He calls me Ella because it means 'come to me' in Greek. He's wishful thinking there!" I said smiling.

"Well, I don't like him! He's annoying," she said.

"Stop being so polite, don't you mean he's a fucking smart-arse?" I said, and she nodded.

I couldn't stop laughing. Dimitri was like a bad cup of coffee to Sharni, he left a bitter taste in her mouth.

CHAPTER 24

CHRISTMAS WAS MY favourite day of the year. It was my universal reminder of the best gift I had ever received on that day, XJ. But lately, I hadn't been feeling it. The city lit up at night with multicoloured lights, giant Christmas trees, and red ribbons. The sheer thought of celebrations depressed me. My ability to partake and feel the festival cheer was no longer there.

"Mum, are we putting up the Christmas tree this year?" XJ asked. "I can get it down from the mezzanine if you like?"

"I don't know XJ, I guess so. If you like, maybe Chloe will help you put it up," I replied.

"But that's *our* thing that we do together every year, and last year you promised we would do it this year…together."

I looked up at him from the sofa where I was lying, my beautiful Christmas gift was now taller than me, and so handsome. I hadn't realised how grown up he looked. I was clouded by depression.

If I wasn't fighting for social justice, I wasn't interested and even that was beginning to fizzle out. I looked over at the corner in the study and saw my files in cardboard archive boxes stacked by the wall. The hours and hours of work I once took pride in was staring me in the face.

"Let me have a quick shower and we can put up the tree." I said. XJ smiled. Even showering became laborious these days.

Dave and I no longer shared a bed. The study had become my new bedroom. That's when my dark nights began, or maybe my dark days. I was lying on my sofa and I had closed my eyes for a moment, and when I opened them, I saw him standing at the end of my feet.

He was a shadow of a man wearing a black trench coat and a hat with a wide brim. He was tall and lanky. He didn't speak, he quietly stood there. Funnily enough, my mind spoke to me. It reassured me not to be afraid as he was there to bring me peace. I was confused, my father taught me only God brings peace and light, not darkness. But I liked this man. He made me feel like I could sink into a dark hole and hide, where no one could find me. He was the man in the hat.

Our home became the Australian Great Dividing Range. Dave and I would strategically avoid bumping into one another at all these days. It was much easier that way. He had his head buried deep in the sand, both of us putting off the inevitable.

I still remember the night I made my acquaintance with depression. It was two years ago when Dave shoved me into a wall during an argument. He was so horrified he cried. I was in complete disbelief he had done what he had. He had crossed the line. I didn't cry, I walked away like I was raised to do, with class and sophistication. That was the first and only time he had shoved me with force, all the other times it was small pushes on the arm or entering my personal space. I knew it was wrong, I knew he regretted it, but it was like we were both caught in this bad habit. They say bad habits take twenty-one days to break when replaced with positive actions. It was too late for me and Dave. Each time we argued it escalated very quickly, there was no forward planning to introduce anything positive or new.

"I'm so sorry Emmie, I can't believe I did that, I'm not an arsehole who hurts women!" he cried.

He was right, he wasn't an arsehole. I still loved Dave.

Chloe preferred to spend her time with her university friends now, XJ still being my shadow preferred to stay at home and watch over me. I think I may have given him a reason for concern, and I didn't want to do that to him ever again. My children were the reason why I was still living with Dave in the marital home. XJ had two years left of high school. I could not afford the fees and he could not afford the disruption to his learning. My son was extremely bright and a high achiever, for the 'shy' kid. Education is a privilege in this country and knowledge was power, it was my son's future at play here.

XJ had recently started at a new school and was thriving. That was no easy task I undertook, *alone*. I had to fight for my son's rights at his school, like I fought for the rights of women. I fought his previous school and won. I fought long and hard, calling for action. I guess like Dave, the school personnel preferred to bury their heads in the sand as well. I wished Dave had supported me in the development.

"You better not get XJ kicked out of this school!" he would say.

"The only kicking will be done by me and it will be up the principal's arse, you elitist!" I would shout back.

Dave loved his fancy-pants school that Chloe had also attended, so prim and proper, it was right up his alley. It was all about image.

Little did he know, Chloe confided in me that she hated going to that school, but she had a mouth and was fearless. Her vibe and energy were prominent, and she was left alone by the other students. I appreciated Dave paying for school fees. His mother couldn't possibly afford private fees as a single parent. He only wanted what he perceived as the best for our kids, but he didn't realise not all that was deemed 'the best' had to have a price tag attached.

I had other parents contact me as their issues of bullying were not being addressed either. The spotlight I shone brightly on his previous school drew out more kids who eventually left. For the parents the cost of changing schools was a small price to pay for their child's happiness, and that made me smile. In effect, I had saved those kids too. They were all now thriving, preparing for university at different schools. I was instrumental in bringing about change to schools addressing the students using social media to intimidate and bully others over a two-year period.

I mentioned the man in the hat to Doctor Rogers once and she suggested I go on anti-depressants, but I wasn't a fan of popping pills. I mean if I could eat pasta fazool (pasta with pork sausage and cannellini beans) as a child without taking anti-depressants, then I really didn't see a need now as an adult, because eating that dish had caused me real childhood trauma.

"Emanuela, I would like you to take some anti-depressants, for a short time to get you over this bump in the road. We can't allow depression to go untreated for too long." She said, as she handed me the signed prescription.

"I'm sure I'll feel better once I resolve this situation involving Xavier and his school, I promise to come back if I don't." I said.

"Mum, are you okay in there?" XJ was knocking on my bathroom door.

'*Oh shit*', I sat upright, coughing up water that had gone up my nose.

"Yes, out soon." I replied.

What the fuck was my problem? Did I fall asleep in the bathtub? Why were my face and hair all wet? I must have slid under the water, why couldn't I remember? Poor XJ, I hoped I hadn't let him down again. I didn't want to be a burden on my children. I didn't want to be hard work for them. I was supposed to be taking care of them, not the other way around.

I quickly dressed, wrapped my wet hair up in a towel, and made my way to meet XJ in the lounge room to assemble the Christmas tree. He looked relieved.

"Ma, I'm home." Chloe called out, as she walked through the kitchen.

"In here!" I replied.

"Hey, can I help too? I never get to do this, I hope I'm not interfering with mother-son time," Chloe said sarcastically with a smile on her face, elbowing XJ.

"Yeah, I'll let you this time, but I get to put the angel on the top." He said.

"That's not fair, you always get to do that," Chloe said.

"Mum gave me that job because I had to wait an entire year for my birthday because I was born on Christmas Day. Plus, you're too short, you've got legs like a Chihuahua." XJ said with a smirk.

"MA! See he's always teasing me." Chloe said, pretending to be offended.

"Besides dumb-arse, we all have to wait a whole year for our birthday," Chloe replied.

I had so much love for these two. Although at times they annoyed me.

I stood back to admire the finished product. I had my moon and my star standing beside me, both shining like the glass coloured ball hanging from the tree. My shining lights leading the way for me in my darkest hours.

CHAPTER 25

I DIDN'T MIND a good sandwich. It tasted even better when someone else made it for me. As a little girl, my mother would make me sprinkle sandwiches, fresh, fluffy, soft white bread with lashings of margarine and hundreds and thousands of sprinkles. Multicoloured madness, fairy bread. She would secretly feed me this 'Aussie' food when my father wasn't around to see. He would not have approved. Italian bread was specially purchased from the continental deli, not from the supermarket. We ate the crust, they were never cut off, in fact, it was the best part. We didn't have margarine in the fridge either, or if she did buy it, she'd hide it away at the back behind the provolone cheese. We only used butter and that was kept in the pantry.

My mother still made me a sandwich when I would pop over for a visit. I personally began to feel like a sandwich these days. I had my young family on one side and my aging parents on the other, and I was the smallgoods smack bang in the middle.

"Emanuela, I have fresh prosciutto let me make you a sandwich, I only bought it this morning when your father drove me to the shop. Get the Australian bread out of the fridge," she said.

"Sure, Ma." I said.

Bless her, I tried telling her keeping this bread in the refrigerator made it hard, but I accepted it. My mother never threw out bread, it was a sin, and she raised me to do the same.

"How are you and papa doing?" I asked on my visit.

"Okay, we go to see the doctor, he takes your father's blood pressure, and we go home." She said in broken English.

"Ma, dad doesn't look well, and he doesn't seem to be eating much either. Why doesn't he go see Doctor Rogers?" I asked.

"Perché (Because) he likes Doctor Tang, he says Asians make good doctors, and he doesn't want to see a lady doctor." She said.

"It's a worry if the doctor is not on top of dad's health needs, should I call and speak to his doctor?" I suggested.

"NO! Your father won't be happy if I worry you with his problems, Emanuela. He said you have too much of your own to worry about already," she said.

"Ma, I'm concerned about dad. I will go with him on his next visit to see Doctor Tang." I suggested.

"Va bene, bella," (Okay, lovely) she said.

I worried about my parents, they were getting older, and I was their only child. I had a responsibility to take care of them. I was concerned Doctor Tang scheduled my father in each week to take his blood pressure, listen to his heart, and then send him on his way, without properly assessing his health. Maybe my father would say he was okay when he was asked? My father was so loyal to this doctor, he respected people like Doctor Tang, and he probably didn't want to be a bother to him.

I had to investigate further. I was going to take my father to his next appointment.

When I arrived at my parent's house to pick my father up for his doctor's appointment, he was sitting at the kitchen table. I thought to myself how frail he looked.

"Dad, are you ready? Let's go to the doctor." I said.

"I could have gone with your mother, you have too much to do, don't worry about me. Mum, you shouldn't have worried her!" he said.

My father called my mother "Mum" in front of me. Gone were the days of personal insults. Old age had finally refined these two.

We had arrived on time for his appointment but still had to wait for over an hour.

"Mr Sopracasa?" Doctor Tang called. I had met him a few times over the years. He was a handsome looking man, smartly dressed, short, with glasses, mid-forties, but I guess I too had put my faith in his hands to take care of my father's medical needs.

"Please sit," he said. He looked concerned because I was there also. I felt his uneasiness.

"What seems to be the problem?" he asked.

"Well, perhaps you could shed some light for me, Doctor Tang. My mother has informed me my father sees you each week, should I be concerned? Is he okay? Is there something I should know?" I asked.

"If there is something you need to know about your fathers' medical concerns, I am sure he can tell you, I don't think there is a need for you to accompany him to his medical consultations." He said.

Was this guy being flippant? His dismissiveness was beginning to irritate me.

"My father places a lot of faith in your hands, Doctor. He will most likely tell you he is fine, but he doesn't look fine to me. I am hoping through your *weekly* observations and notes you may have noticed and recorded any change. So perhaps, *Doctor*, you could share with me any recent tests he may have had, and we could discuss these." I said.

"As I have previously stated, if there is something your father would like to share with you he can," he replied.

"I haven't brought my father to you under duress, he's asked me to accompany him so we can discuss any medical concerns and I would appreciate if you would share these with me. I'd like to become more involved in his future treatment plans so I can ensure he follows through with it at home." I said.

"Can we please begin with looking at his medications, and explaining to me what these are all for?" I asked, pulling out a plastic bag full of prescribed pills my father was taking and held it up for Doctor Tang.

When we were in the car on the way home, he decided to have 'the talk'. Not about the birds and the bees, but about his favourite subject, death. My father respected the dearly departed, maybe he thought he'd finally find respect, peace, and eternity too, one day soon.

"Emanuela when I die, I want you to take care of mum, you know there is plenty of money..."

"Dad I don't want to have this conversation right now, I'm not happy with your doctor and I can't think about death at the moment." I said, cutting him off short. "I have too many other things on my mind right now." We sat in silence for the rest of the way home.

When I arrived back home that afternoon, I rang Dina. I felt stressed about the doctor. He seemed to lack under-standing and bedside manner. I was hoping he would show a little more compassion than he had. I didn't deserve his blasé attitude.

"Are you free next Friday night? I have those free drink cards, let's go for a few hours, if you're up for it. I could use something to look forward to." I said.

"Sure, we can't let those go to waste, now can we! Is it the club by the beach next door to that hotel we ate at once?" she asked.

"Yes, want to meet there around 9ish?"

"Yes, absolutely let's do it." She replied.

The end of the week came quickly, and the evening of Friday drinks arrived. I made my way to the beach club, to meet Dina. I was the first to arrive, the club was dimly lit, it had floor to ceiling windows and was facing the ocean. I could see the water meeting the sand, it was beautiful. The black night sky filled with bright stars that were reflecting onto the water.

Dimitri was standing in the far corner and saw me walk in. He didn't rush up to greet me. He never showed his eagerness when we ran into one another, he preferred to play it cool. I knew by the way his eyes lit up when he saw me, he was excited. I was his spark and he was mine.

Dina has just arrived, and we greeted one another. Dimitri came up to us and kissed us both.

"You girls look fantastic. El, your dress makes your boobs look big and your arse look hot."

"Stop, you always know the right things to say to win over a girl's heart." I said sarcastically.

Dimitri and I shared the exact same sense of humour, sarcasm. Maybe it was our upbringing like he often reminded me of.

"Let's have sex on the beach later, wait for me to finish tonight." He whispered in my ear, kissing my neck.

"What a fabulous idea! Dina, Dimitri has suggested we have Sex on The Beach tonight, let's go order some! I'm charging those cocktails to your account DJ smart-arse." I said as I turned to walk to the bar.

I took my mobile phone out while I was waiting to order, I saw I had six missed calls from Dave. I instantly had an overwhelming feeling come over me, Dave never called me when I was out unless it was life or death.

"Dina, I have to call home, come with me, I don't have a good feeling." Dina stepped out into the foyer with me as I called.

"Emmie, you have to come to your mother's house immediately. She called me earlier on, and I've been trying to call you for the last thirty minutes, come now." He said.

I couldn't hear properly I was trying to find out more, but Dave insisted I left. I was forty minutes away from my mother's house. I was beginning to feel sheer panic. I left Dina in the foyer she insisted on coming with me, but I wanted to be alone. I already knew what loomed. My instincts had kicked in.

When I had finally arrived at my parents' house, I could see two ambulances parked out the front, and the front door to their home wide open. I raced inside. I found my mother sitting in the 'good room' being comforted by her sister-in-law, my cousin Maria, and a paramedic. Renata was with Dave in the kitchen. I went into my father's room, where I saw three paramedics packing up. One walked up to me and held my hand tight. I didn't know this man, but he was holding my hand. "We tried to save him, we tried for an hour, hoping you'd make it in time, but we couldn't. We tried our best." He said.

"Emmie, your father had a massive heart attack. He passed away, and it was very quick. I'm so sorry for your loss, we all are. Your mother rang for an ambulance and your husband arrived as we did." This stranger dressed in green said. I could see the empathy he had in his eyes, they looked teary.

I looked at his name badge, 'John'.

"Thank you, John, I appreciate what each and every one of you have done." I said, as I walked over to my father who was lying on the bedroom floor. I knelt down beside him and held his hand. "I'm sorry, dad." I whispered.

I should have taken him to all his medical appointments. I should have made more of an effort, I was always 'too busy' or had other things on my mind.

Thanks, Doctor Tang, you win. You won't have to see me again unless you refuse to sign my father's death certificate, because no one was going to cut my father up like chop suey. This was one wish of my father's I'd honour.

There are two songs that are ever played at Italian celebrations. One is '*Ava Maria*' at weddings and the second is '*Time to Say Goodbye*', at funerals. I never really liked that song much, it was so sad. My father loved Andrea Bocelli. He'd listen to his music at home, and he would say he had the most beautiful voice in the world.

"He is blind, so he expresses what he sees through his words in his songs. He doesn't need his sight to see what's there, because he can already feel it." My father would say.

Maybe he was right. Maybe if we all stopped looking for what we thought we required in life and began to feel what was inside of us, we'd realise we already have what we are searching for, love.

CHAPTER 26

I ALWAYS BELIEVED it was important for children to grow up in a family with pets. It teaches them responsibility, the pets become part of the family, and they give unconditional love. They experience death and grief when they pass.

One of the hardest things I've had to do in my life is sitting my children down and tell them their nonno had passed. You see, when someone dies it's not about the person who has passed, it's about the loved ones left behind. You remember the good times shared and not the bad. Everyone around me was grieving, except me. I didn't have time to I had to take care of everybody else's needs ahead of my own.

Italian funerals were as extravagant as weddings. There was a lot of planning involved, but in a very short space of time. I had a week to make sure it was going to be the perfect send-off. I had to arrange the flowers, cars, clothes, music, food, and the church. I didn't have time to cry, I was simply too busy.

The day had arrived. When I first woke up and looked out the kitchen window it was drizzling, but by the time I had made my coffee it had stopped, and the sun came out. I'm sure my father was thinking it couldn't possibly rain on the day of his burial.

"Ida and Emanuela would complain about their hair getting wet," he would have said.

The black limousine arrived to take us to my mother's home. When we got there, she had biscotti out on silver trays and liquor glasses filled with different spirits. She didn't say much, she had decided if she was going to speak from now on it would be in Italian, and no longer in English. She had regressed. Perhaps this was her way of dealing with grief.

My mother looked like she had aged so much in a week, she had a black pantsuit on that made her look frail and tiny. Her hair perfectly coiffured.

As I went up to kiss her, she said, "He's left me, that bastardo, he's gone now."

"Ma, we need to go soon, we need to get to the church," I said.

My father always said, "Keep it simple" and simple I did. If I could describe my father's funeral in one word it would be 'elegant'. The lightly coloured oak casket was covered in fresh white roses and green fern leaves. The church had white rose arrangements on the altar and a photo of my father by his casket. I had arranged a soloist to sing the hymns I had chosen. Everything implemented and executed beautifully.

Chloe and XJ read the eulogy, reminiscing about my father's life. These two young adults honouring their grandfather and their culture through the words they had both chosen to write.

We lined up what seemed to be for hours as people paid their last respects, lots of silent tears shed. Rosie and Karl had flown in from Melbourne. Dimitri came too, shaking my hand. He kissed me and whispered, "Ella, be strong."

Strong I was, I had imagined and created another lump in my throat to stop me from crying. I had too much on my plate to grieve.

"Thank you for coming, Dimitri." I politely said.

After the burial, all the immediate family went back to my mother's house for a late lunch. She had it catered for. I sat beside my mother in the 'good room', with Chloe, Renata,

Maria, Rosie, and my aunties. We were all sitting there deep in thought, processing the event that had passed. When I looked up and saw all of the women in the one room, I felt a sense of sisterhood. We all came together, supporting one another in times of adversity and need. It didn't matter if Renata was into threesomes or smoking weed. It didn't matter if Maria was secretly on the internet looking for love and lost money in the process. It didn't matter that I was sleeping in a different room to Dave and we were secretly separated. It didn't matter Rosie was trying for a baby out of wedlock. Because when someone close to you dies and you experience grief, nothing else matters for that moment, all else is forgotten. *I wonder where dad is.*

"Emmie, I know this probably isn't the right time, but there's something I need to tell you," Rosie said. "Can we step outside?" she asked.

"Of course, Rosie, I could use some fresh air." I said.

I found the 'good room' stifling, with the tea light candles burning and the religious statues surrounding a photo of my father.

As soon as we stepped out the door, Rosie blurted out, "I'm pregnant, I'm ten weeks gone." She said, grabbing my hands.

"Rosie, I am so happy for you, you've made me so very happy!" I said tearing up.

"I am so pleased, have you told your parents yet? They must be ecstatic."

"Karl and I are going to tell them tomorrow." She said, I could hear the fear in her voice.

"Rosie. We're adults now. Put your fear aside, you're going to be a mum, fuck what anybody else says or thinks. You and Karl don't need a piece of paper to seal the deal, you already did that when you moved in together. You're already committed. Marriage is so overrated, you're both going to make fantastic, loving parents." I said.

Seriously what did her parents really think? She was in her forties. If she didn't have a child now, she most likely would never experience motherhood because of fear of what her parents thought and their cultural expectations! The mere thought made me angry, and what made me even angrier was that fact *we* still cared.

"Remember Jacinta?" I asked Rosie.

"Yes! I've tried looking for her on social media, but I don't think she has a profile," she replied. "I found her sisters though. I'll show you when we go inside because Jacinta has been named in the comments in some of the photos. She's still as stunning as ever."

Jacinta was Rosie's cousin on her father's side. She also had worked at the continental deli as a teenager in the early seventies. Her family lived next door to the church. Jacinta was the eldest of four daughters, and an absolute natural beauty.

Her father was a very harsh man. He was angry at her mother for not giving him a son. When we came over, he could be found sitting at the table, knocking back home-made wine and abusing his wife.

Jacinta became pregnant at sixteen, word had it, it was Signora Grazia's husband, some disgusting old man. For all we knew she could have been raped and it went unreported, because it had become Jacinta's fault. It's always the woman's fault. Just like Jacinta's mother not bearing a son.

Jacinta was probably made to feel loved by that disgusting old man, because we weren't shown affection by our parents. We were there to be seen and not heard. Jacinta upped and disappeared one day. We were told she had found a job in Italy and was working there.

My mother told me that Jacinta had run away, otherwise her father would have killed her. He most likely would have, I guess it would have been jail time well worth spent for him. Jacinta's mother packed her a suitcase, gave her a hundred dollars and put her on the first flight to Italy when her father went to work one day.

We were never allowed to speak to Jacinta's family again, but we all knew that her father had used her mother as a punching bag in return. She was badly abused, probably up until the day he passed away. That was Jacinta's mothers only saving grace, her husband passed away in his fifties. The rest of Jacinta's sisters wouldn't have much to do with any one of us after that. I mean why would they, we all stood by and watched that happen.

"Poor Jacinta, she wasn't given any support or any options, never mind prosecution for that arsehole who did that to her." I said.

"She had a little boy! He's in his thirties now, he's really a handsome looking young man. I saw him on social media. They're living in Milan." Rosie said.

"She's married now, Em. She met this guy and she works as a translator at the Australian Consulate over there."

"No way! That's amazing. I'm so pleased to hear that. Please don't be afraid to tell your parents about your good news Rosie, I can't wait to meet this little guy! You need to find inspiration through Jacinta's story. Fuck fear, and fuck family traditions." I said.

"How do you know it's going to be a little guy?" she asked.

"Call it a mother's instinct," I said.

As the weeks passed by, I found I was struggling more and more with guilt. I hadn't really felt its presence like this before. My experience with guilt in the past was limited to dieting. If I fell off the wagon and decided to have dessert with dinner, then I might feel guilty for a moment, but this was a different type I had been feeling and it began to overwhelm me.

One night when the man in the hat visited me I asked him, "Why was I feeling guilty?" He told me it was because, when we were traveling in the car I hadn't listened to my father. I had taken him to see Doctor Tang and was heading home. I had cut the conversation short because of my own selfish reasons. He said I should have listened to my father because now I will never know what it was that he wanted to say, and my father was probably not at peace because of it. I was devastated at the thought.

My entire upbringing was based on death and respecting the dearly departed and eternal peace. I wanted my father to be at peace in heaven with God, like he'd always described to me. Not only was my depression clouding my judgement, but so was guilt. I couldn't deal with it, I felt like the pressure cooker had been set on high again. My thoughts were consuming me. They were eating away at me. What if my father had something important to tell me that day? What if there was something I needed to know? He may have simply wanted to get something off his chest. My selfishness had denied him the opportunity. Why didn't I tell him I loved and appreciated him?

Why weren't Italians open with their feelings towards their children? Why, why, why…

I hadn't slept in weeks, I wasn't concentrating at work, and I was always tired. Maybe Sharni was right, maybe each time I crashed and burned it was dramatic.

CHAPTER 27

CHOICES SIMPLY NOT ENOUGH

As A CHILD I wasn't given choices. There weren't any. What you saw was what you got, what was served was what you ate. Direction on the other hand, I was given. I was told I had to go to church, I had to keep my room tidy, I had to help my mother clean each Saturday morning, I had to finish my dinner, I wasn't given a choice. Italians were renowned for believing in signs from above, perhaps if you are given the right sign, then you will make the right choice.

As a teenager I resorted to tossing a coin, heads, or tails, or reading the daily horoscopes. Maybe there was some hidden message in them based on how my week would turn out on what I read. Or Rosie and I would go see psychics, who proclaimed to have an insight into our futures. Or we'd sit around making paper origami fortune tellers where we would number each corner and on the inside are eight flaps, underneath lay a secret message. We'd spend hours making these things, then discussing the hidden messages we had chosen, how it most likely would come true, stories made up in our heads.

"Em, let's go out for gelati." Rosie would say.

"Sure, but you'll have to ask my father if I can go," I would say.

"No way, I'm too scared to ask him," Rosie would say.

I'd take out a coin. "Flip it, heads you ask, tails I'll ask." I'd say.

"Fuck. It landed on heads, looks like we'll be staying here." Rosie disappointingly would say.

"Rosie! I found a blue and white feather with black spots, what are the chances, blue and white! What do you think that means? Do you think we will meet someone soon? I asked the universe for a sign and I saw this feather land at my feet!"

Looking back now it probably belonged to the neighbour's budgies and simply blew over the fence from his aviary.

"Don't touch the bottom of the plate with the knife when you cut the birthday cake, your wish won't come true." My mother would say.

"Don't put new shoes on the table! It's bad luck."

"If a bird poops on you, that's good luck!"

"If you see two white doves, then someone will be getting married or dropping dead, it could go either way." My mother would say.

My choices felt like they were controlled by signs and superstition. Choices and direction had become confusing and hard to distinguish when you are desperate for change.

I remember when I first met Matteo Famoso. He was studying civil engineering at university. He was half Italian half Spanish, and he was simply gorgeous. Matteo and I had become good friends. He would come into the deli to buy fresh ricotta cheese for his mother who'd make spinach and ricotta cannelloni each Saturday morning.

Europeans always seemed to have set menus back then, the same dishes prepared for each day of the week. No choices, you already knew what you'd get when you sat down to eat. It was simple authentic food.

I had developed a crush quickly on Matteo and the feeling was reciprocated. He was the most genuine guy I will probably ever meet in my lifetime. He was kind, considerate, and smart. He was tall, with black wavy hair and brown eyes. He would lean across the deli counter and tell me about life at university. I had Dave on the scene, but it wasn't little Italy official yet.

Matteo would walk me to my car after work and put his arm around me as I would lean up against it. He made my heart skip. He always smelt so good, wearing nice aftershave. He was always beautifully dressed. He had an air of sophistication about him. When he walked, he would take long strides that made him look like he was floating. He never seemed stressed about anything. No one knew about Matteo. I didn't bother telling anyone about my feelings towards him, he was my secret. He wasn't part of the plan, so what was the point, it would only complicate things.

One day he walked me to my car, and he kissed me long and hard. I hadn't been kissed like that before.

"Emmie, you know how I feel about you. I'm crazy about you. I want to make love to you. I want to book a hotel room by the beach. I want to hold you all night." He said as he held me next to my car door.

"I want that too, Matteo." I replied as I kissed him back. I fully trusted Matteo I had no reason not to.

The night Matteo and I were planning on spending together I had told my mother I was sleeping at Renata's house, and I told Renata I was sleeping at Rosie's house. I told her I would pick her up at 5 o'clock and we would go out for a coffee before I headed to Rosie's. I wanted my aunt to see me and I knew Maria would be at bingo at that time so she wouldn't be around to ask questions. Once I dropped Renata back home, I made my way to the beach. It wasn't a hard plan to execute my father was in Italy visiting his mother. Renata kept her bedroom door locked so my aunt wouldn't bother checking. I'd go back in the morning before they woke up to take Renata out for breakfast.

When I arrived at the hotel, I walked up to the counter and asked for them to call Matteo's room, and let him know I had arrived. He came down to greet me. He was gorgeous. Even when he spoke, he was eloquent. He was one of a kind. He wore black pants and a gorgeous shirt. He always wore Italian leather shoes.

He took me by the hand and led me to the elevator. We didn't exchange many words. I could feel my pulse beating in our hands. He took me up to the tenth floor and when he opened the door to our room, there were no lights on, only a soft glow. I saw candles lit and red roses by the bed. The room had a view of the ocean and it was breathtaking. I could see the white foam of the waves crashing onto the sand. Matteo came up behind me and wrapped his arms around my waist.

"Matteo this is so beautiful, I love this so much!" I was so happy, even for a moment, for one night I wanted to feel complete happiness and I was on the right path.

Making love to Matteo was exactly that, no words, only slow passionate love. We didn't require alcohol we had everything we needed, each other. We would stroke each other and feel our soft skin beneath our fingertips, and looked into each other's eyes. We didn't sleep we went on and on and on. He was the perfect lover, flawless and pure, no preservatives, no additives, no MSG, what you saw is what you got.

"Emmie, stay with me, don't go." He said, as we sat on the bonnet of his car to watch the sunrise.

"I have to go. I don't want to, but I don't have a choice." I said.

He had his arms wrapped around me so tightly, God, I wished I could stay. I wished I could have Matteo in my life forever. What was the point of even discussing a future together? I knew Matteo wanted me to be a part of his future. He had confessed this to his cousin who went to my school, and she had told me. Matteo and I would sneak a kiss around the back of the deli now and then, and I loved every single one. He was perfect. My first *true* love.

Was Matteo a sign from God? I wondered later in life. Had I made the right choice? He never married or had children. He moved to Sydney and worked for a large construction firm. He didn't have a social media account, maybe he is still the same unpretentious guy he was back then. I admired a man who chose to keep his life private.

I still kept in touch with his cousin. I would ask her about Matteo on the few occasions I would run into her. God, he was so nice! Apparently, that's the reason why he didn't have a partner. According to his cousin, women found him 'too nice'. He was! That's what I wanted now, nice, not a relationship fuelled by unnecessary nasty drama. Bad boys are so eighties.

Once Matteo had found out my relationship with Dave was in fact official and went viral via little Italy, he stopped coming into the deli. I knew he was hurt, and so was I. I knew I wouldn't see him anymore. We loved one another, and words were left unspoken. I had no choice but to accept it. I processed hurt and pain in the only way I knew, keeping it locked away in my throat.

I hadn't thought about Matteo in years. I think I still have a red rose pressed in-between the pages of a book at home somewhere as a reminder of the pure happiness from that night.

My mobile phone rang and went to hands-free.

"Ma, we need milk and yogurt, can you please grab some on your way home?" Chloe asked.

"Alright," I said.

Why was it that I had encountered every red light and road work possible today? Is this a sign that I'm not meant to get home on time? This was ridiculous each turn I took seemed to take me longer to get to the shops. I wanted to get home early to start cooking dinner. I was driving to the shops for two items. I was annoyed. I should have gone straight home. Chloe would have survived until tomorrow.

I arrived at the shop, parked, got out of my car and I saw him. I saw Matteo standing at the ATM. I was squinting to make sure it was really him. God could not have timed this any better if he had tried. Was this meant to be? Was this divine intervention? I hadn't seen him in over twenty years. He looked so hot, still beautifully dressed in pants, business shirt, and Italian leather shoes.

"Matteo! Oh my God!" I said as I walked up to him. I felt like running up to him.

"EMMIE!" He hugged and kissed me.

"What are you doing here? Don't you live in Sydney?" I asked, still in complete utter shock.

"I do, my father passed away last month. I have a few legal issues to sort out for my mum."

"Matteo, I'm so sorry, my condolences." I said as I was holding his hands.

"Em, you haven't changed a bit, you look great." He said.

"Neither have you, you look so good, Matteo. You still look the same."

I didn't want to leave, I wanted to stand there forever, I didn't care people were walking around us to use the ATM. We spoke about life and family, we stood there holding each other's hands. I could still feel my pulse beating in his hands. Matteo filled me in about a few failed past relationships and his ever-booming career. How he was happy living in Sydney on his own, in a three-storey townhouse in Double Bay with a great social life and friends. I told him about Chloe and XJ, and he told me he heard I had children.

"Just say the word Em, if you ever decide to leave Dave you know where to find me." He said and we both laughed. "It would be nice to share my life with someone one day," he said.

If only he knew. I thought to myself. Dave had moved out of the family home and was renting.

We kissed on the cheek, hugged tight and parted ways. I didn't want him to leave, just like he didn't want me to leave on our special night. My heart pounding all the way home. I kicked myself for not giving him my number.

"Ma, where's the milk and yogurt?" Chloe asked as I walked through the door.

Oh, fuck!

"Sorry I was held up, Chloe. I'll get it tomorrow."

I was standing by the kitchen window still thinking of Matteo.

Why did I ever let the opportunity with Matteo go? I should have put my fear aside and gone with my heart instead. I was on a timeframe growing up. I had to be married at nineteen for fuck sakes. I will never regret my children, but did I make the right choice for *me?* …

CHAPTER 28

VEGETARIAN MOUSSAKA

I HAD A friend once that made the best vegetarian moussaka. He wasn't Greek. I had never tired anything like it before. Who would have thought, an Asian modifying a Greek recipe? I was always too polite to go back for seconds, but secretly I couldn't get enough of it. I was jealous with each mouthful. It tasted so authentic. Maybe that was my first taste of jealousy.

Takeaway food was unheard of growing up at home. My father would not have allowed it. Food had to be prepared from scratch. I remembered my mother tried to convince me as a child she went to the fish and chip shop to buy my hot chips, but instead, she had made them herself and wrapped them up in newspaper. According to my father, takeaway would cause acido (heartburn).

We weren't allowed to eat lamb either. I suspected my father associated it with Greek food. A subject not to be discussed in our home.

"Those poor animals turning on a spit," he'd say.

"That's not a real barbeque, you know!" Maybe that's why my father objected to me ever meeting a Greek boy.

Dimitri loved lamb. He loved eating red meat and couldn't understand the concept of vegetarians. He'd never eat vegetarian moussaka. He and Constantina separated around the same time Dave and I did. His wife was now living with a vegan.

"Go figure, no meat, no animal products whatsoever, she's seriously lost the plot!" he'd say.

"How can you go without cheese or eggs, I don't understand. She hates olives, so I don't know what she'll be eating? Fucking potatoes and onions like they did during the Great Depression I guess." He said.

Dimitri had become quite the entrepreneur, franchising his DJ business. He was still teaching maths and had developed quite an impressive financial portfolio. He was trying to win Constantina back so he wouldn't have to hand over half of his businesses, although he proclaimed, he no longer loved her. He didn't want to part with their cash, which he had more of an attachment to.

I liked hanging out with Dimitri again, we were both free, and we were both good friends. We would catch up like the old days when we went to night school together. He became acquainted with Jess as well in our social outings.

"She's hot." he'd say.

This would annoy me. I found Dimitri annoying like Dave at times. They'd both say stupid things and have little regard of how their words might have an impact on me.

"Ella, I have a gig at this upmarket cocktail bar in the city. Come and see me, bring Jess with you." He said when he called me up.

"Okay, I guess I could ask her, she'd really like that." I said.

I messaged Jess to ask if she was free to catch up for a drink with me and Dimitri and she messaged back, he had already invited her out. He found her on social media.

What was he playing at? Jess and I were planning on going together. I was surprised that I cared. I shouldn't care, it was none of my business what those two got up to.

But I did, and if I stopped and felt my feelings, I would find jealousy under there somewhere.

When I arrived at the cocktail bar, I saw Jess and Dimitri sitting on bar stools at the bar. They were both sipping on Espresso Martinis. Dimitri was sitting close to Jess with his elbow on the counter and his head tilted to one side, both their knees were touching.

"Hi, I'm not interrupting I hope." I said kissing them both.

"Ella, Ella, you made it!" Dimitri said in his animated, attention seeking tone.

"I'll have one of those thanks," I said pointing to the drinks.

Dimitri was very generous he would always pay for my drinks when we were out, no matter what I ordered. It was never a big deal to him.

"Have whatever you want Ella, order up." He'd say.

"I really like Jess, where have you been hiding her?" he asked, as Jess left to go to the bathroom.

"Jess isn't into Greeks, she prefers the surfy types." I said, annoyed.

"That's not what she told me." He said with a smirk.

He was trying to push my buttons. I doubt that Jess would even look twice at him.

"She's not into cultures where the men wear white pleated skirts on their national days." I said sarcastically.

Jess came back and they both sat next to one another. They were giggling and acting like Dimitri and I used to in night school. I began to feel like a third wheel. I felt like I had been taken advantage of, used to bring Jess along, so Dimitri could show off.

"So, Dimitri no pompom shoes for you tonight? Isn't that what Greeks wear when they go out trying to impress women? Where are your komboloi (worry beads)? Wouldn't you like to show Jess those too?" The nasty negative jealousy was surfacing in me.

"I'd like to show Jess more than my worry beads, I'd like to show her how to eat yiros," he said.

Poor Jess, she was caught in a stand-off between a Greek and an Italian, and it wasn't fair on her. She had no idea what was going on around her. She had the biggest blank look on her face, she was happy to be out and away from home having a few cocktails and laughs with friends. Instead, she was smack bang in the middle of a Spanish bullfight. Dimitri, the matador was waving the red flag and I was about to pierce his backside and throw him up in the air with my horns, never to get up again.

"Well, sex with this Greek man can best be described as fucking a fruit and veg guy at the markets, too many boxes to load onto the truck. He can't keep up with the pace, and misses his delivery." I said tilting my head towards Dimitri.

"By the way, Dimitri, I faked it most of the time. It was me being a people pleaser, take it as community service."

Dimitris face dropped. I had hit the lowest of lows. I stood up, got my bag, I said goodbye to Jess and left.

No sooner was I in the taxi Dimitri messaged me.

"Please come back Ella, I'm sorry."

"You used me to get Jess to come out, had a crack at her and then you used Jess to get to me to try to make me jealous. That was disrespectful and you lack integrity, Dimitri. You involved Jess and she didn't deserve that either, I'm done. Ciao." I wrote back. I was hurt.

"El, please come back. I'm sorry, don't cut me out of your life, I love you." He messaged.

I wished he hadn't written that. Those three words that instilled fear into me. He should have messaged "Sorry, come back I'll buy you another Espresso Martini," or "I know what I did was wrong I'm not dealing with the vegan." That would have been enough for me to go back, but not now.

Dimitri spent months trying to apologise. He tried calling me, emailing me and messaging me. Until one day he called me at work and caught me completely off guard when I answered the phone. He put up a real genuine fight to win me back.

"Ella, please don't hang up on me, do you still hate me?" he asked.

"YES! With a capital H and an exclamation mark at the end." I said and I hung up.

That was the last time I ever heard from Dimitri. I didn't hate him. I loved him, with all my heart and soul. We were the same. I couldn't even bring myself to use that word, hate. It was far too strong a word to use. He knew that, that's why *he asked* me, and I simply went along with it.

"I don't use certain words in the English dictionary, Dimitri, and hate is one of them." I'd say to him.

"It's one of those words once spoken is hard to come back from."

Dimitri loved my dramatic nature, it turned him on. He would purposely try to push my buttons. Dimitri knew exactly how to handle me when he'd fire me up. Like Dave did also, he found my dramatic nature very sexy. I wondered at times if he would start a fight only for the makeup sex. Perhaps that's where the recipe formed, stir the pot with a fight, makeup, throw in a sorry or two, and conclude with sex.

There were only ever two men in my life who knew the flip side to my dramatic nature, and they knew exactly how to put it to good use. Others came and went in my life who found drama too intense and proclaimed simplicity, however deep down I found these individuals boring.

"Why wouldn't you want to try to tame the lion in the cage, it's a challenge and I am a master." Dimitri would say.

Love. There's a flip side if you chose to see the positive. If there is genuine love between two people, you can always open that door again if the time is right to have another peek in down the track. There are two doors in life, one at the front and one at the back. I preferred to use the back door, like I was raised to do.

CHAPTER 29

PEAKING DUCK

MY FATHER WAS a good winemaker. All organic, authentic, and preservative free. He liked to drink in moderation. He would have a glass of wine mixed with lemonade with his meal. The Aussie culture liked a drink or two or three, and alcoholism had no class boundaries. The wealthy alcoholics drank expensive wines and the under-privileged alcoholics drank wine out of cardboard boxes. They were all the same, regardless of financial means or what they drank. They had an illness and an addiction.

Dave had been diagnosed with depression and alcoholism. Nguyen had high functioning depression and was a functioning alcoholic. No matter what title you gave it, what spin you put on it, or how some try to disguise it, it means the same thing. Alcoholism. You drink too fucking much and don't know when to stop.

My relationship with Dave was all but over. His drinking had taken a turn for the worse and he was now off on benders, where you just don't stop until you flop. I had become accustomed to late night phone calls from the police asking me to collect him after being found passed out under a seat at a bus shelter or at a random park somewhere.

I had moved out of the marital home. I couldn't afford the mortgage repayments. I rented a little cottage close by so Chloe and XJ could choose where they preferred to stay. Dave and I didn't have rules around custodial parenting, they were old enough to decide for themselves. Besides, I still popped in at home to check on Dave, a part of me saw this as my duty to keep an eye on him. After all, he was the father of my children, and I didn't want him meeting the man in the hat.

The worst part about benders is people think the inebriated person is always the life of the party. That's not the case they're often the ones suffering the most. It's not funny to watch someone make a fool of themselves and then pass out.

The difference between Nguyen and Dave was that Dave truly wanted to change and was seeking help. He admitted to himself and others he had a problem, he owned it. Once I had moved out, he quickly realised the important things in his life, and it wasn't just 'stuff' that completed it. It was his family.

"Emmie, I am seeing my GP weekly now, and I am also seeing a clinical psychologist." Dave said when I went home to grab a few more things.

"I'm glad, Dave. How's the drinking going?" I asked.

"I haven't had a drink in months. I stopped going to the pub as well." He said.

"I've found non-alcoholic drinks that I can have when I am out, and I have started running again. I bought a bike, and I go riding with the boys every Sunday."

"I want you back Em, I love you, this all means nothing without you or the kids in it." He said, as he was waving his hands about.

"I need clarity Dave, it's about me now. I'm sorry you feel alone in this big house, but I'm not getting any younger and I don't know if I want to spend the rest of my life taking care of someone who has a dependency on alcohol and all of the medical conditions associated with it. I don't want to be married to someone who's at a higher risk of developing cancer or alcoholic dementia. I have an autoimmune condition, I need to put myself first now, I should have years ago. Anyway, it's early days to be having these sorts of discussions. I'm starting to feel so much better in myself and my depression is under control." I said.

"I've now recognised the triggers, and I've stopped having late night conversations with the man in the hat," I said with a smile. "I've stopped punishing myself, and I'm putting more focus on the things I like to do without feeling guilty."

I was happy for Dave it took courage to admit he had a drinking problem. No one should live a life where they are reliant on substance abuse to mask deeper issues. It generally didn't end well for the individual if they didn't recognise this in time. Dave chose to drink and didn't know when to stop. He now knew he had no choice but to stop if he had any hope of salvaging any sort of relationship with his children or anybody else that came into his life.

I had reached a crossroad in my life. Two men, both with the same issues. But completely opposite in the way they chose to address this. One had recognised the need for change, the other, had diminished morals and ethics.

Nguyen did not recognise he had a drinking problem. When he drank, everybody else around him *became* the problem.

"Nguyen, are you free to come with me to an art opening? I'd really like to go. It's an exhibition about migrant women who arrived in Australia in the fifties. They're exhibiting artwork reflective of motherhood and the challenges they faced moving to a foreign country," I asked at home one night.

"Sure, we can do that." He replied as he sat down to watch television with his favourite bottle of red.

"I don't know if I should ask Kate if she would like me to take some photos of the exhibition and the artists so we can promote it, but I always stress out when I combine work with pleasure. She might want me to write something up, maybe I should keep it as a private outing just me and you. What do you think? I might wear that new dress I bought. I'm not sure yet, and I'll go get my hair done." I said, really having a harmless conversation with myself and thinking out loud.

Nguyen had heard me and turned around from where he was sitting to answer me.

"Emmie, that's a first world problem. Who cares if you take photos or not, or what dress you wear! People like you in Australia don't know the difference between real problems. Don't bother me with this rubbish you make a big deal out of nothing!" Nguyen snapped back at me and went back to watching his television show.

Nguyen was on a mission to find fault in me when he didn't have enough or had too much alcohol in him, the balance with him had to be just right. Alcoholics are forgetful, moody, and argumentative. But what was my problem? People liked this man, they thought he was fantastic. I became more observant. I took a backseat and I watched each time we were out in a social setting. Nguyen was the life of the party, because of his drinking and his generosity. He would buy people drinks. His unlimited finances allowed him to be the centre of attention. People swarmed around him like desperate vultures waiting for a free top up of red.

Nguyen tried very hard to fit in. He had become so good at faking it by pretending he was this wonderful functioning member of the community, when he wasn't. He would read books on psychology then copycat his behaviour on what he learnt. He would fake it out in public, but at home, it all became too much and the mask would fall. No one knows what goes on behind closed doors. He too, was always buying books and reading for his own purpose, pretending to be someone he wasn't. He had to take that perfect selfie, and post it for the entire world to see to prove there was nothing wrong with him.

Listening to Nguyen tell me I had first world problems were as bad as when he would tell me I needed to practice mindfulness. This had become his latest buzz word.

"Emmie, you need to spend more time alone mastering the art of mindfulness, you're really clueless, aren't you? You stress over the smallest things, you're so dramatic!"

Was there anything that I was actually good at in Nguyen's eyes? Mindfulness to me represented breathing. With each breath I took, I would be present in the moment. To Nguyen I felt like I had to pull a rabbit out of a hat because clearly, I couldn't even master the art of breathing correctly.

Telling an Italian, they were too dramatic or they liked drama was like telling them they're too loud. Yes! To both. How were we any different to Greeks at their wedding receptions where guests were invited to smash plates on the dance floor as a sign of well wishes and good fortune? I wasn't the one who smashed the plates in this relationship.

I didn't mind Nguyen drinking, most of the time he would finish up his bottles of wine in front of the television and go to bed. We didn't have to hang around pubs as I used to with Dave, waiting for last drinks to be called so he got every drop in. Nguyen's drinking became a problem if I said or did something to upset him.

I came home one evening and found him preparing dinner.

"Hi, honey. How are you? That smells so good!" I said.

I went up to kiss him in the kitchen as he was shredding roast duck on a wooden board. He handed me a glass of wine and kissed me. I quickly drank my wine.

"I'm going to have a quick shower and I will be right out. I can help you. I won't be long." I said.

"That's okay, Emmie, I have it pretty much under control. I've made duck pancakes," he said.

When I came out of the shower Nguyen had my plate ready for me with the pancake containing shredded duck and its fat.

"Honey, I don't like duck fat, can you please leave it out of my pancake for me?" I asked, whilst taking a sip of my wine.

I saw the look on his face change. He went quiet and he stiffened up, as he took bits of duck fat out and put them in the bin.

"Honey, why are you throwing that away?" I asked. I was confused he threw my pancake out with the duck fat. I only wanted the meat. I was hungry and now my plate was empty.

"You rejected my food!" he said.

"What?" I asked confused.

I had already had a glass of wine on an empty stomach and Nguyen's behaviour was intimidating. It really reminded me of my dark days with Dave. I didn't want to spend the night under these conditions, and I knew I had to sober up if I was going to plan my escape and get back home. I was trying really hard not to cry in front of him, I didn't want to add fuel to the fire by him saying I was too sensitive or too dramatic.

"You rejected my food!" he repeated.

"It's a traditional dish served with duck fat!" he said.

"I love eating duck, honey, you know that! I am so sorry if you feel like I rejected your food. That was never my intention, I am *really* sorry!" I said with all sincerity.

But the damage had already been done. He was angry, and the only way his body language would improve was with each drink he had. I wasn't going to hang around. I was drinking water as fast as I possibly could to sober up.

I was so intimidated by our misunderstanding I asked his permission if I could use the bathroom. Once I was in there, I splashed cold water on my face. I had hot secret tears streaming down burning my cheeks and I was trying my hardest to stop them.

Rejection. What a harsh word to use to describe someone's food preferences. The only rejection that went on tonight was not between me and the duck, but between Nguyen and me. He had totally rejected me. He threw my feelings out with my dinner. I didn't do or say anything to hurt him, but apparently, I had, again.

I thought of Dina and what she'd do in this situation. She'd kick his arse out of the house, toss him to the curb, and say, "Em, get the fuck out of there and get your arse back home, where you're safe." I thanked God for my intuition and friends like Dina.

I walked out of the bathroom, Nguyen was sitting on the sofa, his arms crossed, still looking like a 'rejected' chef who had been given a bad critique by a customer.

"I think I better spend tonight at home," I said as I got my things and prepared for my departure.

He didn't say a word. No apology for his behaviour, nothing. Did he care? Probably not, he would have had his last drinks before his bedtime and most likely think I was overreacting again. It would be my fault, according to him. As our relationship developed over time it has become tedious and irritating, instead of growing together we were growing apart.

Nguyen and I never had real arguments as Dave and I did. He led me to believe it was always me and my thoughts and what was in my head that created our problems. Fighting with Nguyen was sarcastic and shrewd. He would play mind games. He liked to fight quietly, preferring to be the worm that ate me from the inside out.

Dave, on the other hand, was what you saw is what you got. Put it all out on the table and let's get this over and done with. No winners or losers at the end but instead, compromise. We would eventually reach an adult decision and stick to it. We'd shake hands at the end and most likely go out to dinner or have fun afterwards. Move forward not backwards. My past issues with Dave were beginning to seem a lot easier to resolve.

I had been too ignorant in the past to address these sorts of issues because I was too busy trying to get as much of Nguyen's attention out of him that I possibly could. In the process, I had lost my ability to stand up for myself. I was just like his doormat out the front of his home.

Although his poor behaviour was obvious, even back in the early days, the nice words and smooth talking made it okay. In retrospect, I could see the shortcomings, but I chose to be blind.

I took another look at him as I left, he hadn't moved from the sofa.

CHAPTER 30

I WAS ALWAYS fascinated by magic and magicians as a child, and as an adult, it became a mother-son outing. XJ was exactly like me, we loved to watch the latest illusionists when they came to town, and it became a great source of entertainment for us both. Perhaps it was something still buried deep inside of me as a child, secretly wishing someone would make me disappear from my life.

There were the intriguing magicians who used their charm and trickery to lure victims into the world of the unknown and proposition them with the excitement of something 'better'. And the gypsies who would make promises of being able to look into crystal balls, seeing deep into your future, preying on the vulnerable and desperate.

I was intrigued by this unorthodox practice. The trickery and illusion on your eyes and mind causes confliction on which to believe. What is presented to you in life can be whatever you want it to be, but don't be fooled when the illusion is too good to be true because it could be black magic.

Some magicians would like you to believe they have *real* magical powers, like the ability to make all your worries disappear, or make someone fall in love. But really, it's simply clever emotional and psychological manipulation that abuses our limitations in the way our brains work and think.

I always thought Dimitri was a magician. He would wave his magic wand and I would forgive his misdoings. We had a magical lifeline attached to one another. We somehow knew when we needed one another during trying times. Dimitri was an amateur compared to Nguyen when it came to magic.

While Dimitri was propositioning me with simple card tricks or pulling bunches of fake flowers from his tailcoat jacket, Nguyen would have pretty women tied up in wooden boxes and sawing them in half. There was no comparison between the two. Dimitri liked to think of himself as a Greek stud, a real Eros, but he wasn't. It was his harmless illusion to feed his ego. When push came to shove, he would turn into a little mouse and scurry away.

Nguyen, a philanderer, led women to believe he wasn't a player and was exclusive to one woman at a time. He was the greatest illusionist of them all. He was the grandmaster magician in his field. His costume was the wolf in sheep's clothing.

His illusion was to come across as the innocent, trustworthy man, but in fact, he would turn into Don Juan only to wave his magic wand and use techniques to spin his web of skillful deception and seduction.

His charm reached into my chest, pulled out my heart, and held it in the palm of his hand. He snapped his fingers, and was gone, right in front of my eyes! Looking into his eyes, "It wasn't me it was you," he'd say, waving his wand. Hypnotically, he'd pull the rug right from underneath me.

With every good magician, there must be a good teacher. Dimitri didn't have a problem giving me simple instructions when undertaking a task or seeking his advice. He already had an idea of what the best learning technique was for me and how to help me achieve a resolution. He knew how to get me to listen and follow his advice.

"I'm a teacher, it comes naturally to me. If you don't give kids simple step-by-step instructions, how do you expect them to learn? You can't 'assume' they already understand what I am writing up on the board. I must teach them. Otherwise, it will reflect poorly on me." He'd say.

"I'm struggling today," or "I'm scared," I'd say to him, and step by step he would help me work my way around my thoughts, simple and direct. No talk of, "You have to do what's best for you" or "Sink or swim." His conversations lead me to think a lot clearer and identify areas I wanted to change in my life. I could go back to him over and over if required, until I understood it, securely enabling me to use the right tools and gain confidence. "If you don't ask, you don't get." He'd say. A fantastic teacher, but a lousy magician.

Nguyen, on the other hand, would compartmentalise everything in his mind. He had his family in one box, his job in another, his hobbies, his friends, his goals, and me. All neatly stored and packed into little boxes. I suspect it would be easy to make the boxes disappear when they no longer served a purpose. "Poof" and it's gone!

Nguyen believed in tantalising me with gifts, not direction, or compromise, for us both to be together, because we were never going to be. Not properly. I viewed him as what was best for me. I loved him. I didn't feel worthy of his love. If I was failing to do anything right then I was always going to be in the wrong. I desperately wanted guidance and I wasn't going to get it over text messaging. I was fighting a losing battle.

My mind had become my greatest magician because it was constantly playing tricks on me. I lacked the courage for honesty to tell Nguyen what I wanted in my life, and that was him. I had developed the worst habit of all, overthinking. Nguyen was the master con artist, manipulating my emotions for his own personal gain. He valued himself above everyone else and at my expense.

Nguyen had decided to pack up my belongings one night into a box. I had asked for these in a heated argument via a text message. Perhaps if I was given the opportunity for phone conversations, I wouldn't feel so frustrated and say things I didn't mean. I had resorted to saying anything to get a response. I had hit the bottom of the barrel of communication.

"Nguyen you have misinterpreted my message!" I'd messaged.

"I didn't mean it like that. I don't understand why you are getting so upset." I would write.

Text messaging late at night when one should be asleep is extraordinarily frustrating. In fact, text messaging is generally frustrating. There's no content, there's no body language, and it's vague and distant. We weren't getting a proper sense or feel for each other.

"Can I please call you? I get so tired at night I need to sleep. Can we please talk instead?" I texted.

"No, it's your way of trying to control me," he texted back.

Was a simple phone conversation an unreasonable ask? How was I supposed to get a better understanding where our relationship was headed, without speaking to him, maybe through osmosis?

Silence can be deafening. He was ignoring me, and I already knew why. My instincts were telling me I had been replaced. He had detached himself completely.

"I have your things packed, you can collect these," Nguyen messaged me late one night.

"Can I see you, please?" I asked.

"I don't know I would rather not." He messaged back.

We hadn't broken up, *or* had we? I wasn't sure. We had never had a conversation. I was in a state of constant confusion. I had resorted to the lowest of lows. I wasn't very polite or respectful with my words towards Nguyen, I was hurting. The sorry letters and emails were useless. There was no magic formula to the forgiveness, and he wasn't the forgiving type.

I thought of the box of Italian dinnerware I had found at home when I was packing my stuff to move out. It was Capodimonte dinnerware, the finest Italian china ever to be made. My mother had saved up for months to buy it for me. I was thirteen years old, a teenager, and she bought me a dinner set to stuff into my glory box. I couldn't stand that dinner set, I never used it. I wasn't allowed to take it out of the box, even when I was married, because it was 'too good' to use. I could only use it for special occasions because it was so expensive and delicate. All I really wanted for my thirteenth birthday was a camera so I could have a hobby. Instead, I was handed a big brown cardboard box with crockery in it. I had made my acquaintance with disappointment that day, neatly packed in a cardboard box. Although it now sat it in the garage, I wasn't prepared to throw it out. My mother had invested her love in that dinner set. I simply couldn't trash it, because her love was real. It held sentimental value. Nguyen was completely devoid of sentiment.

I had managed to convince Nguyen to let me see him to collect my belongings. It was awkward at first, I felt like I was collecting some charitable donations for some homeless shelter from a deceased estate.

Nguyen sensed this also and offered me a drink. We were now two strangers, sitting miles apart on the sofa we once shared snuggling up to one another to watch movies together.

My heart sank with each sip of wine I took. I was staring at the brown box next to me thinking *I can't deal with this. I am not ready to say goodbye like this.* Unfortunately, I was still hoping, and this was exhausting because with hope came expectations and I genuinely thought I had a real shot at resolving this. *If I just hope and pray.* I'd think to myself, like my Sunday school teacher had taught me.

Dimitri and I always resolved issues. Dave and I seemed to work around issues, and they had both been in my life for years. We may have parted ways now and then, but eventually we all found our way back to one another. When my mother and father had major issues, he would take off overseas. But they still managed to make things work. I didn't understand the concept of heartache, but I was feeling it.

I asked Nguyen if he was seeing somebody else. He said "NO" and then we had sex. So, I guess it wasn't over just yet.

Nguyen had gotten up to go into the kitchen to get another bottle of wine, and I quickly dressed. I grabbed my bag and left. I couldn't take the cardboard box, I left it behind. I put it in another room when he wasn't looking. He was going to be furious with me when he found it, but I did it for a reason.

Nguyen did find the box and messaged me a week later. He was very annoyed, but I didn't care. I knew he would throw it out eventually. I would rather he did that, than I have it at home as a constant reminder of our relationship and my hurt.

"It's only stuff" he'd say, as he would throw it in the trash. But it wasn't just stuff. It was the sexy dressing gown I would wear around home. It was my favourite books I would share with him, and we would have discussions over. I wanted him to dispose of my belongings, and I was secretly hoping that might resonate something within him. That these items belonged to a *real* person.

I wasn't disposable like trash, I shared a part of my life with him, and that was *real*. I had invested in our relationship, thinking it was leading somewhere.

I realised I wasn't that high up on the list of his priorities, I was shoved into a fucking small cardboard box, that he magically made disappear with any association he had to it, in the trash.

CHAPTER 31

WITH AGE COMES GRACE

A S WE GET older, you'd think we would learn what we're supposed to from life, but that's not always the case. I often wondered why elderly people were grumpy or they didn't have filters when it came to expressing their thoughts or emotions, they said it like it was. How in a way young children did, however, they could get away with it because of their curiosity, innocence, and age.

When XJ was four years old we were at the supermarket and he was sitting in the trolley. I had turned to grab something off the shelf, and he saw a coloured woman walk past. He asked her if she had drunk too much chocolate milk. I was so embarrassed I apologised immediately. I remember the woman patting him on his head and said, "Well in fact, I did drink chocolate milk this morning," and winked at me.

My mother was about to turn eighty years old, and she had discovered her voice again, only this time she let it all out, the filter well and truly gone. She could be offensive and rude, or polite and kind, whatever took her fancy on the day. There was no holding back. When I visited her one day while her carer was cleaning her home, she called me over and whispered, "She's black!"

I nearly passed out. Thank God her lovely carer was vacuuming and didn't hear my mother.

Her other favourite thing had become her lack of patience. No sooner had we sat down in the waiting room attending her appointments, she'd be looking at her watch. Five minutes in she would begin to sigh, and they would become louder and louder. I would have to explain to her that she had plenty of time and there was nowhere else she had to be. She was nearly eighty! She wasn't going to be running late for a committee meeting or the Annual General Meeting for the National Reserve Bank of Australia.

I began to find her frustrating. Sometimes she would get up and make a scene or insist we leave. I had found ways around this, now I would bring along snacks in my bag as I did when my children were little. I would bribe my mother with treats so she would sit quietly and patiently. I liked sitting in a waiting room reading magazines, it was the very few occasions I picked one up and flick through all the trash.

"Don't touch those magazines, sick people have read them," she'd say in the doctor's waiting room. "Germs can kill you!"

"We're here for the same reason, mother. You are seeing a doctor because you are sick too," I'd say. *Sick in the head.*

I had decided I was going to have a birthday party for my mother, and I was going to hold it at her house. She had two kitchens and plenty of room. I loved her dearly, we had a mutual understanding, and becoming frustrated with one another was now accepted. As we both became older, we both swore a lot! In fact, at times I felt like we all had our own secret language, including Rosie.

"Emanuela I tried calling you and that fucking bitch told me your phone is not working!" my mother would say.

"Ma that's a pre-recorded message on my phone, you probably got my voice message, or you dialled the wrong number." I'd try to explain to little or no avail.

"Emmie, my mother is doing my fucking head in!" Rosie would call up and say.

"I don't want to fucking baptise Joshua in a fucking Catholic Church. We're having a naming ceremony, how the FUCK do I explain that one to her?" Rosie would say.

Dave wasn't too impressed with our conversations when we were over visiting Rosie and Karl for the birth of Joshua. He asked Rosie why she swore so much and how un-ladylike it was. So, Rosie told him to shut the fuck up or fly back home. I guess she knew him a lot longer and could get away with it.

I was so happy to be spending time with Rosie again when she flew in for my mother's 80th birthday. I had decided I was going to have a high tea in her good kitchen. Although my mother didn't like to see a mess, we were going to finally party in her barely used near new kitchen. The dining table was set beautifully with tiered trays and platters of food and bouquets of fresh posies. I had ordered lots of spumante because my dear mother liked a drink or two.

"Ma, tells us some stories of when you were growing up," I asked around the table.

"Were there any other boys in the village you liked?" I prompted.

"YES! I was in love with an Americano soldier. The Americano's came to our village and saved us from the war. After the war was over, they still stayed behind to help rebuild our village. I was sixteen years old."

"Tell us more zia," Rosie asked.

"I loved him, Rosie, but what could I do? I was with your uncle. He had plans for us to come to Australia when he turned eighteen, so he didn't have to go into the military."

"The Americano wanted me to move to America with him, but I had to say no. I would go with him on picnics, but

I took your nonna with me too, so people wouldn't talk. I had to be smart about my situation. Then I found out Gino liked another girl in the village, and I got mad, I told the girl to go away he was mine! Quella bastarda (that bitch). She ran to tell Gino not to marry me because I was stupid, so I told Gino she was the stupid one not me, and he believed me. That gave me a little more time with the Americano. I was standing back and watched."

"Watch for what?" we asked.

"I watched if Gino really liked the other girl or was playing games. I even took my ring off my finger that your father gave me, and I threw it in the lake!" she said, miming the action.

"Oh my God Rosie, she played both of them!" I said.

"So, you liked dad more than the American?" I asked.

"YES, of course. The Americano wasn't realistico (realistic) I was young, and I didn't understand him when he spoke. I had to make a big decision. If your father took the other girl to Australia, I would have missed my chance for a life with the best-looking boy in the village. The Americano may have changed his mind about me once he got me over there at least I already knew your father and his family. I didn't know much about the other one. Your father was a very handsome man. He had beautiful green eyes, but he was not easy to live with! But now thinking back maybe I should have gone with the Americano. I regret not going with him because life in Australia was so very hard for me."

"Imagine that Rosie, us growing up in New York, eating all that pizza. Or even better, not even being born at all!" I said laughing.

I didn't take much to heart when my mother relived her past. She would tell me about the American soldier and others who wanted to run away with her, these stories were nothing new. I didn't have bedtime stories growing up. I had my mother's romance stories. Were they real? I didn't care, either way my mother was the best story-teller. She would tell them full of emotion and passion and I could visualise her narrative precisely. We all loved her stories and she would have made one hell of an author. She too, in her day, seemed to be chasing what nearly all of the population was, unconditional love.

As the day wound down, we were now onto the limoncello. My aunt had made it, and it was good. She told us how she bribed her friend's son who was a pharmacist, to get her hands on a bottle of pure alcohol. That was an entirely different story.

Our mothers had no barriers in life, they seemed to fear nothing. If they encounter hurdles, they would snap them in half and toss them aside quick smart. They would keep walking with their heads held high. No fake, no pretend, instead, dramatically beautiful, strong, realistic Italian women.

Growing up, I always had others tell me how lucky I was to have a mother like mine. She was so attentive to others giving them her best advice. Sometimes I would become resentful because I wanted the same attention given to me. I realised then that I was more like her than I cared to admit. I too spent so much time giving others advice and supporting their needs and forgetting about myself.

"How are things between you and Nguyen?" Rosie asked.

"Like a fucking ECG, up and down. Each time I breathe life into our relationship I say something 'wrong' and its downhill hill from there. We went thirteen days straight once without a single word. No text message, no calls, nothing. But now it's worse, it's been weeks without contact."

"I don't know if you know this, but Sharni called me the other night. She said she saw Nguyen out with another woman. They were having dinner and holding hands across the table. When she told me, I hung up on her, I didn't want to hear it. I already knew there's someone else, because the last time we had sex it was different, his style had changed. He thought I was stupid. I tricked him. I asked if he thought there was such a thing as right or wrong in life. I told him I believed there wasn't. He was so happy I said that because he agreed with me, he didn't believe there was either. That was the most responsive he'd ever been in months. Arsehole, I knew at that very moment I had been replaced. I had justified his actions in his mind with that one comment." I said.

"It all depends on what set of values you choose to use, and we had these instilled in us from birth. The universe doesn't tell you what to do, but ultimately, it will make the consequence of your actions clear once you have made your choice." I said.

"Has he told you he is seeing someone else?" Rosie asked.

"No, because he's a coward. He hasn't decided to fully cut ties with me, he's still leaving me waiting until I get sick and tired of his game. But I'm waiting for him to end it. He needs to man up."

"Emmie, I love you like a sister, and I love Dave too. Nguyen will never come close to being half the man Dave is because he has no integrity. Just end it with him. Dave looks so good. He's making a clear effort to improve. He's still around you, he's still fighting to have you in his life. If you had to think of a word to describe Dave what would it be?" she asked.

"Um, consistent, comfortable, compatible, loving." I said smiling, not being able to stop at one word.

"And Nguyen?" she asked.

"Liar, unpredictable, moody, unrealistic, unstable, intense, cheater, unsustainable…"

"Okay, so what happened to your 'smart genes' Em? Did you decide to flush it down the toilet with your self-respect? Did you listen to yourself just then? There wasn't one good word in your list to describe Nguyen. You'll get over him quickly because I'm convinced half of you already has! As long as I have known you, you have been on this constant search mission to find some secret formula to life. If you're not out there fighting for what you think is an injustice then you're giving yourself to people like Nguyen. Em, he doesn't deserve your time or energy. The guy is pure toxicity." She said.

Rosie was right. I had failed myself, and I wasn't taking care of my 'in-between'.

I thought of Dave and amongst some of his faults, he was always so encouraging. He always supported me with my goals, and I realised at times it was me and my expectations, not his. I doubted if Dave cared about having a hot meal waiting for him at the end of the day or if the house was immaculate and germ-free. He was patient, and he was still fighting for me to have his family back and he was still my friend throughout our separation. I admired him.

I remember the morning of my mother's party. I had to collect the platters of food. Continental delis were common now, they were everywhere. We were spoilt for choice. Italian food was now trendy.

When I gave my name to the girl behind the counter, she looked surprised. The men behind the service counter all turned around to look at me.

"Signora did you marry an Australian?" she asked surprised.

"Yes, I did!" I said.

At that very moment, I had realised how much societies perception towards multiculturalism had shifted, and how bloody proud I was to be a Smith. I wished Dave was standing beside me.

It was time to let Nguyen go. The sheer thought made me sad because I still *believed* I loved him. Deep down, I was still a Smith. I wasn't ready to be attached to a Xin, not in this lifetime.

CHAPTER 32

AS A CHILD I was there to be seen and not heard. If I allowed my imagination to take over, I would visualise a magic cloak over my head. If I sat still long enough, I would become invisible to all around me. This allowed me to take in more than just my surroundings, but also my observations. As an adult, if I wanted to tweak certain situations in my life, I would visualise two doors. I would go via the back to open the front and completely take people by surprise. It was a good strategy that seemed to work well for me.

"Hello, hello?" I heard Sharni say at the other end of the phone.

I couldn't speak, I was crying that hard.

"Em is that you? What's so funny, why are you laughing so much?" she asked.

Sharni had never heard me crying like this before.

"Sharni I need my friends, I'm so sad," I said in-between deep sobs.

"Em listen to me. This will take time, you need time to heal, Em. Listen, you will feel better once you cry and get it out." She said.

"Let's go out to dinner tomorrow night. I know this great little pub by the beach. Come to my place, we will go together. But in the meantime, cry, let those tears out, and I will be on the other end of the line for you." She said.

Let it out I did, and thirty minutes later, I felt like I had been hit by a road train. A big mother fucker semitrailer prime mover truck.

Heartache is a real bitch. I was a virgin at experiencing this sort of pain. My life was pretty breezy in hindsight. I realised I put so much unnecessary stress on myself as an adult. I had spent years searching for the meaning of life. I remembered when Dina and I lined up for hours at a book shop in our early days of marital bliss waiting to get our hands on the latest self-help book. Because according to the media, this book was different, it was the one! It contained secrets!

When we finally got our hot little hands on it and paid for it, we centred our entire day on reading this magical manual. After the first chapter and five minutes later, we looked at one another and thought the exact same thing. THIS BOOK IS SHIT! It contained everything we were taught as children and we had it instilled in us. Our values and morals. What you put out there you get back in return, treat others how you would like to be treated, do right by others and they will do right by you. Needless to say, the book ended up in the same place the rest did, collecting dust on a shelf.

I deleted and blocked every possible, conceivable avenue for Nguyen to ever contact me again. Although I doubted, he ever would, most cowards wouldn't. It was to safeguard myself. He was gone, with the click of my fingers. Disappeared.

With grief comes desperation. This hopeless need for answers and the constant mulling over and reliving of the past. Self-torture, and over analysing, I was still shackled to him. I had allowed Nguyen to hijack my mind. I was doing this to myself, no one else. I was forfeiting my own rights at life, joy, happiness, gratitude, and instead introduced sheer exhaustion. Until my mind decided enough was enough, I was dwelling over the past.

It hadn't decided enough was enough yet, I was still fighting it. I was still faking it when asked how I was doing by my friends. I didn't want to bother them anymore with the same old regurgitation of my heartache. I needed help and I turned to the sacrificial lamb for it. I contacted Dimitri.

"Hello Dimitri," I said.

"Ella?" I heard.

"Yes, it's me."

"Ella what's wrong? It's been years, are you okay?" he asked sounding concerned.

"No, I'm not."

"Is it work, home, which is it?" he asked.

"It's my state of mind, I don't know what's real and what's not anymore." I said.

In true Dimitri style, he insisted we meet straight away to talk, and we did. Within the hour I was waiting for him. We had decided to meet at an old church by the beach. I was sitting in the warm sun on the church wall waiting for him.

I was looking around, not sure what car he drove these days when I saw someone walking towards me in the distance. I took off my sunglasses and squinted to make sure I saw who I did. It was Dimitri wearing denim shorts and an oversized shirt held up with braces and a straw hat. He looked like Huckleberry Finn. He had aged so much. He looked like some old ethnic who should be out harvesting and ploughing the field. I was blown away. I had always been attracted to him, but now I was totally off Greek food.

"Dimitri," I said as I jumped off the wall, and hugged him.

"Ella, such a surprise you contacted me. I was not expecting to hear from you after all these years, you still look the same as you did years ago!" he said.

You don't. "Thanks, Dimitri." I said.

"Dimitri, I owe you an apology. I didn't mean to hurt you or offend you when I signed off on our friendship, I didn't mean to. I probably overreacted as usual." I said.

"You didn't overreact, El. You have nothing to apologise for. I knew I would see you again one day."

Dimitri and I spoke. I told him about my separation from Dave and my breakup with Nguyen, from start to finish. With lots of eye rolls, frowns, and sighs he listened. We were now into the new year and my heart was still heavy with hurt.

"Wow, so you turned to Asian food instead then. I'm guttered, I thought I was the best!" he said.

"Shut up Dimitri, this isn't something to joke about. I'm hurting!" I said sounding annoyed.

"Yes, it is, this is a complete joke. You allowed some loser to treat you badly and control you, simple. You should be looking at this differently." He said.

"How so?" I asked.

"Well for starters, stop talking about him, and tell yourself he's dead and gone. Stop making any association to him in your mind. Stop thinking this was all you when you don't know, it may have been him."

"What do you mean?" I asked.

"You're blaming yourself. How do you know it was all you? How do you know for a fact it was the nasty message you sent him that threw your relationship over the edge? How do you know he wasn't already with someone and had you on the side? You don't, so stop thinking this was all your doing. Stop owning his bad behaviour. Stop justifying his actions, choose to own yours instead. He's a loser. You're smart and strong, he gave up not you! Get over it, move on, and don't ever mention his name again."

The lightbulb switch flicked. I couldn't believe it was that simple. I was so blown away I had forgotten the main ingredient, self-awareness. I understood the rest, but for me personally I lost the most important one throughout this process. Instantly, like a massive sugar fix to a diabetic patient, I felt happiness. My brain totally understood what Dimitri had explained to me. No sympathy, he cut right to the chase. Your choice to be miserable, he's a loser, and he's gone.

My brains version of what he said was STOP immediately, LOOK, observe, and LISTEN!

Like my mother had taught me as a child before I crossed the main road. "If you don't want to get hit by a car and die, fermare (stop), guarda (look) and ascolta (listen) for traffic." She'd say.

Bang! I was back in the moment. I was too busy reliving the past in my head that I had forgotten about the present. I was in total bliss. I felt the warmth of the sun beaming on my skin for the first time in months. I was *listening* to Dimitri telling me about his kids and his life without zoning out. I noticed children playing across the road on the playground and I had become aware of my surroundings. I was back in the moment.

I felt like I was able to make snap decisions. I felt an instant surge of emotion throughout my body. I was missing Dave, missing my life, realising and feeling my inner strength. Is this what some would call born again? I felt like I was.

Brains are funny. It took one simple conversation, and I felt like my brain had done a complete turnaround.

"How are things with you and Constantina, are you back together?" I asked.

"Yeah, we are..." he said, sounding hesitant.

"Did you win her back with your grilled halloumi cheese?" I asked.

"No smart-arse, I won her back with a fucking brand-new white Range Rover."

"Good on ya," I said and we both laughed.

"I love you, Dimitri." I said finally.

"Yeah, whatever, I knew you'd call me, eventually." He said and I rolled my eyes.

After all these years, the Greek had finally served his purpose. He was there for me when I needed him the most, although briefly, he had come good in the end. Like the twelve steps of the Alcoholics Anonymous plan to recovery, I had finally made peace with my past and with my cravings for yiros. Arrivederci, Dimitri.

CHAPTER 33

SALUTE! CIN CIN!

ITALIANS EMBRACE THE thought of death because in passing you are never forgotten by those left behind, and you're returning home. Earth is where our life lessons are learned. My father would say, "You are sent here, to learn lessons." So really nothing ever dies, it lives on forever, in our hearts.

Italians are also renowned for a good celebration. They know how to honour the dearly departed. We find ways to move on from pain and grief. Celebrations always involved food and wine and the clinking of glassware, Salute!

Since my conversation with Dimitri, I had felt like I had been resurrected. I was having more good days than bad. In fact, I really couldn't deem any as bad. I had become so self-aware of my emotions I would stop any negative thoughts, even those trying to creep into my mind through the back door. I had found happiness, the type worthy of celebrating. Dave and I had forged a good friendship, I appreciated his company, and our conversations, like I did with all my friends, and I was feeling blessed.

My instincts had returned and so did my self-respect. I was no longer a full-time people pleaser. I began to put myself first and I loved it. I was making up for lost time. Time spent alone had become my quality time. I had found a new sort of love, within me. I began to live my life how I saw fit and I owned it. I was spending my time with the people I appreciated, known as my healthy company.

"You should try dating again." Dina suggested over dinner one night.

Dina and I met for dinner once a fortnight at our favourite wood oven pizzeria. We both joked that the way to a woman's heart was through pizza.

"I did, and it wasn't good. I'm not into time wasters," I said, while taking in the aroma of my Napolitano wood oven pizza the waiter put down in front of me.

"Really, when?" she asked.

"A few months ago. I met this guy at a work function. He was at the same venue as me with his friends. He was nice looking, I mean, he caught my attention. We swapped numbers, and we caught up a few times. He invited me over for dinner one night and he told me he was into role-playing and he thought I could play a secretary! I asked if he meant a Secretary of State like a Federal Government official, and he said, "No, like the one you'd find sitting in an office answering the phones."

"What did you say to that?" she asked.

"See you fucking later! At least refer to me as a personal assistant!" We both laughed.

"Actually, Dina, there is someone I have been seeing." I said pouring our red wine.

"WHO! Tell me, it's not Dimitri. I heard he's back with his wife. Who is it?" she asked.

"It's Dave. We've been hanging out occasionally. We've had a few dinners here and there and we've become good friends. I feel like we've both become better people from spending time apart. He's had to face his fears and I've faced mine. I can honestly say that I feel like I'm at a point in our relationship where we have both learnt valuable lessons, and we have grown to be better people." I said.

"I feel like I can tick certain lessons off my list. There's no rush to get back to where we once were. We've both realised that what we had in the past hurt us both. We have become more focused on the moment and what we can bring from it into the future.

"He builds me up, not brings me down. He's actually a very strong, resilient individual." I said.

"I'm so happy for you, Em. You look happy, not from hanging out with Dave, but you seem happy within yourself and more settled. Now hand over your secret." She said as she began to cut into her pizza.

"There's no secret when it comes to dealing with pain. You do what works for you."

"But like my eyes, which are bigger than my stomach, I went back for a second serve of pain with Nguyen," I said.

"Nguyen found me challenging and dramatic in other areas of my life, it really felt like at times, he was holding up a mirror looking at his insecurities, trying to project them onto me. He had a lot of drama around him. Nguyen only saw what he wanted to in others when it suited him for his own purposes." I said.

"We began to feel on again, off again, there was no real substance to our relationship. His love felt charismatic and sweet, but very shallow. What we had was real to me, because I was fast becoming addicted to the 'makeup' stage of the relationship. He shouldn't have pursued me if he found relationships difficult. They require respect and trust and these go hand in hand. Most times I wasn't trusting Nguyen and respect was quickly vanishing. He simply did not understand the basic fundamentals of human respect and made me feel like I was the crazy one explaining feelings to him." I continued.

"Perhaps this was his way of letting me down gently. Labelling me as insecure, sensitive or dramatic, lacking relationship maturity, and preferring to use his own special modus operandi with his lovers. He was most likely notching up a very impressive bedpost in the process." I said.

"In fact, I felt at times I was pushing him away with my insecurities. I was feeling neglected and isolated from his life. If I pushed hard enough then it might not hurt as much in the end and I could feel the end nearing. His attention span with me was fading. I was becoming less and less important to him. Our relationship became a game of tug of war." I said.

"Em, he didn't build you up. We were all worried about you. We all thought you had made a big error in judgement there," she said.

"Well for me to overcome it, I had to find my gratitude and accept what it was. I'm so bloody grateful I've learnt from my heartache and not wallowed in self-pity for too long. I won't refer to Nguyen as a mistake, because I don't see him like that. That relationship had challenged me to look at the way I saw myself and it wasn't easy identifying what I needed to change. Although he detached very quickly, that's his stuff and not mine. He chose to replace me." I said.

"Have you forgiven him?" she asked.

"I have forgiven myself and made peace with me and my past, does that mean I have forgiven him? Not all the gifts in the world could compensate for 'crazy'. I had to keep reminding myself of the torturous, manipulating, and confusing games that came with that man." I said.

"I'm transitioning onto better things now. I don't know if that constitutes forgiveness, I'm not sure. I don't feel a great need to, this is about me, not him. I've thanked my strength and resilience, the two things that Nguyen felt intimidated by and that's what I truly believe he is searching for in his life," I said.

"I understand now why his ex-girlfriend sent him a thank you card. I said.

"What would you write in your hypothetical thank you card?" Dina asked, smiling.

"It would be, 'Thank you for not being there for me because from day one, you weren't real anyway.'

'Thank you for not holding my hand when I needed you the most. It shows me you know very little about team effort'.

'Thank you for showing up only when it was convenient for you, because it showed me you have very little understanding of relationships and commitment'.

'Thank you for teaching me about disrespect and making me cry, because I deserve someone who wipes my tears away not bring them on'.

'And thank you for leaving me for her, because you're now her problem, not mine'. Fucker." I said.

"I can safely say the lump I created in my throat has gone, it no longer serves a purpose, and neither does Nguyen," I said.

"Didn't he tell you to sort yourself out?" she asked.

"Our timing was all wrong, I met him when I was still living with Dave and things became very complicated very quickly. I was dealing with my loss of identity. I saw it as death, and I was grieving. I lost what I thought at the time as being the most important relationship in my life." I said.

"That's all we have known, Em. We pride ourselves on being good mothers and wives. That was our dream growing up. We were always putting others ahead of ourselves. He knew you were still living with Dave, if he perceived that as complicated, he shouldn't have pursued a friendship slash relationship, loser." She seethed.

"Didn't he tell you that you had to spend time out on your own?" she asked.

"They say history has a way of repeating itself. I spent years sitting at home alone when Dave and I first got married. That forced me to appreciate my alone time, not to fear it. Remember night school? I became independent." I said smiling.

"For me, it's not a big deal. I enjoy alone time. I truly believe Nguyen can't stand being alone, that's why he's constantly looking for someone. He likes having a backup plan. He's searching for something that I don't believe exists, he's in a constant state of limbo." I said. "Italians call these types of people vagabondo (vagabond)."

"Do you think about him?" Dina asked.

"In the beginning I did, that's a given. I was mourning a relationship that I made up in my head. My mind was trying to heal my heart through the only way I knew how to, and that was a make-believe story, like I used to do as a child." I said.

"I heard a song the other day on the car radio that took me back to my teenage years sitting in my bedroom listening to music and reading my books. Always wishing my life to be different than it was. Now that it is, I have realised the one thing I was wishing for I already have, my freedom. Why would I want a man, I want to enjoy *me* for now?" I said.

The waiter came and took our dessert and coffee orders. We ordered limoncello. I ordered the rum baba and I thought of my mother who made the best version.

I began to think about my childhood beliefs. I only saw the good in others and wasn't equipped or savvy enough to recognise people like Nguyen. He was a predator who preyed on women like me. We didn't share the same head set. He had a deceitful mind. I was vulnerable and open to all of his moves. I had a big heart and I trusted people. I was genuine.

"Remember when we'd freak out each time when we'd find someone had left tissues in their pockets after we pulled the clean clothes out of the washing machine? It was frustrating, time consuming, cleaning up mess. But we did it and moved on. We all make mistakes. The trick is to learn from that and not beat yourself up over it. People become tired of listening to the same old story, and so did I." I said.

"Sounds like you're on the right path, Em." Dina said.

"I'm so ready to move on. I'm really looking forward to going to Sydney to catch up with Matteo and seeing some of the local sites." I said.

"I was so happy when I ran into him." I said.

"He seems lovely, Em. It's nice you two have been able to reconnect again. Telephones and real grown up conversations are such a wonderful thing in this day and age." She said and we both laughed.

"Unlike the day, I almost ran into Nguyen. I couldn't believe it, I instantly felt an unsettling feeling in my stomach."

"Has he changed much? What did he look like?" Dina asked as she sipped her limoncello.

"No, he hasn't changed one bit. Honestly Dina, he looked like a dissatisfied little duck. A heavily burdened, desperate, lonely, lost person."

"Maybe I should write a children's book about him one day and call it *The Angry Little Lost Duck!*" I said, and we laughed.

"He would create the ultimate plot to that story, that's all he's good for," said Dina.

"I mean how hard could it be. That would be a lot more creative than any boring old thank you card!"

"Silly Quack!" I said as we picked up our glasses to toast. Cin Cin!

THE END

ACKNOWLEDGMENTS

Writing this book came very naturally to me. With each draft I wrote, I found myself on a journey of growth and self-discovery. This would not have been possible without support and encouragement from my friends and family, whom I take great pleasure in mentioning and thanking below. I am eternally grateful and sincerely appreciative to you all.

I would like to thank from the bottom of my heart, Shireen Khemlani, for the suggested ViNo addition to the front cover. For believing in me and encouraging me to keep writing even on bad days. ViNo, just like people, can leave a bad after taste. Thank you for always helping me make smarter choices in life.

My beautiful editor Bianca Iovino, who put my book on a diet and still managed to keep all my work intact, genius.

My friend, Donna Orchard, our philosophical conversations about life, and our problem-solving skills have been inventive, and highly entertaining. Thanks for holding my hand.

My beautiful family, Alysia Thomas, Patrick Thomas, Joel Caon, Rosa Roocke, and Yule Watts for your constant support and encouragement. I thank you from the bottom of my heart. You're always there for me. For the endless hours of listening to my chapters, to reading my drafts, and offering me feedback. Patrick for helping me behind the scenes, you saved me many hours of work and your insightfulness a blessing.

This book would not have been possible if it weren't for the stories I was raised listening to. My cultural upbringing is something I am very proud of, as well as the family values I was raised with. I would like to thank and honour their memory in passing, my father Domenico Severino and his mother Maria Vicario. I would also like to thank my mother Elvira Severino. I love you mama. I would like to remember and honour my beautiful Dutch mother-in-law Trudy Eerden, a true example of strength. Without your cultural influence I wouldn't have stories to share and I promise to keep these alive through future generations.

Lastly, Peter Thomas, thank you for the freedom to explore. There's always one who insists on following the other, and is hard to lose along the way. You're still here. It's a toss-up between Boo Radley and Atticus Finch.

Finally, to all my friends and family and for all of those who I have met along this journey. Your loyalty and friendship are something I hold very close to my heart. Thank you for choosing to take this ride with me. Bon appétit.

AUTHOR'S NOTE

Thank you so much for reading MSG FREE.

As an independent author MSG FREE is my debut novel.

I feel like I have developed true and meaningful relationships with all the characters. I hope you can too. The book is set in Australia. Although I have mentioned Melbourne, Canberra and Sydney, the scene can be where ever the reader chooses.

I have chosen to introduce the character Emmie in the present day, through her past experiences and how she has grown forth from that.

I wrote this book to reflect the strength and resilience within the main character, hoping to resonate with the reader by giving examples of various life lessons.

Please follow me on Facebook: Eleonora Thomas Author and Instagram. I would like to share more of my experiences with you, new editions and future novels. Thank you again for reading my book and meeting Emmie. I hope you love her as much as I do.

Eleonora Thomas.

ABOUT THE AUTHOR

Eleonora Thomas lives and writes in Adelaide, South Australia. She likes to surround herself with good food, music, and great company. She believes wine is a food group and that creative revenge is an empowering tool. She drinks her coffee extra hot and likes watching reruns of old American sitcoms from the '90s. She likes to make people laugh. She cherishes her friends and family. She is a protective mum who will attack like a vicious one-eyed Chihuahua if anyone threatens her family. She has two adult children who are her best friends and her greatest teachers in life.